Larkwood Academy

SCREAMING

JAYCE CARTER

Screaming
ISBN # 978-1-80250-499-6
©Copyright Jayce Carter 2022
Cover Art by Kelly Martin ©Copyright November 2022
Interior text design by Claire Siemaszkiewicz
Totally Bound Publishing

SCREAMING

Dedication

To my little sister, whose existential dread and
anxiety make me feel less alone.
I can't offer you good advice, but hopefully some
werewolf orgies help.
Now go forth and make today your bitch!

Chapter One

Hera

I might have escaped Larkwood, but I couldn't shake the feeling that they were right behind me, that if I let my guard down for even a moment, they'd grab me again and drag me back to hell. Every sound, every person that passed, it all put me on edge.

"Here." Knox made me jump when he caught my hand from behind and pressed something into my palm.

I glanced down to find a couple of folded twenties there. I frowned, then offered him a questioning glance.

"Don't worry—I didn't do anything weird to get it. I just used my powers to convince someone to hand over his wallet. Given the very nice sports car he was driving, I doubt he'll miss it all that much."

I let out a relieved breath. If it were Brax, I'd have worried he might have left a body behind. With Knox, a fear that he'd done something he hadn't wanted to get the money had hit me. Hearing he hadn't soothed my fears.

It had been nearly a week since we'd gotten out of Larkwood. The first trek through the open desert had been the worst, and we'd moved fast, pushing ourselves to our limits. Thankfully, with my hearing, I'd been able to identify helicopters and patrols before they got close. This was the second town we'd stopped at, since we hadn't wanted to stay long in the first. We'd only remained in the first long enough to get a change of clothing.

We'd picked up some items from a thrift store, paying for it all with money Brax had — I sure didn't ask him how he'd gotten it. It had left me in a baggy cable-knit sweater and jeans with large rips in them — far more casual than I'd been used to in my old life and yet not the clothing I'd had in my life at Larkwood.

Wade had found a pair of slacks and a long-sleeved shirt, Brax a large hoodie and jeans, and Knox wore a rather loud Hawaiian button-up short-sleeved shirt, a windbreaker and a pair of shorts that made him look like a surfer. We resembled hopeless fashion rejects, but at least we didn't look like escaped prisoners. The long sleeves allowed us to hide our Larkwood bands as well.

I tossed food into my basket as Knox walked beside me, picking things with a good shelf life and plenty of calories. I had no idea what the future held, where we'd go, what we'd find there, which meant we needed to make the best out of what we could find when we got the chance.

I peered behind me, wondering where Brax and Wade had run off to. It was best for us not to be too close in public since a group of four brought more attention than a pair did, but I struggled not to worry when I couldn't see them.

"They're picking up some goods at the general store down the street," Knox said. "I gave them some of the cash I'd gotten."

I nodded to acknowledge the information, then reached for a pack of cookies from the shelf. They made me pause as I looked at them, the same brand that Brax and Wade had fought over in my room before.

"You sure we need those?"

I thought back to Larkwood, to the chaos we'd left behind. I remembered the way Wade had stood between me and the shades who had wanted to kill me. Next, I recalled Brax fully changed into his berserker form, blood dripping from his huge body, the way he'd taken out everything that risked me before he'd rumbled out "*mine*."

We'd gone through so much, suffered so much pain to get us here. Cookies seemed a small price to pay.

Knox set his palm over mine, which made me realize my hand still hung in mid-air. He guided me back to drop the cookies into the basket while offering a kind smile. "Comfort food is important, right? In fact…" Knox pulled away and walked toward the end of the aisle for a moment. He plucked something from a shelf, then jogged back and tossed it into the basket.

I peered down to find a king-sized chocolate bar.

"You complained about the lack of chocolate before. I figured you deserved something nice, too."

I couldn't stop my smile, not just at the thought of tasting the candy but also at Knox's sweetness.

Now is not the time to act all smitten.

We had bigger things to deal with than my feelings toward Knox.

"You haven't been sleeping well," Knox said, the words so unexpected I frowned at the change in topic.

I tucked the basket into the crook of my elbow so I could sign. *"What?"*

"You've been waking up from nightmares. Are you reliving what happened?"

I gulped but shook my head. *"I'm tumbling into this endless void of darkness. It feels like I'm drowning, and no matter how I kick, I can't reach the surface."* Even admitting the dreams that had plagued me every night made me shudder.

"Kit."

That took me by surprise, and I jerked to a stop.

Knox, however, kept speaking as if the topic weren't awkward at all. "Your bond with Kit. I'm going to guess he's trying to reach you through it, and when you resist, that's why you get that sinking feeling."

"He wouldn't hurt me like that." I might not be certain of many things, but that I knew for sure.

"No, he wouldn't on purpose, but he might not realize it's causing you any distress. It might be like…being blindfolded and screaming for someone, not realizing they're right next to you. He might be reaching for you but have no idea you can feel it."

Now *that* sounded like the man I know. *"What should I do?"*

"Talk to him." At my look, he laughed softly. "If Kit wants to find you, he can. You need your sleep, though, and you won't get any if this keeps up. So talk to him." After a moment, he added quietly, "You'll probably feel better after checking in with him anyway."

Which was true… Leaving the way I had without a real goodbye to either Kit or Deacon hurt. The memory of Deacon's face, the way he'd stared at me as if I'd broken his heart, was almost as bad as the nightmares.

In fact, no matter how much I wanted to ignore it, the feeling encompassed more than just the two of them. I'd left so much back at Larkwood, so many people hurting. Why was I free when they had to stay there?

Instead of dwelling on it, I told myself that I'd brave that conversation when I fell asleep that night. I'd force myself to confront that darkness and Kit.

I owed him that much, didn't I?

"Shit." Knox's curse took me off guard, pulling me from my little pep talk. He wasn't the sort to swear much, and I hadn't done anything to earn a reaction like that as far as I knew.

I pulled back enough to peer at his face, finding his gaze not on me but up and to the left.

I turned, my blood running cold when I realized what he stared at. On the television a breaking story ran, and above the newscaster's shoulder? Knox's, Wade's and Brax's faces stared back at me.

The words that ran along the bottom edge of the screen talked about the escape from Larkwood, though they only mentioned the other three. Nowhere did they imply a fourth person had participated.

Why doesn't it include me?

"We should get going," Knox said, his voice low. "You check out, and I'll head next door to grab Wade and Brax. Meet us on the side of the building."

After I nodded, he headed out, his face down. Thankfully, the three looked different enough in regular clothing than the sweats the pictures showed. Besides, most people ignored news reports like those, assuming that such things would never touch their lives.

I paid quickly, a gesture toward the large scar at my throat when the cashier had tried to strike up a conversation. My fingers ached from the heavy bags, but just as Knox had said, I found all three men around the side of the building.

And boy did Brax look angry. Still, the expression fit rather well on his face. In fact, if he really wanted to hide who he was, the best way would have probably been to smile. No one would recognize him like that.

Brax narrowed his eyes before swiping his hand out and taking the bags from me without asking. "No idea what you're thinking, but I don't like that smirk."

I shrugged rather than admitting or denying anything.

"Looks like this might be our last family outing," Wade said.

"Why wouldn't they include Hera, though?" Brax asked.

"It has to be a ploy." Knox pressed his lips together for a moment. "Maybe the Warden hopes that will get us stuck, that it'll force her to act alone so guards can look for Hera?"

Maybe…though the more I thought about it, the less that made sense. *I think she doesn't want it known I'm at Larkwood at all. She's keeping it secret to leverage that information, which means she can't admit I'm not there anymore. She probably can't even tell my parents, because if she did, they'd stop helping her.* Even saying that hurt, making a deep spot inside my chest ache, the part that still craved a family.

Wade reached for me and entwined his gloved hand with mine, his tight grip reassuring.

His touch made his point loud and clear—whether or not my parents ever accepted me, I had people. No matter how hard it had been to lose my voice, it had taught me how much a person could say without ever speaking a word.

So I squeezed back as we headed off toward the empty store we'd broken into the night before to sleep at.

Things might look bad, and they might just get worse, but I wasn't alone.

* * * *

That horrible sinking sensation took over me again when I went to bed, made me cry out in fear. Even asleep, even locked in this dream, Knox's words came back to me.

This was Kit's call. Now that I knew that, I could feel it. That darkness, that cold, it was exactly like him. After almost a week outside of Larkwood, I couldn't avoid him anymore, could I?

No matter how difficult it was, how much I wanted to avoid this, I couldn't any longer.

So rather than trying to run from the connection, from the bond that tugged at me, I followed it. I walked through that door I'd discovered during my first dream, when I'd spoken to him after the forming of our bond.

And the moment I saw Kit, I nearly collapsed. He looked so much as he had before, the sight threatening to yank me backward, to Larkwood, to the hell of that place, but also to *him*.

He lifted his gaze to mine, and his black eyes widened. Any doubts I had disappeared in that moment, in the hunger there that said he wanted to consume me.

He came forward in such a rush that I backed away — not that it mattered. He slid a hand behind my neck and yanked me against him, lowering his head until he took my lips in a kiss that was nothing like the ones he'd given me before. Those had been innocent and sweet, but now I suspected he'd held himself back the other times.

He held *nothing* back this time. His mouth took mine, deep and aggressive, not letting me have an inch of space, and even though I didn't feel his touch as I did in person, even though the tingle from it wasn't quite right, it made my heart speed and my body crave so much more.

Except I couldn't lose myself in this, not when we had important things to discuss. I set my hands on his chest and pushed away.

Not that he let me go. He broke the kiss but left his large, strong hand on the back of my neck, keeping me up against him as if afraid I'd get away again.

Staring up into his fathomless black eyes managed to blank my head, to steal all my thoughts.

"You should have told me." His voice was dark and so similar to that terrifying one he used to command others.

I dragged my tongue over my bottom lip, missing the taste of him but glad I could at least speak with him here. "I'm sorry."

"Sorry?" He let out a harsh snort before yanking away from me and moving to pace. It seemed he had energy he didn't know what to do with. Perhaps he thought doing that would keep him from grabbing me again? "What does sorry matter? You could have been killed! I knew you were planning something, but never would I have suspected anything like *this*. All the years at Larkwood I've spent, and you managed what no other shade ever could." He paused to stare at me as if he couldn't understand me, as if I were something different all of a sudden.

"It wasn't me," I said.

"No? Because it sure seems like it to me, seeing as you are not here."

"It wasn't *just* me," I clarified. "The only reason we pulled it off was because I wasn't alone. The Warden could anticipate any one shade, but she couldn't keep ahead of us when we worked together. That's why Larkwood worked so hard to pit us all against each other, but because otherwise, we're too powerful."

Kit took a deep breath, his chest rising then falling as he exhaled. Finally, he faced me again. "That's what you don't understand. Only you could have done that. Brax, Knox and Wade had been here for years, but they never managed to work together. You brought them together—you gave them reason enough to put aside their petty disagreements. I don't think you understand just how amazing that is."

His praise made my cheeks burn, so I turned my gaze from his, unable to hold that scrutiny. "You and Deacon didn't get into any trouble, right?"

"No. Your trick with Deacon worked to throw suspicion off him. Larkwood is already almost back to normal. It seems as if nothing at all happened. A new bridge was put up the next day between the North Tower and the main building, and with the reinforcements, the Warden gained control again by noon. It's strange how such a violent event can so quickly be swept away." He shook his head, then offered me a hard look. "Are you really okay?"

I nodded, struggling with how to answer. "We're all safe. I won't say the escape went without trouble, but we got out uninjured." I paused, then forced myself to go on. "You know, I would have taken you with me if I thought you'd come, right?"

He offered me a smile that lacked humor. "I wouldn't have gone. I didn't believe it possible to do what you did. You know what they say about old dogs and new tricks."

But now we were at the point I couldn't turn away from. Even if I wanted to keep things like they were, I owed him the truth. "I need to tell you something," I said.

He furrowed his eyebrows, as if the very words were unpleasant. "That doesn't sound good."

And it wasn't good. Kit believed his daughter was human, that she lived some normal, happy life somewhere, completely ignorant of the horrors of Larkwood and shades. While he missed her, no doubt, her living the happy life she wanted to no doubt eased him.

Discovering that wasn't the case would hurt him, but he still deserved to know.

"I was taken to the North Tower," I explained, unsure how to start the conversation. His expression pressed me to continue. "I saw what Project Corrander was. You probably saw it, too."

"Those shade soldiers," he responded. "A few showed up to guard the Warden until reinforcements came."

I nodded, rubbing my hands together to try to ease the anxiety inside me. "I also met the shade who created them."

He went still at that, a frown appearing on his features as he put it together. Leave it to Kit to figure things out so quickly. "A few shades can do that, but if you're talking to me, I assume it's a wendigo. To think they had one so close and I never knew..." He shook his head. "No, I suspected, I think. Sometimes, I felt a presence, but I brushed it off as nothing more than a desire to find another like myself." He went still, and when he brought his gaze to mine, anger rested there.

"I remember something before the escape, this anger that struck me, and someone trying to pull you away."

"You said '*mine.*'"

His eyes widened. "So that wasn't just a feeling?"

I shook my head. "It was real. The wendigo wanted to turn me into one of those soldiers, had expected to, but when they felt your bond with me, they decided not to."

He approached more slowly than the last time, as if once again worried about frightening me after that story. He cupped my cheek in his large hand. "I'm sorry you went through that, but I'm glad our bond saved you. I don't know what I'd do if some other wendigo broke that, if they tried to claim you, to take you from me."

I let myself melt at his words for a moment, enjoying that connection between us before forcing myself to tell him what I needed to. "That's not all."

He pulled back enough to stare down at me, waiting for me to go on.

"The wendigo they're using there is a young girl with long black hair."

He went impossibly still but didn't interrupt me.

"She's lived her entire short life in the North Tower."

"You don't mean..." He didn't finish the thought.

I nodded, swallowing hard once before speaking. "She said she remembered someone calling her a name once — Lilianna."

Kit yanked away from me, his face a mixture of pain and anger. "She was so close? All this time?"

I grabbed his arm, fear overtaking me at what he might do. I didn't want him to go charging in, to try to do anything without thinking it through.

He peered down at where I touched him. I expected him to throw off my concern, to tell me it wasn't my business. Instead, he set his hand over mine. "Don't worry, I'm too old to react carelessly. She has been this close her entire life, and I never realized. A little more time to plan carefully won't change anything." He opened his mouth as if to ask something, then closed it again.

"Do you want me to tell you about her?"

He nodded, but before I could, he pulled me against his chest, wrapping his strong arms around me. "You know this isn't over, right? I don't care where you go, or how far you run, I won't just give up on you. I wasn't kidding. You are *mine*."

I let myself rest against him, nodding instead of answering.

Kit pressed a kiss to the top of my head, then released me. "Okay, tell me about my daughter."

* * * *

Brax

How was it that even now, wearing clothing that didn't quite fit her and with no makeup, Hera could still manage to tempt me so much? I'd seen women all dolled up who had barely gotten an eyebrow raise from me, yet here Hera was, checking to make sure she had everything, not trying in the least, and she had me pathetically smitten.

She turned toward me as if she'd sensed my gaze. The way she smiled warmed me, especially since there weren't many people who would smile when they saw me.

"Getting ready to go?" I asked.

She nodded, patting her hands down her sides as if to check for everything.

"I don't like you going by yourself. I'm not good for a lot of things, but bodyguard is a readymade role for me. It pisses me off that I have to stay behind."

She smiled wider, as if charmed by my pouting. *"We can't risk you or the others getting seen. I'm just going to pick up the last of the supplies for the next leg of our trip, because we can't stay here any longer. Don't worry,"* she signed.

"How can I not worry? Sure, you weren't mentioned in the news, but that doesn't mean the Warden doesn't have people looking for you."

She frowned, and it took a moment for me to realize why. The moment I did, I jerked my gaze away, ashamed that I'd been so stupid as to make that mistake.

Her hands flew a second time, signing faster than the first. *"You could understand me, couldn't you?"*

I let out a long sigh at my frustration with my own idiocy. I'd stupidly opened my mouth and admitted something I'd never planned on admitting. Still, with no good way to get out of it, I nodded and answered truthfully. "Yeah, I can."

"For how long?"

"Not long. Couple weeks before we left?"

"Then why didn't you tell me?"

I rubbed the back of my neck, not caring for the scrutiny. "I'm not very good at it yet. In case you haven't noticed, I'm not really a studying sort of guy— never was. Turns out that learning sign language isn't all that easy. Didn't want to say anything until I didn't embarrass myself, especially if I couldn't get the hang of it."

"So you started learning a couple weeks ago?"

And here went the part I'd not wanted to discuss. "No. I started a few months ago, after our first night together. I just couldn't get a good grip of it for a while."

I stared at the floor, now wanting to see her disappointed when she realized just how hard it was for me to grasp some more delicate information. I wasn't stupid, but unless it had to do with tactics or warfare, my brain just didn't like to convert it into long-term storage. It meant that learning ASL had taken months of study at night with that damned book, sitting up late while I tried to beat the information into my thick skull.

It had burned that I'd needed Wade or Knox to translate for me for so long, when no matter how many nights I worked toward it, I just couldn't understand with how quickly her hands moved. But I'd kept going, wanting to communicate with her on my own.

A warmth on my cheek made me lift my gaze again. She said nothing — with her hand on my cheek it wasn't as though she could sign — but the smile she gave me said more than anything else could have. She came closer and leaned up, onto her tiptoes, then brushed her soft, warm lips against mine.

It reminded me of when I'd been in my berserker form, the memories fuzzy as they often were after I returned to myself, but *this* I remembered. She'd pressed her forehead to mine, the touch so unbearably gentle that it had reached past the haze of my bloodlust.

And just like the time before, it made me shudder and give in. How could she do that to me so easily?

It hit me especially hard when she crossed that line, when she reached out for me. Too often our relationship had been me crossing it. I'd gone to her room. I'd touched her. I'd craved and she'd given in.

That meant when she made the first move, when she showed that she didn't fear me, that she wanted me in some way, it completely took me down. Any resistance I might have mustered went away immediately. She had a line past all those other feelings, right down to something deeper, to the real me that rested beneath my berserker.

So I kissed her back, taking her first move and running with it. I pushed her until I had her trapped between the wall and my hard body, wanting to keep her still. She felt like something that kept slipping away, like holding her was trying to grasp smoke, but for the moment I had her.

I had to let her go out alone, because my face was plastered on every TV screen around. I'd caused her far more trouble than I'd help her with, which meant no matter how much I hated it, I had to keep my ass planted right where it was.

And I *really* hated it.

I kissed her deeper, tasting her, slipping my tongue past her lips. I ran the hand not behind her neck down her, tempted by her soft and giving body. She wore another outfit from the thrift store, something that didn't quite fit but made her look better than women who wore expensive tailored gowns. It was just her, though, and she drew me as no other had. I didn't care what she wore. I didn't care how she styled her hair—I wanted her no matter what.

I reached beneath her sweater to find her warm skin, dancing my fingertips over her stomach, her ribs, the sensitive flesh beneath her the line of her bra. It all made me want to strip her bare right then, to forget others were in the shop, that we had things to do, that dangerous problems plagued us. We could toss that all aside and just lose ourselves in each other for a short while. When I did that, the rest of the world didn't seem so overwhelming or imposing.

A door opening farther back in the shop woke her up, at least. I didn't know if I cared—if Knox or Wade walked in, what did that matter? We were all adults, and we were well aware of what happened between adults.

Yet, it seemed Hera was less willing to let others walk in on us naked and tangled together, because she pressed her small hands to my chest and pushed.

I broke the kiss but rested my forehead against hers. "Saved by the incubus, huh?" I knew Knox's footsteps as if they were my own, so as soon as he got close enough for me to catch them, I easily knew who approached. "Normally incubi lead to more sex, not less. Figures my brother would end up being a cock-block."

I leaned in and pressed my lips to her throat, not willing to let her go without something. I sucked hard at a spot on the side of her neck, a place difficult to hide.

She arched against me, pulling in a harsh breath at what was no doubt a sting, but I didn't stop.

Finally, I released her, pulling back. I stroked my fingers over the red mark I'd left. "If I've got to stay put here while you go out, you damn well will wear my mark when you go." A hazy memory of myself from my other form, when I'd thought of her as my mate, hit me.

I'd never felt that way before, never wanted any one female over another, had never really cared, but clearly Hera wasn't like anyone else.

Was that why a rush took over me at the sight of the darkening hickey on her neck, the sign that she had someone? It felt like a huge warning signal to anyone who would dare even consider touching her.

And it soothed me. It let me take a step backward before Knox walked into the entryway where Hera and I stood.

"Not gone yet?" Knox asked the question with a grin, as if he knew exactly the reason and it amused him.

Then again, as an incubus, he could probably *smell* Hera's interest, could taste the lust in the room, and Knox didn't take sex seriously as a lot of others did. He didn't give a damn if I slept with Hera—he'd made that clear enough after the first time.

He wanted her, of course, but me having tasted her, me being with her, that didn't change his feelings about her.

His gaze moved to her neck, to the mark, and his smile widened. While the thought of anyone walking in on me fucking Hera didn't bother me, as it turned out, Knox seeing the mark made me shy.

Maybe because I'd never wanted to leave proof on anyone else, never wanted to claim anyone else, it felt far more personal, more special.

I ignored the heat in my cheeks and pulled back from Hera, putting distance between us. "Be careful," I warned her again. "If you run into any problems, don't face them yourself. Just get the hell out of there and back to us."

"You worry too much," Knox told me.

"I saw her tear down the bridge to the North Tower, then take down damn near every shade between there and you. Trust me, she can manage some shopping on her own." Wade walked into the room, a cup in his hand. "In fact, next Black Friday, I'm taking her with me to score the best deals. She'll be able to clear out any competition."

I frowned and gestured at his coffee. "Where'd you get that?"

"Gas station."

"You aren't supposed to go out." I shoved the words out through gritted teeth.

"It's *fine*," he assured me before taking a drink of the coffee. "Whereas you two look like the type people notice, I am unfailingly forgettable. It is one of my few redeeming qualities. I look like any young college student, or even like a high school senior trying to look older. No one looks twice at me."

"And you didn't get me any?" Knox managed to look downright offended. "I thought we were friends."

"You share women with your friends — not coffee. Come on, now, some things are sacred!"

Knox reached out and snatched the cup from Wade, who gasped and pressed his now empty hand to his chest. "You just wait, buddy. The next time you want to quiet your incubus, I'll leave you flat on your ass!"

I turned from the two and back to Hera, trying to ignore the bickering of the children. "You should just get going. They'll keep this up for a long time."

Hera nodded, fumbling with the strap of her bag as if uncomfortable. It made me chuckle, that oddly innocent sweetness she had.

She nodded, then took a step toward the door. I stopped her with a hand around her arm and tugged her back to me, not giving a damn if the other two saw. I offered one more short passionate kiss before pulling back to look into her eyes. "Be careful," I repeated.

Hera's tongue touched her lip, as if she missed my taste, and I forced myself to let her go and step away before I took her right there.

She turned away and left, a quickness in her steps that suggested her cheeks were bright red.

I twisted to find the other two no longer bickering, but instead staring at me with wide grins, as if they'd just gotten treated to the most amusing sight they'd ever seen.

I glared, then flipped them both off before storming back into the main area of the empty shop.

And I tried my hardest to ignore the laughter from behind me.

Chapter Two

Hera

Finding the items we needed proved rather easy. The list didn't have much left on it. A bit more food — mostly jerky and other non-perishable items — a few bags and some other camping items.

We needed to head north. I'd heard Canada had fewer restrictions on shades and more people willing to help. They might have similar laws on the books, but it seemed they had less of an interest in enforcing them. Their travel rules were more relaxed, which meant getting out of the country would be a far cry easier than here.

So our gear would allow us to make that long trip safely in case we had to camp along the way. Knox could get us a car — people tended to offer him whatever he wanted when he turned on that charm — and the farther we got from Larkwood, the safer we'd be.

It was strange to think that we could be past this in just a few weeks. If all went well, if we moved quickly and didn't run into trouble, we could get out of the Warden's reach.

Then what? Act as if it had all never happened? Pretend to be human? Live our lives looking over our shoulders in fear that Larkwood would still find us someday?

I sighed when I didn't have an answer to that. Getting out of Larkwood was my only goal, but now? Now I didn't know what life could be like after that.

I finished getting the items on our list, reusable totes slung over my shoulder to carry it all. A pad of paper along with a pen tucked into the side pockets of the leggings I wore had allowed me to communicate, when needed, though I'd mostly tried to avoid dealing with anyone.

I tried to remain as unremarkable and forgettable as possible.

Now, I could head back to the shop. We'd pack up and be off, headed for a new life, for freedom. I couldn't picture what that meant, what it would look like, but I wanted to find out.

A young girl ran past me, bumping into me as she went. It was impossible to not notice the fear painted across her features.

She turned down an alleyway, her clothing dirty and her face streaked with dirt. She was only nine or so, if I had to guess. Behind her came two men, though they avoided running into me—good thing, since they'd have easily knocked me down if they had.

"Where did she go?" one asked before the other gestured down the alleyway the girl had disappeared into.

The man's voice bled into me, a plethora of images assaulting me. The man smiling around a table with others, him working a job on computers, him kicking a man on the ground who wore a band on his wrist identifying him as a shade. He threw out insult after insult, and even after the man on the ground had stopped moving, he didn't stop the attack.

I blinked, building up my shields, stopping the wash of images, and my feet moved before I had to consider it. I only transposed the image of that young girl and what the man had done before, and I sure as hell wouldn't let *that* happen if I could stop it.

Brax getting angry, Knox and Wade lecturing me later, those things didn't matter.

I rushed forward, dropping my bags at the opening of the alleyway.

Down farther, the two men approached the girl who cowered, her back to a fence that blocked her escape.

"Leave me alone," she begged, her bright blue eyes red already, her long, dark brown hair tangled. That was when I noticed a black eye — clearly not new.

It seemed this was far from the first time she'd been in a dangerous situation. Her terror wasn't the kind from surprise, but rather from someone who had experienced this before, who knew exactly what could and would happen.

"You aren't welcome here," the man at the front, the one I'd seen memories from, snapped. "You know the rules — you don't come to this part of town."

"My friend needed medicine," the girl said, pressing herself as flat against the fence as she could. "This is the only pharmacy that has the medicine."

"Don't care. Guess you need a reminder of the rules."

Oh, fuck that.

The man went forward, and I'd reached my limit. I snapped my fingers, then swiped that sound forward and to the side. Just as planned, the wave smacked both men back and shoved them against the wall of the building to our right.

The girl jerked her gaze past the men to me, her eyes wide as if she wasn't sure who the bigger threat was.

Then again, I'd seen the darker side of shades as well, had witnessed what they were willing to do to each other when backed into a corner.

I moved to the side, giving the girl a wide berth to move past me.

She moved her gaze from the men to me, the back and forth as if deciding what to do. "Who are you?" she asked.

I lifted my chin to show her the scar at my throat, but I wasn't sure if she was old enough to understand the meaning. She certainly wouldn't come close enough for me to write her a message, given her hesitancy.

I gestured toward the end of the alleyway and jerked my head that way, trying to tell her to go.

And that battle in her eyes restored some of my faith in people. It was her not wanting to leave me to whatever would happen, not wanting to make me face the danger alone.

I offered her as kind a smile as I could and shook my head.

One of the men rose, using the wall as support. It was the one who had spoken before, the one whose memories I'd seen. He paid the girl no mind, focusing on me instead, fury in his dark blue eyes. "You bitch," he spat, red trailing down his chin from a split lip.

The girl tried to dart past him, but it seemed he hadn't fully forgotten about her, because he reached out to grab her.

He'd have gotten her, too, if I hadn't moved so fast. It seemed using my power was becoming second nature to me, and I didn't have to even think about it. Instead, I snapped and sent a wave right at him, using it to slam him against the wall and hold him there.

Kit would be so proud to see how fast I did that.

I focused on the man as I stepped between him and her. The other man hadn't risen again, though he breathed which suggested I hadn't killed him. He seemed less seriously injured and more unwilling to become a target by fighting anymore.

The man stared at me with so much hatred it nearly made me sick. He hated me for what I was, not giving a damn about who I really was. Men like this, people this twisted with hatred, couldn't change. They didn't *want* to change or learn.

"You're making a *huge* mistake," the man said, his voice all ignorance. The bulging of the muscles at his neck said he struggled, but I held him so tightly he couldn't do a thing about it.

I gave him a cruel smile, feeling like a person holding a rattlesnake behind its head. It didn't matter how he bared his fangs—he couldn't do anything to me, not until I decided to release him.

"You think you saved her? Hardly. You shades think you're so damned smart, so powerful, but the truth is that humans keep winning. We keep putting you in your place, and I don't give a fuck who you think you are, *what* you think you are. You'll end up on your knees like every other one of your kind." Bottomless insanity swam in his eyes, so deep it reminded me of Kit, of that same black hole that could drag a person in.

And it reminded me that no matter what happened, no matter what I went through, I could never let myself turn into that. I couldn't let my own anger consume me.

I released him, letting him collapse to the ground like the trash he was as I took a step backward. While I had more confidence with my powers, I wasn't stupid enough to let him too close. I'd learned my lesson with how much damage a knife could do the hard way.

He fell to his knees, bracing himself forward as he coughed. It seemed I might have pressed a bit hard on his chest.

No guilt assailed me at that. It seemed I'd changed quite a bit.

He lifted his gaze to mine, his lips curling into a cruel smirk just as the sound of gravel crunching behind me made me realize I might have made a mistake.

Sure enough, when I twisted, I found another group of men, this time a few in police uniforms.

The first man let out a rough, confident laugh. "You think I'm on my own? I'm not the only one who knows how the world really works."

I twisted, finding myself just as trapped as the girl had been. *It doesn't seem like I helped things that much.*

The flimsy wall of the abandoned building beside the men caught my attention, and I recalled the way I'd dealt with the soldier on the bridge.

I kept the girl behind me, away from the eyes of the advancing men. I pushed her down, to press her into the space behind a dumpster, the small, protected area that should keep her safe from any falling debris.

As soon as she was there, I met the gaze of the men before me, feeling like even if I was outside of Larkwood, I faced the same problems, the same violence. It had been so easy to think that Larkwood was this terrible island, that the hatred existed only inside those walls, but this reminded me that the same danger existed everywhere, that I couldn't escape it, that hoping it would all go away once I had escaped was foolish.

I took a deep breath, wishing I had a better idea, a plan I felt confident would let me return to Knox, Brax and Wade, but I was where I was. None of them would blame me for valuing a kid's life over my own.

Well, maybe they would, but that's fine. I'm not sorry about it.

I listened for the sounds others couldn't hear, the scurrying of rats in the abandoned building, of traffic, of voices blocks over. The building was empty — *perfect.* I took all those sounds and lifted my hands, yanking them toward me.

The men twisted their heads toward the abandoned building, but they were far too late. The deafening crack as the wall gave way, as the sounds caused it to topple toward us, said they had nothing they could do to stop it.

The man who had spoken, the one who had chased the girl, turned his eyes to mine.

And me? I grinned. I flashed him my best smile, wanting him to *know* that I'd done this, that while he'd looked down on me, while he'd thought me incapable and pointless, I'd ended him.

No, more than that, I'd sacrificed myself to save a child *from* him. His death wasn't some brave stand but embarrassingly incidental.

The wall collapsed, somehow managing to move slowly as I watched it tip, bricks falling away from the rest to come flying down first.

I didn't close my eyes. I'd learned in Larkwood that closing my eyes and pretending the world was different from how it really was didn't do a damned thing. Monsters would still take a bite whether or not I looked them in the eye, so I'd rather go while staring them down.

The men tried to scatter, but I didn't move. I readied myself for that crushing sensation, hoping it took me out fast enough not to suffer. Sometimes that was all a person could hope for.

Except, that didn't happen. Something struck me, but not *nearly* as hard as it should have. It knocked me to the ground, and the crashing of the wall reached a thundering pitch.

To my side, I found the girl on her knees, her hands raised, a shimmering barrier between us and the falling debris. The barrier wasn't perfect, and dust covered me, smaller pieces still falling through and striking me, as if her powers kept the brunt from hitting me but couldn't resist all the force.

The world clouded over, and my eyelids became far too heavy. Before I knew it, unconsciousness took me, and I collapsed into the darkness.

* * * *

Deacon

I'd had years working at Larkwood, years of meeting with and talking to the Warden without caring. I didn't like her, but I never figured I needed to.

Why was it that now, every word from her lips forced me to grapple with my temper?

Because of Hera. I snorted softly at the obvious answer. I'd seen firsthand the suffering the Warden caused, had watched her target someone more important to me than anything else in my life, so of course I struggled with my anger.

And the presence of Kit beside me said she didn't plan a random, friendly conversation.

Not that I expected such a thing from the Warden.

"Good work bringing order back to Larkwood so quickly," she said, somehow managing to appear just as calm and collected as she had before, as if she hadn't lost control of the entire place a week ago.

Thankfully, Kit responded so I didn't have to. "It was necessary to prevent any further loss of life."

Which was true—I'd told myself that as I'd helped to put down fights, as I'd worked to calm tempers and regain control. I'd reassured myself about the greater good as I'd locked down the more rebellious shades who hadn't wanted the riot to end. I didn't do it because I wanted the shades beneath the Warden's thumb, but because with the reinforcements the Warden had brought in, if I didn't help to bring order, they'd do it by destroying each and every shade who even looked at a guard wrong. A riot emboldened the imprisoned and made those in power quick to anger and retribution.

Kit, no doubt, felt the same. Our actions had saved many shades, had protected ones who would have otherwise been slaughtered, even if everyone at Larkwood saw us as the enemy over it. That was a place both Kit and I should be used to by now.

"This is what I like about you two. You help to bridge the gap between people and shades."

Her use of *people* rather than *human* chafed, as if shades were animals unworthy of basic consideration.

Still, I kept my face carefully blank.

"You're both pragmatic enough to understand how the world works, to accept both your place and that of others. I appreciate that in a person, which is why I have given you both a lot of leeway. I will admit, I was worried when the riot broke out where your allegiances would rest."

Neither of us spoke, just waiting. The Warden had never cared for back-and-forth conversations anyway, so I doubted she wanted a response.

"I'm aware that you both spent time with Hera, more than what is normally appropriate. When she somehow managed this little rebellion of hers, I wondered which side you two would come out on. I'm not usually unsure about a person's allegiances, since predicting the behavior of others is one of the reasons I've managed to achieve as much success as I have. However, it seems she left you behind. Perhaps she realized neither of you would betray Larkwood or your own best interests, so decided you served her no further good? The fact remains that neither of you took part in the riot, that you both worked toward restoring order when it was over. For that reason, I have a task for you."

Tension shot through me at that. The Warden didn't hand out tasks from the goodness of her heart. When she wanted something, it was never anything good.

"What task?" Kit asked, his words slow but devoid of feelings.

"I need you to return the four of them to Larkwood."

"Why us?" I asked. "You've got more than enough regular guards to do it, especially with the reinforcements you called in. Kit never leaves Larkwood, and I don't do it that often. What good would we do?"

The reality was that I didn't want to be the one to drag her back. Someone would—they'd find her and bring her and the others back here—but I couldn't bring myself to be that man.

She'd never forgive me, never look at me with that soft sweetness again. Even if a part of me wanted the job just to protect her, to make sure she made it back safely, I couldn't have her look at me like that.

The Warden smiled, a coldness there that made my skin crawl. "Kit can find her, right?"

Kit didn't answer outright, staring back without speaking.

"You bound her to you, did you not? That was why she was conscious during the last Medical trip. It also means you can find her, doesn't it?"

Still, Kit didn't respond. What the hell was that about? Why didn't he deny it? Normally, Kit played the game well, managed to convince the Warden of whatever he wanted, but right now, he said nothing.

"There's no reason to deny it," the Warden said. "I know the truth already. That's why you'll go, why you'll venture out and bring her back, because she's yours."

"If she is sent right back to one of your pet projects in the North Tower, how would that benefit me at all?" Kit asked, a bitterness to the question.

The Warden leaned in, placing her forearms on her desk. "What if she didn't have to? I'm not convinced she could be useful there given your bond with her. What if I gave her to you? I'm quite certain you could keep her under control if you needed to." She turned her gaze to mine. "And for you? After she made a fool of you, don't you want a little payback? Dragging her back to where she belongs would go a long way toward soothing those wounds, wouldn't it?"

I clenched my hands on top of my thighs to keep myself silent. This woman understood *nothing*. Even if I hated Hera, even if I still believed that she had betrayed me, I couldn't imagine willingly hurting her like that.

"I'll do it," Kit answered before I could say a word. I whipped my head in his direction, hardly able to understand his words.

"I thought you would," the Warden said, her tone saying she'd expected this outcome all along. "You are my favorite dog, you know? I've been here for thirty years and since we came to our understanding there at the start, you've never failed me." Her gaze moved to me. "But if he wavers, do not hesitate to put him down."

I swallowed hard, then nodded. There wasn't another answer to give to an order like that.

Which meant, for whatever reason I couldn't understand, we were going to go find the woman who had left us both.

Chapter Three

Hera

I clutched my head as I woke, air escaping my lips in as close to a whimper as I could manage. I remembered everything that had happened instantly — the young girl, the men, the falling building.

And that girl saving me.

I squinted after opening my eyes, the light far too bright.

And in front of me I found the face of that young girl, her blue eyes still amazingly bright, only inches from mine, so close I jerked backward.

She did the same, scurrying away as if *I'd* been the one acting oddly.

"Are you bothering our guest, Soshi?" came a bright male voice.

The girl shook her head. "She just woke up."

I rolled over to find the man who spoke there, and without thinking, I put myself between him and the girl.

The man paused and tilted his head, as if I were someone he couldn't quite understand. After a moment, he chuckled. "As vicious as you might look, you can give it a rest. I wouldn't harm Soshi—she's part of our little group here."

At his words, I frowned and looked more closely at him. He appeared to be in his thirties with black hair that was short but curly enough to appear messy. His eyes were a dull blue, so light they appeared gray. He wore a pair of slacks and a button-up shirt, rolled up to the forearms. He had an easy air, somewhat like Wade, but I'd learned that lesson before. Underestimating someone was stupid when based on how they looked. If I hadn't learned it the first time, Lilianna sure had driven the point home.

Kit's daughter looked young and innocent, but that was far from the truth about the wendigo who had the same terrifying powers as her father.

It meant, despite his outward appearance, I wasn't about to blindly trust him.

He sighed, as though my reluctance annoyed him.

"My name is Bowen. That makes us friends, doesn't it? A name is rather important, so me giving mine is a gift to build bridges. You helping Soshi is the reason I healed you."

Healed me?

He nodded. "While Soshi is learning shields, she still has a ways to go before she's fully capable. It means you took some damage, and I went ahead and took care of it for you."

I froze when I realized I hadn't moved my hands. How did he know what I was thinking?

Bowen chuckled and sat beside me on the edge of bed, ignoring any idea of personal space. "You really are new. Despite what Soshi said about your skills, you don't have a clue what I am, do you?"

I shook my head.

"I'm a brownie. No, not a girl scout, though I'm not opposed to putting on a uniform if the mood is right." He winked, though I sensed no actual lust behind the statement. Rather, it seemed more his general personality. "A brownie is a house spirit. We're bound to those who live with us. In order to take care of them, we can read their minds, especially if those thoughts are about things they want or need. We can also heal and create shields."

I'd heard of no such shade.

"We aren't the sort of things found in Level 1."

At that, I grasped at my wrist, the reminder of what they could have found on me when unconscious. I knew better than to trust anyone, especially when they could buy themselves a lot of favors by turning me in.

Except, I found my wrist bare. It astounded me that I hadn't realized how much that metal band had become a part of me. I'd had it on me for nearly a year.

"Popped it off you," Bowen explained. "Not hard to do with the right know-how. Figured you'd have an easier time of things without it."

I glanced at his wrist to find he wore a band still. If he could remove them, then why?

"We don't remove them from Level 3 or 4 shades who are out free. They make us targets, but if someone gets picked up and the authorities realize they took off their band—let's just say the consequences are a lot worse. You, though, you'll be screwed if you're picked up either way."

I made the sign for thank you, then frowned as I realized he wouldn't understand. Except, he'd healed me, right?

I frantically pointed at my throat, a question in my eyes. Could he fix that? If his skills went beyond just regular medical procedures, maybe he could give me my voice back.

Bowen's smile dimmed, turning oddly kind. "No, I'm sorry. The damage is too great, and you've healed too much. I can't do anything about that. I can only speed the natural healing processes, aiding a bit in what it can do on its own." The sorrow in his voice surprised me, as if he really was sorry that he couldn't do more.

So I shrugged, since it wasn't his fault. I hadn't even thought something like him could help, so I hadn't had long to get my hopes up.

Soshi moved from behind me. "What is she?"

Bowen grinned at the girl, a sweet familiarity between the two. "A siren. They control sounds, can hear things others can't and bend those sounds to their will. Rumor has it they can hypnotize others with their voice and even kill with just a song."

"Why doesn't she talk, then?"

Ouch. I reminded myself that children had no understanding of things that should and should not be said.

"Some monster maimed her. See the scar at her throat? She had her vocal cords cut. Judging from the jagged scar, I'd guess it wasn't done as a medical procedure, though the scarring says she received help in the healing process."

I nodded, to tell him he was right.

"Could we have helped her if we found her sooner?" Soshi asked.

"Perhaps. We can help the body heal, but some wounds are beyond even our powers."

Our. I peered at Soshi.

Bowen chuckled. "Yes, Soshi is a brownie as well. She's still young and untrained, but I suspect that given a few years, she'll easily surpass me."

"I will!" Soshi said, pulling her shoulders back. "I'm going to become a great brownie and help so many shades. You'll see!"

I couldn't stop my smile at her attitude, at the spunk she showed. It was so much better than when she'd cowered before. I much preferred her like this.

"I'm sure you will. Why don't you go make sure everyone has food?"

Soshi puffed her chest out at the important task before taking off, leaving Bowen and I alone.

"So, you're behind the upheaval from Larkwood?" He stared at me with a bit less friendliness than he'd had with Soshi in the room. It wasn't outright hostility, but more caution at least.

I swallowed hard, wanting to deny it, but what was the point there? He'd seen my wristband—it wasn't hard to make the leap that right after an escape happens, when a shade shows up with that wristband, they might have been involved.

So I nodded.

"Interesting that I haven't seen your face on the news. Then again, I did hear some rumors about a search for a siren—I guess that means you, huh?"

I shrugged, my way of saying, "So it seems."

"Normally I wouldn't touch you with a ten-foot pole. Staying alive for Level 4s has to do with flying under the radar. I don't want or need the problems of harboring someone like you that Larkwood would bring down on us."

I reached for my writing pad, only to find myself not wearing what I'd been in. Did that mean Bowen had changed me?

My cheeks heated at the thought, especially because I wore a sundress, something feminine and totally different than how I'd lived my last year.

He waved me off. "Feel free to use sign language. I won't understand it, but it might help to visualize your thoughts more clearly so I can understand them. As long as you're here, you're considered one of those under my care. Oh, and don't worry, I didn't do anything while you were unconscious."

"Then why did you change my clothes?"

"Because they were filthy? Plus, I need access to a wound to heal it, and you had scrapes and bruises all over you. You even managed a broken femur. Lucky for you, I'm a damned good brownie, and I patched you right up."

That made me jump to my feet as it reminded me of something important I'd somehow forgotten.

Brax, Knox and Wade would be beside themselves with worry, and they were the types to cause problems when worried.

"How long have I been out?"

"Six hours or so."

Yep, they'll be pissed.

"Don't worry, I already sent someone to find your friends."

"How do you know about them?"

Bowen let out a hearty laugh. "You know, you keep winning me over when you get all protective like that. You were trying to talk in your sleep and that was enough for me to pick up your thoughts. I sent someone to the shop you were staying at to bring them here. I expect them to show up in the next hour or so. We're a bit out of town, here."

I frowned as I considered something else. *"Soshi is tiny. How could she even move me?"*

"We never send her out alone. I was just around the corner in one of the shops." He paused, his eyes clouding over, the first real spark of anger I saw there. "I should have kept a closer eye on her, but she wanted to check out the park, and I sometimes spoil her because I want her to have a normal life."

I understood that feeling, the desire to have or give what wasn't possible, and the anger when it didn't work.

He turned an empty smile on me, the sort that said he was used to smiling even when he didn't feel like it. "So when I found her, and she told me what you'd done, well, I went ahead and brought you back here. Call it a moment of stupidity, due to my gratitude. If you hadn't been there, Soshi would have been hurt— maybe even killed—and it would have been all my fault. So I figured I owed you this much."

"Thank you." While I didn't trust him, not by a long shot, I sure as hell was willing to admit that he'd saved me.

"Just don't make me regret it, okay? My place in life is to protect those around me, those who reside with me. I'll do whatever it takes to do that. So if you endanger us, I'll make a formidable enemy."

And I couldn't help a shudder that ran through me at his not-at-all subtle threat. When hearing the name brownie, or the idea of a house spirit, I'd expected someone who cooked and cleaned and cared for the residents of the house.

I sure hadn't expected the violence of his threat, but I couldn't deny that was exactly what it was. In fact, he even made me believe he could follow through on it.

So I nodded in agreement. I wanted to get out of there, wanted to take my men and get to freedom, to

live a happy, quiet life together. I wanted to put Lakewood and all that pain behind us all.

I wouldn't tangle with an angry house spirit and risk messing that up.

* * * *

Kit

Deacon hadn't spoken a word since we'd left Larkwood. He drove—I'd never learned how, since I'd gone to Larkwood before cars were around.

He didn't need to speak for me to know exactly what he thought. It reminded me of our last exchange, when I'd told him to think, to stop and use his brain to figure out what Hera had been doing.

Of course, now we were here, heading off to go find her. It was strange how my entire life had somehow wrapped around that girl.

"Direction?" Deacon asked as he pulled up to a stop sign.

I closed my eyes, feeling the ends of that bond, the one that led to Hera. I pointed to the left. "North Eastern."

"How far?"

"No idea. The bond doesn't tell me that."

Deacon's knuckles went white as he gripped the steering wheel, a sure sign he didn't much care for me, or the bond, or probably a million other things. Deacon wasn't the sort of man who needed much of a specific reason for his anger.

He was a lot like Brax in that way. It confused me, made me wonder what it would feel like to experience life in that way. Perhaps that was what Hera needed, why she ended up with men so full of passion. From

Brax and Deacon, both run by anger, to Knox who let self-hatred and lust control him, to Wade who used humor to rule his life. If that was what she wanted, what she desired in mates, why would she spend time with me?

I had brief moments of emotion, like when I'd seen her through the bond after the escape, when the need to touch her and have her had overridden all the calm I usually lived with, but that was it. Otherwise, the world always seemed distant, like something I observed but didn't belong to.

"Would you like to simply come out and say whatever it is you want to say, or would you prefer to wait until after you break the steering wheel?"

Deacon pressed his lips into a tight line, then yanked the wheel to the side and slammed the breaks, skidding the car off the road and onto the shoulder. Dust kicked up around us as the car shuddered to a hard stop.

Deacon turned toward me, and I wondered if I'd get another punch from him. He might have been the only person I'd allow to hit me *twice*.

He didn't, though. Instead, he stared me down. "I thought you cared about her."

"What?"

"*Hera,*" he growled out, as if the answer were obvious. "I thought you gave a damn about her! It's why I ignored you two, why I asked you to help her, why I accepted the idea of your fucking bond with her, and now you'll break her heart like this?"

"Like what?"

"You'd drag her back? She did the *one* thing she wanted, the thing neither of us thought possible—she got out of Larkwood. How can you tolerate the idea of stealing that from her? What? You think she'll just go along with it? That she'll happily play the part of the little woman for you when you get back?" Deacon bared his teeth as he spoke, his purple eyes brighter than usual. Metas really were troublesome, weren't they?

"No, I don't expect that."

"Then what? You'll rip away her free will? Turn her into just a shadow of herself? Just a puppet for you to play with?"

Him even asking nearly caused a rush of anger from me. Perhaps it was less anger at him and more fury at the idea that it had nearly happened, that my own daughter had almost destroyed the woman I loved.

Still, I kept that to myself. I hadn't quite come to terms with the fact that Lilianna was a wendigo, that she was at Larkwood. I didn't doubt the information at all—a part of me suspected I'd known already, that I'd just refused to let myself believe it. I just didn't know how to handle it. I couldn't break her out, not yet. I wouldn't leave her there forever, either. Hera was in the most immediate danger, though, and I could do something about that.

That was a benefit of living a long life—I had time to think about things, to develop plans. I didn't have to rush into things with Lilianna. She was far too vital to the Warden's plans for her to do anything to my daughter, which would keep her safe, at least for the moment.

Deacon made a rough sound, full of annoyance, and I realized I'd let myself become so lost in thought that I'd failed to answer his question.

So I shook my head. "No. Believe what you'd like of me, I'm not about to steal Hera's free will."

"So what *are* you doing going after her?"

Deacon might be connected to Hera, might even love her, but that didn't mean I planned to divulge my personal feelings to him. "That is my business," I said, leaving no room for argument or ambiguity.

Deacon didn't wilt at my sharp words. "I know you might be at the top of the food chain, but make no mistake, I'll do whatever it takes to take you down if you threaten her."

I offered him a chilling grin. "I'd expect nothing else. In fact, if you weren't willing to do that, you wouldn't be worthy of our troublesome siren, and I might just turn you to dust right here."

Deacon snorted and put the car back into drive. "At least we agree on something, huh?"

This was going to be a *very* long road trip.

Chapter Four

Hera

Seeing so many shades together outside of Larkwood felt odd. I'd grown up with an intense fear of shades, with the voices of my parents and everyone else around me warning me just how dangerous they were.

Seeing them together would have sent me screaming.

While I didn't bolt, my unease said that, despite my year as a shade, I hadn't quite shaken that fear.

None of the shades who wore identification bands were high level, telling me they hadn't escaped from any academy. Instead, they either were Level 3 or 4 or wore no band at all.

They all lived inside what looked like an old, rundown church, and as I went through it, I found all sorts of rooms.

Where I'd woken seemed to be an infirmary, and beside that, a school room, a kitchen, a living area, and in what seemed to be an old classroom area, with lots of smaller rooms, the living quarters. I didn't walk into those, of course.

In an odd way, it reminded me of Larkwood. Well, not exactly. The general threat of Larkwood, the intense unease, that wasn't here. These people lived together out of necessity as well, but their daily lives were their own.

Though, at the same time, they lacked many of the amenities. Windows had boards over them and the floors were aged and rough. Everyone wore clothing that had seen better days and there were far more people than space. In short? They might have some level of freedom, but they had little else.

And yet these were likely some of the luckier shades in the world.

The reality caused an ache in my chest that refused to go away.

The main space was the auditorium, and many shades sat in groups there. The pews had been removed, and instead some tables and folding chairs filled the room. Even then, many of the shades simply sat on the floor. Across the large room, Soshi carried a small bowl of food to an elderly man who didn't seem able to rise himself. It made me wonder why Soshi was here instead of with her family.

"Her mother kicked her out," Bowen said, his voice catching me off guard. He appeared out of nowhere too easily.

"But she's so young..."

"The government likes to say it's rare for shades to turn so early, and it isn't as common, but it happens, especially with certain types. Brownies tend to change earlier. Soshi was seven when it happened. Her mother called the authorities who came and picked her up, tested and categorized her, and when they released her? Her mother refused to let her come back. About a year ago I found this tiny thing eating out of a trash can and couldn't just leave her be. She was eight at the time."

That burned, made me rub at that same ache in the center of my chest. The idea of Wade growing up inside Larkwood had been bad enough, but I hadn't considered much about the life outside of an academy, either.

Low-level shades weren't always kept at academies, yet they were often too young to work or unhireable due to that band on their wrists. The government stripped them of every ability to take care of themselves, stole everything from them, then threw them out to survive or perish on their own. Worse, they pointed to the inevitable disasters and crimes as proof that shades needed regulation rather than proof that the current system didn't work.

"You didn't have that sort of experience, did you?"

I shook my head, my hands moving as I answered. *"I was nineteen when I changed, getting ready to leave for college. Some men attacked me, and I guess that spurred my change. They sent me to Larkwood."*

"You don't look much older, so you couldn't have been there long."

"About a year."

"It only took a year to plan an escape from Larkwood? That's impressive."

Was it? As I looked out over the room, at little Soshi running errands for shades, after being kicked out of her home, I wondered if it was impressive at all. Larkwood was horrible, but was this world really any better? We were trapped everywhere, imprisoned by our genes, by what we were, viewed by the world as monsters who didn't deserve to exist.

Whether in Lakewood or out here, was it all that different?

Again, I wondered about a future, about what exactly I was running toward if *this* was the world I had to look forward to...

A sound from behind me made me turn, especially because I recognized a gruff, growling voice. "If anything had happened to her, you won't live through the day."

Ah, good ol' Brax, threatening people wherever he goes.

Sure enough, Brax stalked into the large auditorium area, his hand wrapped around the arm of a young man who couldn't be older than seventeen. Funny that he wasn't much younger than me, yet I saw him as a kid. His eyes were wide and he didn't struggle at all.

Bowen let out a sigh as though reminded that we were all far too much trouble. "So you have a berserker with you?" He narrowed his eyes as he peered past Brax. "Along with an incubus and a void? I suppose you broke out of Larkwood Level 1, why did I not expect companions such as these? It isn't as if they house the cute and innocent shades there."

Despite the slight annoyance in his voice, he didn't seem afraid.

Which was more terrifying than it should have been.

And judging from the way Wade had removed his gloves, I suspected the men had all anticipated the risk of a fight.

Brax swung his gaze around the room with the intensity of a man prepared to deal with any threat in the room.

At least until he stopped when he saw me.

I smiled and waved, which in terms of appropriateness might have been a strange reaction. I just wanted him to understand that no one had harmed me, that we had no reason to worry.

Bowen strolled toward Brax, Knox and Wade, showing no fear of them despite the very real danger the three posed. "Could you please release Thomas, there?"

The sharp edges of his face showed he walked that edge of control. "I'd rather keep my leverage until I'm sure Hera's fine."

Bowen gestured toward me as if to ask, '*Do your eyes even work?*' "As you can see, she's fine. I'm sure Thomas told you that as well. She was hurt saving one of ours, so I brought her here and healed her, then sent for you all. Consider it a gesture of goodwill to repay hers. Bloodshed now would be unfortunate and a waste of my work to save her."

Knox pushed past Brax and approached me. He grasped my chin, tipping my head up, a hunger in his green eyes that shook me to my core. Not only he stared back at me, but his incubus, too. His gaze traced my face, my body, studying me as if gauging whether Bowen spoke the truth or not. The tension in the air was choking, violence simmering just beneath the surface, and not just from the three who had come for me.

The other shades, the ones who had been run down earlier, all seemed to ready themselves for a potential fight.

"You okay, songbird?" Knox asked, his voice quiet despite the harshness.

I nodded.

"Is what he said true?"

Again, I nodded.

He let out a slow breath before leaning in and brushing his lips to mine in a gentle kiss. When he pulled back, the tension broke, as if that was what it took for everything to relax, for everyone to take a step backward and breathe.

Brax released Thomas, who stumbled over to Bowen's side. Bowen didn't examine him the way Knox had with me—and I didn't mean in that possessive, sexual way. Rather, it seemed it only took a glance from Bowen to recognize that Thomas had no injuries.

That was probably due to his being a brownie.

"Now that we've all almost killed each other," Bowen said, "why don't we sit and eat? Nothing like testosterone-fueled near-misses to spur the appetite."

Wade turned his gaze from Bowen to me, then broke into a grin. "I think I like him."

Which was the last thing we needed. One smart-ass was *more* than enough for our little group.

* * * *

Wade

Sitting beside Soshi made my stomach tight in an altogether uncomfortable way.

It took me back to when I'd been a kid, to when I'd been uncertain and afraid and alone. Changing into a shade was scary no matter what, but it was far worse when a person had so much growing left to do. I never got the chance to learn who I was before finding out even that wasn't solid.

I saw that same feeling of disconnect in the young girl who stitched a patch to the ripped knee of a pair of pants. They were too large for her, which told me she did the work for someone else.

"You keep looking at me," Soshi said, not lifting her gaze from her work. "If you even *think* anything weird, Bowen will kill you."

I fought the urge to recoil from her suggestion, and worse, from the reality that a girl of her age would even *know* about that sort of thing let alone seriously consider it.

Acting offended would only make the situation more awkward, though, so I went with what I knew best—humor. "Sorry, but young and scrawny isn't my type. Besides, pretty sure she'd kill us both." I gestured toward where Hera sat with Bowen and Brax.

Soshi furrowed her eyebrows, the look strangely adorable on her young face. "She saved me."

"She does that. Want to know a secret?" I lowered my voice as if admitting something forbidden. "She saved me too."

"Really?" Soshi's eyes widened. Then again, people tended to see voids as boogeymen. Being able to steal power from others was an understandably terrifying skill.

I nodded, giving her my most solemn expression. "That's right. It was when we were escaping. We ran into a bunch of people who wanted to stop us, and Hera had to make a path for us."

"She doesn't even know me, though. She had no reason to help me."

"It sounds like Bowen didn't know you at first either, but he helped you."

"Yeah, but Bowen is a brownie. He's made to want to protect people."

I shrugged before taking the next piece of clothing from Soshi's pile and going to work sewing the ripped seam. I wasn't the best seamstress, but mending clothing was a useful skill in Larkwood, where getting replacements could prove challenging. "I think everyone wants to protect people."

Soshi shook her head, the certainty there breaking my heart. "Trust me, they don't."

I focused on the needle as I spoke, letting our easy motions distract us both. "They do, it's just that sometimes they're wrong about what protect means, or what they want to protect. Think about animals. A wolf will kill a rabbit, but they're doing it to protect their cubs by feeding them."

She pressed her lips together as if considering my words. "So people target us because they want to protect their families? But I'm not going to hurt them."

"We know that, but they don't. They think we're a threat to them, to their way of life, to their friends and family."

"And that just makes it okay?" A tremble in her hands made her task more difficult, but she seemed determined to not let it stop her, to not even acknowledge it.

"Not a chance," I assured her. "But sometimes it helps me to remember that because it gives me hope that there's still a good future out there. If we can convince them we aren't so bad, that they don't have to fear us, well, there might be a better tomorrow, then."

She shifted her hand, that shaking causing her to stick the needle into her finger. She hissed and brought the bleeding wound to her lips, a grimace there and a shine to her blue eyes that said she held back tears.

Bowen appeared in front of us so quickly I hadn't realized he'd even moved before he dropped to one knee in front of Soshi. He took her hand in his, a reminder of how much larger he was than her. "You need to be more careful," he gently scolded her as he peered at the welling drop of blood. "I won't always be here, you know."

That made her bottom lip tremble just as Bowen blew a breath across the wound, the skin knitting back together before my eyes.

As soon as her finger healed, Soshi tore her hand away and bolted, a glimpse of those tears she'd held back running down her face before she disappeared through the door.

Bowen sighed, still on his knee. "She doesn't like the idea of me not being here."

"She's already lost a lot," I guessed. "I don't think she can stand the idea of losing anyone else."

"Maybe," Bowen agreed, "but she doesn't have the luxury of pretending about life."

"Is it pretending? I'm pretty sure she knows exactly what could happen. She's just not willing to let it cause her pain now because later, when it does happen, it'll hurt enough."

Bowen tilted his head as he stared at me. "You're not as stupid as you look."

"I get that a lot. In reality, it's just that I changed when I was even younger than her. It's different when you're that age. I find the younger they change, the better adjusted they are to this life later, though. Silver lining, huh?"

Bowen rose, brushing off his knees. "Probably true. I doubt it's much of a reassurance to her at this point, but it makes me feel a little better."

"You might be the first person who has ever felt better after talking to me."

Bowen chuckled then nodded toward where Hera, Brax and Knox all sat. "Come and take a seat."

I sighed but forced myself to follow. I'd take sitting and talking to kids over hearing adults argue any day of the week.

Knox

The speed with which Bowen moved forced me to acknowledge him in a new and wholly unwelcomed way. It was easy to think of him as just a house spirit, as something cute and innocent, but each time he did anything, he made it clear that he went far beyond that simplistic description.

He had helped Hera, though. Even if I might have been tempted to remove him — especially because he knew about us and could turn us into Larkwood if he wanted to — him saving her made me begrudgingly allow him to live.

At least for now.

"Not that I'm rushing you, but just how long do you plan to stay?" His words proved he was rushing us.

Which was fine by me. The quicker we could get out of here, the better. While he seemed willing to help us for a short time, I couldn't shake the feeling that he'd turn on us if it served him better.

"Tonight," Brax said. "We'll get out of here before the sun's up. We'll need a few hours to make sure we're ready. Fair?"

Bowen nodded. "Fair enough to me. In fact, I'll offer you a vehicle to make it a quicker process, and we will remove your bands. You can eat, rest for a while then get packed up. I'm thankful to Hera for her help, but I'm sure you can understand why I might not want the sort of scrutiny you all are under to upset our lives here anymore than it needs to."

I nodded, sitting back in the chair that rounded the large table. "Understandable. You've got enough on your plate."

He rose from his seat. "I wish you all the best of the luck, and if I can give you some advice—head north. People are far friendlier to our type in that direction." With that, he nodded and took off.

Brax stood next, the same tension he'd had since we'd arrived wearing on him. "I'm going to take a better look around." No doubt, by that, he meant that he'd find all entrances and exits as well as scoping out all weaknesses and potential strongholds. Brax's berserker side was always on alert for danger, always expecting a fight, which meant when somewhere unfamiliar—especially when surrounded by people he didn't know or trust—he'd find himself eased by making preparations.

There just wasn't any getting around that.

After he left, Wade peered slowly between Hera and I, then muttered out a half-assed excuse about needing to count cactus spines before he went as well.

Which left Hera and I alone in the room, the first time we'd been alone in what felt like years.

And that gnawing hunger inside me roused at her closeness. It had grown since before the escape, since Wade had put that side of me asleep and I'd lost myself in Hera's warmth.

"You're hungry, aren't you?" she signed.

I swallowed down my immediate reaction of telling her no. I didn't care for discussing this, but I disliked the idea of lying to her even more. So I nodded, admitting the ugly truth to her.

She sighed, her shoulders dropping. It didn't take any powers to know exactly what went through her head. She wanted to help me, to let me feed from her, but the thought terrified me.

However, even I couldn't deny the urge strengthening. It wasn't *just* directionless hunger, either. It was as if the idea of feeding from her specifically interested me. My incubus had started to take note of her, had started to crave her. Maybe because I'd denied it, because I'd kept it away from her, it craved her more?

"I can't," I said softly.

She let out a long sigh, then dropped her gaze to the table. The longing on her face drew me closer, made me want to wipe it away, to give her whatever she wanted just to see that smile of hers again.

Or, perhaps that was just a way to make my actions feel altruistic, to make my desires into something about her rather than about what I wanted. I cupped the back of her neck and pulled her in, kissing her soft, warm lips as deeply as I dared.

She tangled her fingers into my shirt, using the grip to draw me closer. I knew her aggressiveness was a sign of her own desire, of the moment catching her in the same current that held me.

So I gave in, at least a little. I tilted my head, sliding my tongue along the seam of her lips until she parted for me, until she let me in. When she did, I forced her neck to arch, so I could take her as deeply as I wanted, my thumb on her jaw to hold her still. She tasted of passion and music, like some symphony I could listen to all night and never tire of.

Every touch made me crave more, though. It pushed me closer and closer to the edge of my control, to the place where I feared my ability to pull back.

At least until my incubus surged forward, until my aggressiveness made me yank away. Was I changing? Becoming what she wanted? That had to be why I wanted her this badly, why I felt so out of control, why I wanted to lie her down and mark every last inch of her.

Hera stared at me, worry on her features. That only made me feel worse, the way she looked at me as if afraid she'd done something wrong, as if an apology perched on her lips that she couldn't utter.

It wasn't her, damn it, but she kept trying to take the blame for it.

I rubbed my hands over my head, frustration coloring each movement. "It's not you," I said, even if I knew she wouldn't believe it. "I just can't do this."

"You can't just starve yourself."

"No, I can't." I didn't sugarcoat it, staring at her, waiting for her to come to terms with the reality.

And when she dropped her gaze again, when the pain raced across her delicate features, I knew she'd figured out my meaning.

I'd have to feed from others. It didn't matter how much I loved her, how much I hated being with anyone else, I couldn't sleep with her unless Wade put my other side to sleep. That meant my incubus would keep starving, and eventually, that would endanger her.

"Why?" she signed, her hands trembling.

I swallowed hard and sat beside her, taking her hand in mine, needing the touch of her skin to give me the bravery to answer. "I change when I'm with someone. You felt it, didn't you? The way I was rougher, more aggressive. I don't want to be anyone else, to turn into something else. I don't want that between us."

I let out a long breath then squeezed her hand tighter. "You matter to me, but I don't have a choice in feeding. I can swear it won't change how I feel about you. It won't have anything to do with what we have."

Even saying that made me want to scream. It was cowardly and felt like slashing at her to make myself feel better.

She met my gaze, and the strength in those hazel eyes of hers made me glad I wasn't facing off against her as an enemy. The girl had shown her backbone more than once, and I was thankful I hadn't been on the receiving end of it. She extracted her hand from mine to sign a response. *"What if that's just who you are? How do you know you don't just feel that way?"*

Her question caught me off guard, but I couldn't accept it. I shook my head. "I always change. I'm not blaming you—you aren't doing anything wrong. You just want what you want and I'm helpless but become that."

She puffed her cheeks out then blew the breath out slowly. *"I don't want anything except what you are, Knox. I'm not in a position to tell you not to be with anyone else. I won't push you or try to force you, but I will say that I'm not asking you to hold back. I know you and I trust you – every part of you, which includes your incubus. I mean, if I can tolerate Brax when he becomes his berserker, and can allow Wade to render me powerless, do you really think your other side is any more terrifying?"*

When she said it like that, I understood her point.

Still, I reached for her, wanting her to understand. "It's *never* been that I'm afraid you'll reject me. I just reject myself. I'm afraid of myself, of being someone other than who I am with you. I've never cared about someone like this, never wanted them just because I wanted them, and I'm sure it makes me a coward, but I don't want any of that to change. It isn't you I'm worried about not being strong enough — it's me."

Just as my hand came to rest over hers, she pulled away, her warmth slipping away. "*You know, it wasn't until I changed into a siren that I realized how afraid I really was before. I thought I was brave, but I wasn't. I avoided everything uncomfortable or scary, and I realize now how much I missed out on. In fact, I never said what I wanted to say. I kept quiet because I didn't want to cause problems, because I was afraid of what might happen if I spoke my mind, and it wasn't until I lost the ability to speak at all that I realized how stupid it was. I hope you can learn to be brave before you figure out that lesson the same way I did.*"

She shook her head and walked out, leaving me alone in the room, her words ringing in my ears.

Even if she was right, I didn't think that I was brave enough to actually follow through.

Chapter Five

Hera

I only had on a sundress, but the warmth of the night still got to me. That was probably due to my time in Larkwood, because I'd grown used to the steady temperature of sixty-eight that they'd kept the academy at.

Of course, maybe it was also a residual unease after my fight with Knox.

No, it wasn't even a fight. A fight implied we'd yelled or tried to come to some common ground. That hadn't happened. Instead, Knox had shut a door in my face and locked it. He'd given me no middle ground, no 'maybe someday' to hold onto.

And I could hardly blame him for it. Boundaries were important, and Knox deserved to set his.

But didn't I deserve to set my own as well? To decide what I could and couldn't accept? The idea of having some half-assed relationship where he hid a huge part of himself from me felt wrong, like a perversion of what I actually wanted.

But we hadn't figured anything out in the past year, so why did I think a magical solution would pop up now that we had escaped?

Or maybe I'd hoped that he'd see me differently, that he'd realize I could handle him, that I was strong enough to be his partner in every way.

Clearly, that hadn't happened.

I'd promised Brax I wouldn't go far, had explained I'd just needed a walk to clear my head before we all piled into a car for days together.

He hadn't liked it but had agreed—probably because he knew I'd go whether he gave me permission or not. He, Knox and Wade were packing the vehicle Bowen had offered to us, getting ready to leave as we'd promised.

The quiet and solitude lifted my mood. Believing that every problem I had would disappear right after leaving Larkwood had been foolish. As it turned out, my life didn't become perfect just because I'd escaped.

A sense behind me made my steps slow. It wasn't a sound, not anything so specific or easily identifiable. Rather, it was the sense of being watched, of having something dangerous and predatory stalking me.

I turned, narrowing my eyes, but I saw nothing in the dimming lights as the sun set.

I chided myself for the paranoia, angry that I'd let myself get fooled by something so stupid.

I tried to shake away that sense before taking another, louder step, as if to assert dominance against whatever false thing my brain had created to frighten me.

Then it happened—I turned again, drawn by another of those senses, only to find the large, shadowed form of a person.

My heart raced at the sudden appearance, my body taking a large step backward from the imposing and frightening presence.

As soon as it happened, they rushed toward me. I snapped and tried to shove a wave of sound toward them, but they ducked to the side, avoiding it.

And without time to send a second blast, with my feet sinking into the damp dirt beneath my feet as I backed away, the person struck me hard.

They took me to the ground, though amazingly despite the large body over me, it didn't hurt. I didn't slam down, didn't strike my head. It seemed as if they'd cushioned me.

After the world settled, when I opened my eyes after the abrupt fall, what I found above me terrified me as much as it reassured me.

Kit.

He was here, outside of Larkwood, but boy, did he *not* look happy. That was what made me snap my fingers again, my hands pinned by his larger form but far from useless. This time, the wave struck him, and because he was so close, he couldn't avoid it. It knocked him off me, sending him flying backward.

When he hit the ground, the motion as graceful as it was frightening, he twisted. As he rose, he took on his wendigo form, his limbs elongating, his fingers tipped with claws that caught the light, his face shimmering until just that flat bone remained, those deep, pitch-black eyes locked on me.

I swallowed hard as I scrambled to my feet, torn between wanting to run to him and wanting to run away. Of course, him having turned made me lean heavily toward the get-the-hell-out-of-here option.

"You left me," Kit said, his voice so deep it seemed bottomless.

My fear had grown too much, my hands shaking and far too focused on readying myself for another defensive move to even consider trying to sign a response.

Kit stretched his hands out then curled them again, the light of the setting sun catching on his claws. He stood tall, the first time I'd seen him not slouching, not making himself smaller to fit inside Larkwood—in so many ways.

In fact, he was stunning with the deep reds and oranges of the setting sun behind him, the trees reaching up around him, making him appear entirely at home. He'd never belonged inside Larkwood, not under shackle and key, not in the unnatural brick and plaster walls.

So often I'd thought of shades as unnatural, but seeing him like this? It was clear that he belonged here, that it was the human world where he didn't fit.

Kit barreled forward again, dodging my next attack even more easily than he had the first, as if without the encumberment of his human body he was even further away from anything I could counter.

He tackled me again, pinning me beneath him until I could do nothing but stare up into those black pits that threatened to pull me under.

"You ran away from me," he said, his voice anything other than the cold emotionless one I was used to.

He came closer, and for a moment, confusion hit me. His face was a skull. Kissing wasn't an option, not like this, so why did his face near mine?

I thought that until his body twisted against me as he turned human again, and his warm, soft lips took mine. He kissed me like he had in the last dream, rough and aggressive, and I melted into it.

It was the first real time we'd touched like this, the first time we'd crossed this line in such a way. The way he kissed me said he'd wanted it, that he was as consumed by the desire as I was.

It shattered the view I'd had of him as someone who had no connection to anything, as entirely disinterested in the world around him. The way he'd viewed himself, as an elder who didn't care about the world, that wasn't the man who kissed me. This man cared greatly, at least about this.

His hands — thankfully human again — traced up my side, over the fabric of my sundress. He cupped my breast, though the touch was odd because he refused to pull away from me in the least. His confidence surprised me the most, given how careful he usually was when he touched me.

And I responded with just as much desire. I wrapped my arms around his shoulders, tugging him closer, writhing against him because I didn't want any space between us. I had feared that I'd never see or touch him again, so I wouldn't hold back now.

He braced himself on one elbow, then reached down, grasping the hem of my dress to pull it up. He let out a feral growl before something sliced through the hip of my underwear. Since he had no weapons that I knew of, I had to assume he'd shifted his fingers to claws. It also screamed the same lack of restraint I'd suspected from the rest of his actions.

And somehow, that aggressive nature infected me as well. I should have been afraid to have so much of him focused on me, to feel the way he lost his control, but even if I was, my want outweighed it by a longshot.

He shifted his hips away from me as he reached between us, brushing the back of his hand against my bare skin for a moment as the sound of his zipper seemed impossibly loud.

He broke the kiss and lifted himself enough to stare down at me. "Tell me yes." The desperate edge to his voice excited me. He could force me, could demand my compliance, but he didn't. Instead, he gave me the choice.

Did I want to go this far? Did I want to cross this last line, to have him like this?

The answer was so simple it almost made me laugh. *Of course* I wanted him.

I wanted his flaws and his strengths — all of it. I wanted that deep coldness inside him, and the loneliness, and the years he'd lived, the power and the fear. I wanted to taste it all, everything that made him into who he was.

So I nodded as I curled my fingers into him, gripping the back of his vest, the dichotomy of his nice outfit and the dirt from where I'd thrown him to the ground, the coldness of his eyes and the heat of his touch, it all drew me deeper into our shared madness.

Strong, agile fingers ran up my drenched slit, the intimate touch making me arch against him.

"Be still," he growled. "I'm on the edge of my control, here. You're *mine*, bound to me, and yet you ran from me. You endangered yourself. Do you have any idea what that does to me? I don't want to hurt you, but I have to have you, and I can't wait long."

He said it like an apology, but he didn't need to apologize to me over that. I was fine with it. I wanted him as much as he wanted me—maybe more. I didn't need nor want slowness or romance. I wanted *him*, the real him.

But I didn't dare pull my hands away to sign that. Instead, I reached across the thread of out connection to push a thought to him as I had before. *I need you, too.*

His eyebrows raised, one of the rare moments of true surprise from him.

He groaned out a sound equal parts frustration and pleasure before he sank two of his thick fingers into my waiting pussy.

And it was so much more than I'd ever thought I'd get from him.

Kit

Hera was impossibly hot. My life had been bathed in coldness, in a never-ending appetite that wanted to consume everything. Nothing but that hunger had existed inside me, yet Hera pushed all that aside.

The snug grip of her cunt drove me mad, made me crave nothing but her. I wanted to burn alive with her.

The way she'd told me she needed me even managed to push aside my hesitancy, my fear of moving too fast, of not doing this right. I could say all day long that Hera deserved romance, that she should have had me take my time, to have her in a place better than the dirt outside like this. I would have wanted to take her in a bed, to strip her slowly and discover and worship every inch of her perfect body. I wanted to show her what she meant to me, that even though I could be cold, even though I struggled to find connection with much or care about much, she mattered to me.

I pulled my fingers out of her. Wetness clung to me, proving she was ready, that she wanted me. I needed her, but not at the expense of causing her pain. I needed her to think back on this positively, to not regret it just because I'd rushed and fumbled and hurt her.

The touch of my own hand to my cock drew another deep groan from me, but it was nothing compared to the sensation when I ran the head along Hera's drenched folds. I allowed myself a brief moment of teasing, of savoring how soft and giving she was against me. I'd wanted this from the first day I'd seen her, when I'd found her cowering after a face-off against Brax, and this desire had shown then.

I hadn't expected it, hadn't even really recognized it at the time, but now, looking back?

It was as if fate had told me it was time to move on, time to rejoin the world, to wake up after slumbering for so long.

And that was miraculous on its own. When little else could have moved me, she had.

So I took one last breath before shifting forward, before sliding into her and reveling in the way her tight heat wrapped around my cock.

She seared me, reaching into those cold spaces inside me and warming them.

It made a mockery of the times we'd touched through our bond, when I'd only felt the spark of electricity instead of her true skin. Now that I could taste her, now that I experienced every wonderful bit of her actual body, I knew before had been just a cheap imitation.

And it snapped all my control — or what little I had. I took her lips in a possessive kiss, as if I could feed directly from her. Instead of consuming everything, I wanted to feast on her, to take her apart and gorge myself on her. The intense desire terrified me.

She roused my hunger, but she sated it as well like some endless cycle. And I gave myself over to the feeling. *As if I could resist.*

I slipped my tongue into the sweetness of her mouth as I pulled my hips back and plunged into her harder. I took her as roughly as I dared, wrapping one of my arms under the small of her back to pull her tightly against me.

Her running from me, her trying to resist the bond between us, it ate away at me. I wanted to prove to both of us that we belonged together, that no matter what, she should have been with me.

I tried with my body to silence the doubt inside us both, to prove to her that she should never run from me again no matter the reasons.

I knew she wasn't running *from* me, but that didn't change the way I wanted to own her.

This tiny part of me, the part that was an elder shade, the part who by its very nature was used to turning people into tools to be used, to stripping away their personality and free will, it wanted to do that to her. It wanted to force her to my side, to make it so she could never leave me again, but I easily resisted.

If I did that, I'd break her. She wouldn't be this woman, wouldn't make me feel the way she did. I craved that smile of hers, the spark of fun she brought to my life by behaving in a way I could neither predict nor understand. She made my life interesting, made it worth experiencing despite the years I'd already lived, the years that had made me grow bored with existing.

So I held her tightly, rewarded by Hera digging her blunt nails into my back. I didn't care that I dirtied my clothing, that I gave in, that I showed a part of myself I had never exposed to another person. My carefully cultivated exterior shattered, the darkness lighting up, the coldness warming until we melted together.

I took her with frantic, deep thrusts, drowning us both in the pleasure. I left no part of her untouched, no part hidden from me.

It didn't last that long, all things considered, but that didn't matter. She broke apart beneath me, her lips parted on a silent scream I could hear in my head through our bond as she clung to me desperately. I doubted I'd ever seen a look like that, that I'd ever experienced something as beautiful as she was lost to sensation.

So I followed her over that edge, diving deep into her and the pleasure right along with her. I spilled into her, biting gently at her bottom lip as I did so, humbled by her offering me something so precious.

I remained over her, having her small, soft body trapped beneath mine, even as I softened and slipped from her tight cunt, reluctant to lose any of this. I broke the kiss enough to stare down at her, to see her hazel eyes even in the darkness — the sun now having fully set.

What shook me more than what we'd just done, then the way that she destroyed the calmness I'd lived so long with, more than how deeply I still craved her, was the trust in those eyes.

I wasn't sure if any other person in my life had ever fully trusted me. I'd have called it stupid before Hera, would have chided her for doing something with so many risks and so few rewards.

Except…wasn't this what had made me fall for her? That she did as she pleased without reservation? She loved with her entire being, she cried with her whole heart and she did so no matter how it might have terrified her.

It was a form of bravery I'd never felt myself, that I'd never experienced or even witnessed.

And maybe that was exactly what had allowed Hera to do what no one else had been able to do. Maybe that was what had let her best Larkwood, and it was what would end up saving her.

The same action both risked her and offered her salvation. Her trust would either kill her or save her.

I could only hope the latter happened.

* * * *

Hera

Talk about awkward... No wonder people had sex just before falling asleep. It removed the uncomfortable moments afterward, when people had to talk about what had happened or stupidly pretend it hadn't happened.

It seemed Kit and I would go with the second option.

"I'm not taking you back," Kit said, his voice low.

At that, I swung my gaze toward him.

He didn't look at me as he matched my pace, walking beside me. "The Warden sent Deacon and I after you, but I wouldn't bring you back. I came because I needed to see you, to be with you, to ensure your safety."

"What about your daughter?"

"We live long lives. Once I'm certain you are safe, I'll go back and get her. For the moment, she is at much less risk than you are." He swallowed hard, then added on, "I thought you would be more relieved that I wasn't going to take you back."

"I never thought you would."

"Then why did you throw me?"

"You charged me," I signed, then added on, *"Sorry,"* at the end.

"Don't be sorry. If anyone—including me—makes you feel unsafe, I'd expect you to do the same thing. If anything, you held back. I've seen what you can do when you want to truly hurt someone."

His words made me shy and uncomfortable in a way that made my heart speed. That was nothing compared to my reaction when he paused and caught my chin, forcing my eyes to his. "You have to protect yourself. It doesn't matter who your enemy is, you need to use all your sills to keep yourself safe. Tell me that you understand."

I nodded. The response wasn't because he'd forced me from any command in his voice. Instead, I agreed because of the honesty in his voice, the way he meant every word of it.

I'd responded to his threat because he'd startled me, because a part of me had worried I'd pushed him too far, but the moment I'd had time to think, I'd never suspected he'd take me back.

Kit leaned in, his lips softer than before, less frantic, as if he'd tamed that side of himself.

"Seems you found our runaway siren." Deacon's voice caught me off guard and I jerked back from Kit's touch.

When I turned to find Deacon there, his face carefully blank, I struggled to meet his gaze. All I could see was his expression when I'd shut the door in his face, when I'd left him behind.

If Kit was angry, it couldn't compare to Deacon, right? Deacon had stood only feet away from me, had begged me to not leave him, and I'd done it anyway.

When he came forward, I flinched, worried about his reaction. I didn't think he'd hurt me, but I couldn't bear to have him hate me. Instead, his strong arms wrapped around me and pulled me against his solid, familiar chest.

The steady thumping of his heartbeat eased me somehow, and I hadn't realized how much I missed it, how much I needed the reassurance. I inhaled, breathing him in, letting his soothing smell wash over and through me.

He didn't kiss me, didn't pull away, just held me tighter as if he needed it as much as I did.

I went to respond, but Deacon only tightened his grip around me, cupping the back of my head with his large hand to keep me against him. "We'll fight later, Hera. Just let me hold you for a minute."

And that sounded fine with me. Despite all the times we'd told each other that, when we'd tried to push off our problems, it had never seemed more important than right now.

I shuddered, relaxing into his embrace, into the fact I had him back, that no matter how long it lasted or where things went, I could touch him again.

A sound caught my attention and made me jerk my head in that direction. Neither Kit nor Deacon moved, but then again, I could hear far better than either of them.

The sound was the firing of a tranquilizer gun, the soft pop different than a regular bullet, and it came from the direction of the church. It would be far too quiet for anyone else to notice.

I shoved away from Deacon's chest, and he let me go. When I took off, the two men followed—no complaints, no hesitation. Even if they couldn't hear, even if they didn't know what was going on, they still trusted me enough to come without question.

Before we reached the church, I found Wade, Brax and Knox at the van, packing their things. The car Bowen had given us was parked about half a mile from the church. They all stood straighter upon seeing Deacon and Kit, but my expression must have made them realize those two were not the cause of my panic.

An angry shout to get down from someone in the church drew everyone's attention, now that we were close enough for them to hear it as well. It was the sort of command we all knew well, the tone of a person used to saying such things, used to others obeying.

Which meant Larkwood had tracked us to the church, and I sure as hell wouldn't leave Bowen and the others to fight them in my place.

Chapter Six

Hera

I burst through the doors of the church, fear gripping me. What if someone had gotten hurt, and I'd let it happen because I hadn't been there? What if one of the children was killed because the Warden wanted me back?

The sight inside the church chilled me. A few shades already lay on the floor unmoving with Bowen standing between them and the people who held the guns.

All the men were humans, but they all wore black clothing but no identifying badges or marks. Of course, that didn't matter—I could easily guess exactly who they were. These weren't local policing forces, not with the tranq guns they carried. They had to work for the Warden.

At least they didn't send Lilianna's toys...

Bowen turned his head toward us, his eyes sharp, proving again he wasn't the weak house spirit it was easy to mistake him for. Instead, he had the expression of a man ready to take on the entire group himself to protect those he cared for.

Except, his gaze moved from me to Kit and Deacon. His mouth flattened. "Normally, I'd toss you all out, but I think I'll make an exception this time."

I peered at Wade, then gestured toward Soshi and the other shades huddling in the corner. Wade was more fragile than the others, and he couldn't do anything against the human soldiers. He would do the most good focusing on getting the more vulnerable shades out of the way. Even if a few of them could help, they were more risk than reward compared to us.

He nodded, rushing over to the cowering people while Knox, Brax, Kit, Deacon and I all placed ourselves between the soldiers and the other shades, beside Bowen.

These men had shown up ready to do serious damage, but they hadn't realized exactly what they'd face. Judging from their gear, I doubted they expected us to be here. They were used to individual shades, to people who would run from conflict, who were so isolated that even when they snapped, they fought alone.

Now they faced shades who were willing and able to fight together.

They had no idea the trouble they'd brought down on themselves.

Brax

Energy ran through me at the violence hanging in the air. There was always this spice at moments like this, when bloodshed was inevitable, and it spoke to my berserker.

I stood to the left of Hera, opening and closing my hands, ready to destroy anything in my way. In this case, it was fifteen human soldiers with their weapons at the ready. They held tranq guns, meaning the Warden wanted us back alive. That was probably all for Hera's benefit. I doubted the Warden gave a fuck about the rest of us.

Of course, that made it all the easier for us. They weren't willing to use lethal force, but I had no problem with it. I wasn't like Knox, wasn't a man who struggled with what I was much. I didn't give a damn about my violent side, about my desire and willingness to kill. It didn't bother me, didn't make me wish I was something else. This part of me had allowed me to keep Knox safe for years, and now I could use it to protect Hera.

And to protect these other shades, to keep safe the ones who couldn't do it themselves. I'd never given a damn about what I was, but now I appreciated how useful it could prove.

"Hera Weston," one of the soldiers said, stepping forward. "Come with us and no one else has to be hurt."

Hera pulled her shoulders back and stood tall. She truly wasn't the same women I'd met that first day when she'd arrived. She'd cowered back then, afraid of the world and of herself. Now, though? She held her head high, willing to face down any threat rather than running away.

It took my focus away for a moment, distracted me by how lucky I was to find a woman like that, to watch her find herself and fight for shades when so many of them had rejected her already.

"So, plan?" Bowen asked in a far too casual tone.

"Kill 'em," I responded, my words rough since my mouth and throat had already started to shift to my other form.

"A fan of the simple, huh?"

"Why go for complicated?" Knox added.

The soldier who had spoken narrowed his eyes when he spotted Deacon. "The Warden won't be happy to hear about this."

"The Warden can go fuck herself," Deacon said, no hint of regret or hesitation in his voice. While I struggled to trust Deacon far, his voice left no doubt about what side he'd picked.

And given he was a meta, something that had no real place, it wasn't a shock he wouldn't stay sided with the humans who continued to use and hate him.

Surprise flickered across the soldier's features, as if he hadn't expected the harsh reaction. But why the fuck hadn't he? Even if I couldn't stand Deacon, it would have taken a fucking blind man to not see how Larkwood treated him, to not notice how the guards and staff looked at and spoke to him. He might have been above the shades there, but they'd made it clear he was far below humans.

It made me realize why he would throw that all away—for Hera.

She was the only person—shade or human—who seemed able to fully accept people, to know who they were and still want them. Fuck knew she'd done it for me, for Knox, for Wade. It wasn't a stretch to think that Kit and Deacon stood beside us for the very same reason.

"Well, if you love the shades so damned much, I'm sure when we drag you back, you can join them. Have you been missing the North Tower? Because you'll be back there soon—just another filthy lab rat."

Deacon held his hands out as if the idea didn't worry him in the least. "You're welcome to give it a shot, but bigger and tougher men than you have tried their luck and lost."

And that reminded me that despite Deacon appearing mostly human, he really wasn't. I'd never seen him go all out, never watched him in a real fight, but it seemed I'd get to witness it now.

Still, I held myself still, unwilling to jump the gun, to rush into it until I was sure we had to. I didn't normally worry much about that, but there we had others who weren't nearly as indestructible as I was.

"Now!" yelled the solider who had spoken, and as a testament to their training, all the soldiers raised their guns at once.

I reached for Hera, ready to push her behind me—a few tranqs weren't much to me, but just one might incapacitate her—but the shots happened before anyone could do anything.

Or so I thought.

The tranqs struck something that wasn't flesh. Instead, they slammed into an invisible shield inches away from us, then fell to the floor. To my side stood Bowen, his eyes bright and burning and locked on the soldiers. He jerked his chin up, and the soldiers flew backward, the barrier he'd erected flying outward.

And that was my cue. I sank into the rage inside me, gave in to all that coursing power, let it wrap around me and fill every last bit of me. The strength and rush of power made me feel like myself again.

Even before the soldiers rose again, I threw myself forward with a roar, but I was far from the only one. Deacon rushed forward, as did Kit. Bowen remained in his place, though his focus said he worked hard. Sure enough, when one soldier came forward, instead of striking Deacon, he hit a wall. It seemed Bowen's defenses worked against them but we could pass through them.

I'd never realized that a brownie could be this useful.

My brain clouded as my body shifted, my thoughts slowing and simplifying until they were locked on nothing but removing the threat.

So I trusted myself and let go.

* * * *

Wade

I got the remaining shades out through the door at the back of the church, then had them hide in an attic space Bowen had set up above the infirmary. I'd have never known about it, but Soshi had taken over and ushered them through.

Despite her age, the girl was tough and capable. I could tell she helped Bowen, that she'd had to grow up quickly and had thrown herself into the role. She grabbed a pack with food and medicine and handed it off to one of the others as they helped one another into the small attic space, moving quickly, suggesting they'd practiced this all before.

The sound of fighting in the other room drew both Soshi's and my attention. What if something happened to Hera? What if she was bleeding out in the other room?

I understood why she'd sent me here, why I needed to help these people, but it didn't mean I liked it. I had so much power, but it was also extremely limited. On my own, against humans, I was no stronger than the others. In fact, I was weaker in many ways, especially because I didn't have a clue how to fight nor had the physique to win by size and strength alone.

So letting the other handle the fight while I escorted the more vulnerable away was the right call, no matter how much I hated feeling sidelined. We didn't need these shades to turn into collateral damage or hostages.

"Up you go," I said cheerfully to Soshi despite the lump in my throat. I needed to get her safe before I could return, before I could check on Hera and see what was going on.

Soshi hadn't looked away from the sound.

I saw her plan a moment before she did it, before she darted past me and back toward the main room.

I reached out, ready to snatch her arm, to force her into the safety that I knew she needed to go to, but she flinched away and my hand encountered an invisible barrier rather than her.

Damn brownie...

She avoided my grasp, darting past me, and it made my choice easy. I peered up and into the frightened faces of the hidden shades. "I'll go get her, so close it up."

They nodded, then pulled the string, which shut the door and pulled up the ladder to the attic space. Once closed, it was nearly impossible to notice, which should keep them safe so long as they remained silent.

I didn't need to see Soshi to know where she'd gone. It was the worry on her face, the matching worry inside me. I understood her actions perfectly because they were what I would have done in her place.

It meant when I arrived back in the large central room, it didn't surprise me to find Soshi there, on the outskirts of the violent skirmish.

And *boy* was it violent.

I'd witnessed a lot in my life, had seen so much bloodshed, so much death, that it rarely bothered me. I didn't even think about it anymore.

Maybe it was because it happened in front of Soshi, but it suddenly took on a more sinister feeling. She was too young to have a front-row seat to such violence, to have to worry about this in her life, and the barbarism I had grown used to took on a new light.

Deacon moved like Brax, both large and hitting hard, though given that Deacon was smaller than Brax's berserker form, he was quicker. Brax swiped his claw-tipped hands, able to knock down enemies without trouble. A spray of blood splattered the wall and left a long, red streak.

Since Deacon lacked the claws and fangs, when he struck a soldier with his fists, the hit was hard and loud. They fought, but Deacon outmatched the soldier with ease.

Kit had transformed into his other form, the tall ceilings of the main room allowing him to stand at his full height. Had I ever seen him like this? I'd seen sketches before, had heard of what a wendigo looked like, but I'd never seen it myself.

I kind of wish I still hadn't.

He was something out of a nightmare, and he moved in a way that was wholly unnatural. It was fluid and ethereal and terrifying. His claws made Brax's seem like dull stubs, and he used them with a practiced motion that suggested he was extremely comfortable with them. In addition, when he cornered someone, those elongated hands of his would turn the body to dust in moments.

Knox didn't move like the others, not by sheer strength. Instead, he slid through the fight with lethal grace. Where the other three men hit hard, clashing, Knox moved with a fluidity that felt more like a dance. HIs green eyes were incredibly bright, and each time he neared anyone, the person stumbled as if distracted by his presence. Then again, it only took one sniff to know the room was bathed in his pheromones.

Incubi were scary in a different way than other shades. They were less obvious, less brawn but more sinister. They hide beneath the veneer of seduction, able to turn people mindless with nothing more than their bodies and a promise of something more. Beneath that, under all that temptation, rested a beast just as willing to kill as anything else.

Knox showed that side of himself then. He didn't need claws or fangs, didn't need brawn. He moved so fast, it was as if he anticipated anyone else's moves. When they swung for him, he bypassed it, almost faster than I could follow. When one charged him, he easily grasped their wrist and rolled over the other's back like some acrobatic feat. It meant that after avoiding a strike, it took little for him to maneuver the enemy into slamming their own face into the wall, by using their momentum against them.

It gave me a good reminder that incubi were nothing to laugh at.

Hera stood behind the rest, her hands moving quickly. She snapped, then directed a blast in one direction or another, focusing on wiping up those who got past the men or the occasional stupid soldier who tried to get in behind one of the others.

Bowen was beside Hera, creating barriers with an ease that said he'd done so many times in the past.

And Soshi stood behind Bowen and Hera, her blue eyes wide. She'd been targeted before—like the time with Hera—but I doubted she'd seen a true fight like *this*. There was as fair difference between how Level 4 shades were treated—especially outside Larkwood—and the sort of response four escaped Level 1s would get. As much as I hated the idea of her feeling fear, it was probably good for her to see exactly how dangerous the world was.

Not that I'd let her get hurt for it.

Before I could reach her, one of the stray soldiers caught sight of her. He probably thought her an easy target, someone he could grab without much work and use as a bargaining chip against the rest of us. It meant he knew deep down that we valued one another, that we weren't just animals out for ourselves as they liked to pretend.

He dove forward, headed for Soshi, but I wouldn't allow that to happen.

I rushed ahead at the same time, not giving a damn about my own lack of skills against him. I'd been that child before, frightened and unsure of what to do, of how to react. I'd survived alone against people who had hated me for no good reason.

I struck the side of the soldier hard, taking us both down just before he reached Soshi. We hit the floor, the linoleum rough from years of use and lack of maintenance. The soldier was far stronger and better trained than I was, and when his elbow struck my cheek, I hissed. It shook me, made it hard to think for a moment, but I still didn't release him. Instead, I struggled for control of his weapon.

My focus remained on the gun, which let him land another hit on me. Because I didn't resist it or protect myself, I got hold of the gun and shoved it aside, skidding it across the floor.

He went for it, but when he rose, something struck him and threw him to the side. His body hit the wall hard, and when he fell, he didn't move. I twisted, finding Hera offering me a smile, a clear sign she'd been responsible for it.

And here I thought I couldn't fall in love with her any more...

I didn't let the help go to waste, though. I scrambled to my feet, ignoring the pain in my cheek, the way my thoughts felt sluggish, to search for Soshi. I found her on the other side of the room, her gaze on Bowen. He hadn't seen her, his attention on the fight, but she hadn't gone unnoticed by the enemies. She seemed like a beacon for them, but then again, they were cowards.

They used weapons to prove how tough they were, willing to inflict any sort of pain they needed to in order to get what they wanted.

Which was Hera and us back in their custody.

I bent low as I crossed the fight, narrowly avoiding when Deacon and another soldier barreled past me, then again dodging Brax—who I'd bet hadn't even recognized me—until I reached Soshi.

"We need to get you out of here," I told her.

She shook her head. "I'm helping. This is *my* home, and these people are my family. I won't just leave them."

"Don't you think Bowen will be in more danger if he has to protect you, too?"

"I don't need him to protect me," she argued, standing her ground.

"Soshi!" Bowen shouted the name, forcing me to look over and see what had alarmed him so. Not only had he realized that Soshi wasn't hiding, as she should have been, but a soldier across the way stood there, his rifle trained on the young girl.

I didn't even think about it—I didn't have to. I threw myself in front of the girl, grabbing her and pulling her against my chest. My skin didn't touch hers, which meant I didn't steal her power, and the noise of the room meant I didn't hear the shot before something stuck me in the back. It wasn't the first time I'd had tranqs used on me, and I damn well recalled that sinking feeling as the drugs took effect. I collapsed to my knees, careful to fall to my side to ensure Soshi could escape my unconscious form and run.

Except, when she pulled back, she didn't leave. Instead, her gaze held the same harshness I'd seen in Bowen. They really were the same, weren't they?

She lifted her hands, and the air around us shimmered. Another tranq headed at us, but it struck the bubble she'd created and fell. She offered me a strained smile, as if to reassure me just before the world disappeared around me.

Hera

I wanted to rush to Wade's side, but we hadn't quite finished yet.

Not that we were far. Despite being outnumbered, the fight wasn't all that dangerous. A tranq in Soshi could have been—she was little, and those dosages were made to take down enraged, adult shades — but Wade had taken the hit for her.

And in return, Soshi stood her ground and threw an impenetrable barrier up between them and the rest of the chaos.

Kit turned to face me, offering a quick nod. We needed to end this now. He called out, his voice taking on that other tone of his, the dark one, "Down!"

Each of the shades dropped to the ground, controlled by his voice alone, leaving only the humans upright.

I took the chance to clap once, then sent that power flying out toward the ones who remained upright. It slammed them against the walls and everything went silent afterward.

Kit, Deacon, Brax, Knox and Bowen rose slowly afterward, the dust heavy in the air from the fight.

Bowen glanced around, then rushed to the barrier that surrounded Soshi and Wade. "Drop it," he ordered her.

Soshi blinked slowly, her uncertain gaze moving to Wade.

The action confused me, but Bowen raised his palm to me to let him handle it. "She's a brownie. She's driven to protect those she takes under her protection, which is him right now." He spoke directly to the girl next. "Look at me, Soshi. That's right. It's me — you know I won't hurt him. I need to check him, though. I'm a better healer than you still, aren't I?"

She swallowed hard, then nodded. Her hands fell, which seemed to sap her remaining energy. She collapsed to her knees, and Bowen crouched beside her. His gaze was hard but careful, and despite not touching her, not checking her closely, I got the feeling he could tell if she was hurt or not. He nodded after a moment and turned his attention to Wade.

From that point on, we all moved. We had left no survivors, not after the violence that had happened. I ignored the way Kit destroyed all the evidence, turning the bodies to ash, and especially the way he seemed healthier each time.

I knew he consumed others, but I hadn't considered what that really meant. It seemed he fed off them when he turned them to ash like that, when he decimated them. Somehow, killing something felt dark, but not nearly as dark as feasting off them. It felt like some strange form of twisted cannibalism.

Yet, I hardly had a reason to feel uncomfortable. Vampires fed from humans and so did Knox.

Still, I turned my gaze from Kit as I checked on the others. Brax chuffed and brushed his forehead to mine before heading outside, no doubt to calm and gain control over himself again. Deacon collected the weapons, but I saw no serious damage to him. Wade was asleep, but Bowen and Soshi watched over him. Knox sat across the large space, on a chair, leaning forward.

I went toward him, but he lifted his head and nailed me with a look I'd never seen on his face before. It made the one when he'd been starving appear downright friendly.

There was nothing of the man I loved there—I looked directly at his incubus, now.

He shook his head once, a harsh jerk that made me go still. Clearly approaching him right now was a bad idea, so I let him be. It was probably similar to Brax, where he had to take a moment to gather himself, and I owed him that much.

So, instead, I went to Bowen to check on Wade.

"Everyone is safe," Bowen said, his voice low as he held his hand over Wade. "A few shades were hit with tranqs, but it could have been far worse. That not happening is thanks to you all."

"They targeted you looking for us. I couldn't just leave you to deal with it."

"Others would have," Bowen answered. "I might have even done it if I were in your position. We aren't your family or your problem. If you'd taken that distraction, you could have snuck out and been a long way off before anyone could have caught you. Are you trying to tell me you weren't tempted?"

I shook my head at the easy answer. *"Not even a little."*

"Why not?" He turned to look at me, his gaze hard as if he couldn't understand me.

"I spent a year at Larkwood, and you know what was constant? The Warden, the guards, the staff, they all wanted to keep us fighting each other. I realize now, looking back at my life before then, that it was the same. People in power tell everyone that shades are vicious, and they put us all against each other. They tell the Level 4s that the Level 1s are dangerous, and they tell the Level 1s that the Level 4s are lucky and privileged and we should hate them. It took me a while to figure it out, and it wasn't until my escape that I really understood — they did that all because they want us focused on each other and not the real problem, not on them. When we work together, they lose that power."

"If I heard that a month ago, I'd have laughed at the idiot espousing such a fantasy. You're not the first person to offer up such a stupid idea." Even though his words were cruel, they didn't come out mean spirited. He tilted his head, staring hard at me. "But you might be the only person I'd actually believe..."

Though, that made me question my own words. I sat there and talked about how I couldn't leave Bowen and Soshi to face the danger alone, but hadn't I already done that? I thought about the shades in Larkwood, the ones still suffering, the ones left to clean up the mess I'd left behind. Why was this church different? Why were *these* shades any different than those I'd abandoned already?

Because you were responsible for these ones being targeted — the ones in Larkwood were just unlucky. You can't be responsible for everyone else in the world. Even as I told myself that, I struggled to understand or believe it.

Before I could say anything else, he went on. "Because you helped us and risked yourselves for us, I'm going to offer something. I like to pay back my debts, after all. Wait here."

I knelt beside Wade, who had his eyes open, though he clearly wasn't all there. I set my hand on his shoulder, trying to reassure him. His lips quirked into a happy grin that lacked any of that cutting edge of wit he usually had. He twisted, his cheek brushing my palm as if he couldn't bear to not touch me.

It took a moment for me to realize what was wrong. I felt no pull, no sinking of my powers. I still heard everything around, still felt that noise of the world. Why wasn't Wade taking my powers as he normally did when we touched? It was strange to feel the warmth of his skin alone, to not have him take my powers at the same time.

Was it the drugs? Perhaps he needed to be fully conscious to do it?

He blinked slowly, his eyes trusting and open as he stared up at me.

"I told you he was fine. Voids shouldn't get involved in fights like that, though."

"He's tough," I argued, as if his words had been some insult against Wade.

"I know exactly how scary voids are, but they don't do much against humans. They're more of a specific weapon against shades."

"His powers aren't working right now. Is that something you did?"

Bowen cocked his head to the side. "He isn't in danger, so why would his powers work right now?"

"His powers work all the time. Anytime he touches someone, he draws their power from them."

The press of Bowen's lips into a tight line said he suddenly understood something he didn't care for. "I knew he was an odd one, but I hadn't realized he was quite that broken."

I frowned but said nothing, unsure how to respond.

"Voids use their powers like any other shade. It isn't automatic normally. Some of the time, though, it can be like a dog that bares its teeth — a warning. So I've heard of cases where a void experienced trauma and they stopped being able to control that impulse because they felt driven to protect themselves."

So Wade was capable of controlling his powers, but he simply didn't trust me enough to do so?

I squeezed gently at his hand, unsure how to react or what to say back. It made sense, and I couldn't pretend that Wade was the picture of perfect mental health. Still, it also caused an ache in my chest. He had locked himself away from people, forced himself to wear gloves, and none of that had to happen? It was all due to his inability to feel safe?

Would he someday come to trust me enough to not do that? Could he ever learn to let down his guard, at least with me?

"Here." Bowen's voice drew me out of my thoughts, and when I turned, he had a business card held out to me.

I took it, letting go of Wade to focus on what he'd handed me. An address was written on the card, one scrawled in messy print along with a symbol I didn't recognize. I lifted my gaze to Bowen, my eyebrow raised.

"Consider this my debt paid in full. It's the contact information for a group who help smuggle shades out of the country. I've already contacted them so they know you will all be coming. You've got a meeting tomorrow night at that address. Show them this card so they know I sent you."

I clutched the card, the first glimpse of real escape I'd found. Despite getting out of Larkwood, despite avoiding the guards and soldiers sent to find us, I'd still had no real idea how to create a life. I'd had no concrete plan as to how to get out of the country, away from those who tracked us.

And now Bowen had handed me just that.

I nodded at him, the closest to a thank you I could muster. One more long drive, and we'd be safe. We'd get out of the country, away from our pursuers, and hell—maybe we'd get that quiet life we all deserved.

But at what cost?

Chapter Seven

Deacon

I would have rather kept going until we reached the meeting place, but it became clear quickly we'd require a stop or two. While the drive itself could be done in about four hours, none of us were at our best and we had to take smaller roads to avoid the highways. Besides, our meeting wasn't until the following day.

Hera and I were the only two able to drive. Wade, Kit, Knox and Brax all had been in Larkwood during their older years, meaning they'd never learned. Besides, they seemed exhausted from the fight.

It meant they'd all piled into the back of the minivan Bowen had given us for the trip, the four of them stretched out like some weird puppy pile. Hera remained awake – probably too keyed up to sleep since she wasn't accustomed to such violence – and sat in the passenger seat beside me.

It was funny how quickly things could feel normal. We hadn't talked since she'd escaped. In fact, we hadn't really spoken since the morning after she'd crawled into my bed, when I'd spent the entire night with her in my arms.

Strange to think that one of the best nights of my life could have transitioned into the most difficult.

And yet, I didn't have a clue what to say.

She squinted as she glanced out of the windshield, then gestured at a small cafe with a bright neon sign.

"We should pick up some food."

I nodded and pulled the car off the road. "Yeah, you're right. After injuries, it's best to give shades plenty of calories."

Even though the van bumped along the poorly maintained parking lot, none of the others stirred. I guess that showed just how rundown they all were.

Then again, we'd all had a rough few days.

I put the van into Park and glanced back to find Kit awake, staring back at me with his black eyes. Then again, despite his eyes having been closed before, I suppose wendigos didn't actually sleep.

Still, he jerked forward with his chin, a sign that he'd stay behind.

Was he giving me time alone with her?

Judging by the way I'd found the two of them — by the dirt on both of their rumpled clothes — clearly they'd made up when they'd first found each other in that forest. It seemed he wanted to give me the same chance.

Which I wasn't about to turn down.

I got out of the van, Hera following suit. We went into the cafe and placed an absurd order from the curt waitress. Then again, who wouldn't be curt when someone ordered twelve burger meals at eight in the morning?

The waitress told us it would be a forty-minute wait, then waved us toward an empty booth.

Hera sat beside me in the corner seat, and my heart pounded faster than it had in the fight.

I really am pathetic, aren't I?

Yet, knowing that didn't change my reaction at all. She managed to make me ridiculous, to make me unsure when I'd always been confident in my world and my place in it.

"I'm sorry," she signed.

So, it seemed we were going to talk about this. Then again, expecting us to just move forward without even addressing what had happened was probably a stupid hope.

"I get it," I said even if I didn't quite feel that.

A warmth covered my hand, and I dropped my gaze to see she'd set her hand on mine. Her gaze was soft, as if asking me to be honest, to tell her the truth.

And as it turned out, I was all but helpless against her. "I get why you did it, I do. I don't like it, and I'm still terrified that it'll get you killed, but I get it." I sighed and stared out of the window. "I was never really angry at you for it. Maybe the problem's that I never had any freedom, so I don't get the draw. I was raised in a lab, learning that I never had a future, that there's nothing else for me, but you didn't. You tasted real freedom, so I get that you'd want that. Maybe I'm just a coward, but I get it now. Being out here, I think I understand what you were craving."

She pulled her hand from mine to respond. *"Will you stay with me, then? Will you come with me?"*

I frowned, surprised that I even needed to say it. "If I wasn't willing to do that, do you really think I'd be here? I made my choice, Hera, and it's to stay by your side. Wherever that is, I don't care, as long as I'm with you." I kept the rest inside, the pathetic words like, *'please don't ever leave me alone again.'*

Still, the lines between her eyebrows implied she heard them, that she knew exactly what I couldn't bring myself to say.

Her gaze darted from me and to the side, to a restroom off the side of the cafe, before she lifted her eyebrow.

And again, I wondered exactly why she thought that was even a question. I craved her like nothing else, wanting to taste her, to feel her against me and wrapped around me.

So I took her hand in mine and pulled her toward the bathroom. While I'd prefer to have her in a place where I could really enjoy her, I'd take what I could get. I wanted to reacquaint myself with every inch of her, to lose myself in her, to remind myself of the reasons I was willing to risk everything and throw my entire life away just to have a little more time with her.

She was worth it. No matter the danger, I just wanted her. I wanted the life she offered me, the way she made me not feel so alone, as if I had a place in the world.

So I took her with me, pulling her into the small bathroom, flipping the lock before sitting her on the sink and kissing her with a passionate aggression, not hiding or controlling any of it. She'd accepted me, so she deserved to feel every bit of desire I had.

Because I loved her, and I'd make damn sure she knew it.

* * * *

Hera

Hours later, I stretched my hands out to ease the cramping in my fingers. Gripping the wheel for so long during the drive, when as tense as I felt, made my body ache.

Perhaps my time with Deacon had been a mistake, since I'd already been tired even before that, but I couldn't bring myself to regret it. With everything so uncertain, his touch had made me feel at ease and accepted.

Being back in the town I'd lived my whole life in felt strange. No, it was more than that. As I drove down the long, winding street with Kit, my chest tightened. I hadn't expected to ever return here, to see the familiar buildings and the streets I'd driven down countless times before.

"Are you all right?" Kit asked, his voice soft.

No, I really didn't think I was. It was too strange. It bridged who I had been with who I was and forced me to confront both.

With my hands gripping the steering wheel, I couldn't say that, so I shook my head instead.

Deacon drove the van with Knox, Brax and Wade in it. We didn't want to draw unnecessary attention to ourselves by piling so many of us into a car together. That meant we'd grabbed a sedan from a shady-looking bar. The person driving it hadn't owned it—I'd easily heard it from his voice—so he hadn't been willing to argue much when Kit had demanded he hand the keys over.

Kit set his hand on my thigh, the touch as comforting as it was stressful. Perhaps that was a result of us having had sex, because our relationship had changed after that. I'd gotten a look at the real him — not the wendigo, but the passionate man he hid — and I actually liked it. Still, it made me unsure about how to act.

He was so much older than I was, so different. I'd nearly believed him before, that he didn't care about anything, but looking at him now I realized how wrong I'd been. He was deeper than others, had more years that had shaped him, but he wasn't without feeling. Instead, those feelings rested under all that, so it took longer to reach them, but once I had?

I could easily drown in them.

So I offered him a tense smile in return.

He sighed but didn't remove his hand. "Did I frighten you?"

At that, I frowned and lifted my eyebrow at him.

"You seem uncomfortable around me now. I understand I behaved rashly before, no doubt rough, but I hadn't ever intended to frighten you. I wouldn't want to hurt you, not like that."

I pulled the car to the side of the road, unable to sit there while I couldn't respond. Deacon had taken another route, which meant Kit and I could talk without worry about others getting involved.

"I'm not afraid." I signed.

"You've behaved strangely toward me since we had sex. What else could it be?"

Heat crept up my cheeks at Kit's blunt words. Why was it that having sex was so much easier than talking about it later?

"It's not uncommon for people to get a little weird afterward."

"You aren't the sort of person to worry about things like that. You've had sex with Knox, Deacon, Brax and Wade, but you don't have this same discomfort with them. That means this is about me specifically."

I sighed. *"I've had a while to get more comfortable with them. I haven't had that with you."*

"You don't need to spare my feelings. I know what I am, and I understand the reaction people have to me."

He really wasn't listening, was he? It was almost funny how hard Kit worked to make this all his fault.

"I'm not surrounded by wilting flowers, you know? The men I love, they're all rough, they're all demanding, they're all dangerous. If a little roughness scared me, I'd be terrified all the time."

Kit didn't respond right away, his black eyes locked on me. "Love?"

Fuck. I realized my mistake almost instantly. I usually tried to stay away from that loaded word, but I'd gone and said it out loud and now I had to deal with it. Worse, I'd said it to Kit, who wasn't the type to let that go. He wasn't a man to let me pretend it hadn't happened.

No, he would stick with it until I admitted everything.

"Are you including me in that group?" He asked the question with a quiet flatness, as if he didn't dare allow himself to hope.

Which was an impossibly dumber question than I'd realized. He wanted to understand if I loved him, but he seemed unwilling to accept such an idea.

As for myself, I didn't have to think much about it. Of course I loved him.

Even if it had taken time for us to figure this out, for us to get to this point, I'd fallen for him a long time ago. It was in the way he'd remained with me, in the way he watched out for me, in how he'd bared his past and his pain to me.

I'd fallen for him before I'd ever realized it, and keeping it from him, when he looked at me with that expression, would have been impossible.

"Of course I love you," I admitted.

He said nothing at first, his face that expressionless mask as if he needed the words to sink in, as if he needed to test them before he could accept them. Finally, he furrowed his eyebrows. "Jasmine never really loved me," he whispered. "I loved her, but I never let her see the real me because I knew she couldn't accept me if she saw it. If she witnessed my darkness, the emptiness inside me, how could she? So I kept that hidden, kept myself under control at all times, which never allowed her to know me enough to love me. I find it difficult to believe or accept that after all you have seen of me, that you could."

"I couldn't, not unless you'd shown me that," I tried to explain. *"If you'd hidden yourself, I couldn't have trusted you enough to fall for you. I don't need you to be some pretty, safe version of yourself. I only need you to be you, to show me the real you, and you have. I haven't lived an easy life the last year, have gotten to see the world for what it really is, and I don't need that gentleness I used to."*

He frowned, as if he didn't care for that. He placed his hand on my cheek, and I leaned into his touch as he spoke. "You should demand those things, Hera. I wish I could give them to you, could let you have gentle romance, could show you what you deserve."

I shook my head but kept the contact of his warm palm. *"I might have needed that before, but I'm not the same person I used to be. I think I finally understand why people say that shades aren't the same people they were when they were human, because I'm not. It wasn't turning into a shade that changed me, but the fact that the world changed around me, people looked at me different, so I couldn't be the same person. You wouldn't have fit with the girl I was before, but you fit with who I am now."*

His expression softened, a strange thing to see on such a frightening and severe man. He rubbed his thumb across my cheek, the touch gentle, before he leaned in and offered me a kiss that was nothing like what we shared in the forest. He'd been aggressive then, dominant, where this was an exceedingly soft kiss. His warm lips brushed mine, and I returned it. It was funny that for a man who assured me that he didn't have this in him, who was so sure he was too harsh and aggressive for me, he could touch me so carefully.

He broke away far too soon, stealing the touch before I'd had my fill. His quiet chuckle filled the car. "We should get going or Deacon will come looking for us."

Right. He'd so distracted me with his words, with his kiss, that I'd totally forgotten we were headed somewhere important. The burning of my cheeks that he'd managed to blank my mind, that I'd wanted more, and he'd been the one to remind me of our actual purpose, made me want to cover my face and hide.

Kit dragged his thumb over my bottom lip as he offered me an exceedingly sexy smirk. "We'll finish this later."

And that was a promise I could get behind...

* * * *

Hera

I walked into the small general store, my gaze hard as I listened for any sign of a trap.

I didn't distrust Bowen, but I sure didn't trust him, either. I doubted he'd set me up on purpose, but that didn't mean much for those he knew. I'd learned that people always had a price, and the price for us would be high. I hadn't even known him long, knew little about him. It was easy to believe he'd betray me if it suited him.

I had Kit and Deacon flanking me, with Brax, Wade and Knox remaining outside to keep an eye for any danger. Having us all come in together would pose too big a risk.

I went to the front of the general shop, then held up the card Bowen had given me.

The man behind the counter studied it, then darted his gaze up at me. He quickly dismissed me, instead moving to study Deacon and Kit. Given both of their surprising eyes and intimidating stances, it wasn't a shock that he'd peg the two of them as the bigger threats.

The man nodded and gestured toward a door at the back of the shop. "Back there. They're already waiting."

I nodded back, then headed toward where he'd indicated.

Kit went first, moving past me to twist the handle. It placed me between Deacon and him again, ensuring that if someone surprised us, the men would take the brunt of the attack.

I might have been upset by the behavior before, but I'd accepted that different people had different skills. I couldn't take a hit as well as the two of them, but I could do a hell of a lot of damage so long as I could stay on my feet.

I followed Kit inside, and Deacon shut the door behind us. Past that door was a smaller room, one with couches and cabinets along the outside wall. There was a door on the far wall, and from inside, I could pick up the soft steps of a single person approaching.

It didn't seem like a setup or an ambush.

Sure enough, the steps came toward the door a moment before it opened.

And standing there, the savior Bowen had promised, the one who was supposed to offer us a path to freedom, was someone I recognized instantly.

Moa stood there, her eyes widening when she spotted me.

The past never stayed put, did it?

Chapter Eight

Hera

Sitting with Knox, Brax, Wade, Deacon and Kit reminded me that while I wasn't alone as I faced my past, boy, was my old life over.

Moa sat in a chair, having said little after we'd stared at each other for a long, silent minute.

I'd grown up with Moa as my best friend, a connection to my past. We had spent countless nights staying up late, talking about boys and gossiping until the sun came up. There had been a time I'd have considered her the closest person to me, yet now we sat across from each other with a year of pain and uncertainty between us.

No matter how strange things were between us, I didn't think she'd trick shades into danger. Even before I'd changed, most of our fights had been about her wanting to help shades and my distrust of them. I couldn't bring myself to think that could have changed.

For that reason, I had called in the others who had waited outside, and it left us all sitting on the couches along the wall, pressed together and quiet.

Even if I was wrong, even if Moa wasn't as trustworthy as I wanted to believe, she was still just a human against six shades.

"I can't believe you're really here," Moa said, her eyes catching the light from unshed tears.

I swallowed hard, unsure how to respond. How had it been so long since I'd seen her face or heard her voice? It took me back to the night everything had changed, to when we'd walked around the mall and gotten those charms together.

What happened to mine? I hadn't had it when I'd woken in Larkwood, figuring it had been thrown away at some point, people thinking it worthless. I hadn't really thought about it before, but faced with Moa, her own charm on a chain at her chest, I couldn't stop thinking about it.

I pictured it in the trash somewhere, nothing more than a testament to everything else I'd lost.

"It's been a while." As soon as I signed, Moa's frown told me she didn't understand ASL. A quick look in Kit's direction had him nodding and repeating me.

Moa glanced between Kit and me, then swallowed hard. Was it fear of Kit, of me, or just pity?

Were any of those better than the rest?

Probably not...

"Bowen didn't tell me who was coming, but I never expected you." She peered at Knox, Brax and Wade. "I knew those three escaped—it's been all over the news—but I didn't know you did."

"Bowen just said I'd meet someone to help us. I had no idea you were doing work like this."

Moa shrugged. "You knew I'd worked with some groups to help shades in high school, but after you were taken away, I couldn't sit around and do nothing. I couldn't do anything for you, but I thought about how many others there were, so I got involved with a group who helps smuggle shades out of the country." She dropped her gaze, as if ashamed. "I wanted to help you, I really did, but there were roadblocks everywhere. Every time I tried to do anything, I couldn't find any information. Your parents said you'd gone abroad, and it was like every trace of you was gone. Even when I tried to contact Larkwood after you called me, they claimed you weren't there. I'm so sorry, Hera. I didn't know what else to do."

I shook my head. *"It's not your fault. I know you did everything you could."*

Even as I told her that, the words stuck. Here Moa was risking herself to help shade and she wasn't even one. Me?

I was running away from everything, ready to put it all behind me and act as if it weren't my problem. It took me back to the selfish girl I'd been before everything had changed, the one who hadn't cared about anything but myself.

Maybe I hadn't really changed at all…

"I never thought I'd see you again," she whispered, a tremble to her shoulders, the actions making her seem so young.

Wade pushed my arm, his touch insistent, and I offered him a glare before realizing what he wanted from me.

Had it really been so long since I'd lived in the real world that I'd forgotten basic things like compassion? I sighed and did as he wanted, rising from the couch and going over to her. When I neared her, she all but threw herself from the chair and against me, wrapping her arms tightly around me.

Tears muffled her words. "I missed you so much. I didn't even know if you were still alive. I just kept thinking about everything that could have happened, about where you were, about what I could have done differently. If I hadn't gone home, if I'd kept an eye on you, maybe it all would have been different."

I rubbed her back, unable to respond. Even if I could have spoken, what would I have said? I had no idea. In all my thoughts, each time I'd focused on my own pain, on what I suffered, I'd never really considered anyone else.

I hadn't thought about Moa hurting, hadn't thought about those left behind without answers, especially after my parents hadn't seemed to give a damn.

"Why don't we step out?" Wade rose to his feet, an unbearable kindness in his tone. "You two can have a minute to yourselves."

"She doesn't speak ASL," I signed quickly as I looked away from Moa.

Deacon held out a writing pad and pencil, as if he'd been prepared for such a situation. I gave him a tense smile in thanks as I took them. The five men left, heading back into the general store, leaving Moa and I alone.

Her gaze followed them, locked on the door after it closed. "Are you safe with them?"

I scribbled on the first page of the writing pad. *"I thought you didn't judge shades like that."*

"I'm not judging shades—I'm judging five men I don't know who are following you around. I want to make sure you're safe."

That made me pause. I hadn't had to consider it much. Larkwood was so twisted, so strange, that the idea of having a relationship with five men hadn't fazed me. Nothing about my life was normal, so why would my relationships be?

Yet, it seemed more difficult to explain. It was like losing my virginity. Doing it was easy but admitting to it was far more difficult.

Still, I trusted Moa, knew her like no one else, so I gave her the truth I could. *"They're the only reason I'm alive. We escaped together, and I'd be dead or still in Larkwood if they hadn't been there to help me."*

"So it's just convenience? Because you seem a lot closer to them than just that…"

I took a deep breath, then put it all out in the open for her. *"I love them."*

Her eyes went wide. "All of them?"

I nodded because that was clear enough to me. I had no reason to pretend it wasn't true. My life was a mess, but I knew damn well I loved them all, each for a different reason.

She blew out a slow breath, then nodded as if coming to terms with it. "Okay then. I can't say I understand it, but I trust you."

"So will you help us?"

"Of course I will."

"How does this all work?"

"That depends on the shades. Most I've dealt with are low level and no one is looking for them, so it's not that hard. We make sure their bands are removed, then we get them out of the area. Usually another state is more than enough. You, though? You all are a different story. Not only are some of your faces plastered all over the news, but I've heard a lot of troubling rumors."

"Like what?"

"Like soldiers without identification showing up randomly at a few of our other meeting places, the sort of shadowy people backed by money and power who don't answer to anyone. The escape from Larkwood has put people on edge, and even regular citizens who normally would stand up for shades are quick to call in anything suspicious. Moving shades is a lot more difficult right now, and you all are sitting at the top of the list of problematic."

I sighed, my shoulders dropping. *"I don't want to put you in danger. We can go."*

I pulled back, ready to go, to figure it out on our own. I risk Moa or to force her into anything she didn't want to do. I couldn't use our connection like that.

She wrapped her hand around my arm, pulling me to a stop. "I didn't say no, Hera. Do you really think I'd send you away? That I'd leave you on your own? If I'm willing to risk my life and my freedom for any shade, what do you think I'd do for my best friend?"

I gulped at the honesty of her voice, unable to stop the way her words reached into me. The men were one thing. We had passion between us, romance, but Moa?

She was my friend. She'd known me most of my life. Her standing by my side made me want to hug her again, to thank her for being a rock when I'd drifted for so long.

Except, before I could say anything else, the back door opened and someone else rushed in who I wasn't in the least bit prepared to deal with.

Aaron.

If seeing Moa was hard, it was *nothing* compared to coming face-to-face with my ex, with the man I'd expected I'd spend the rest of my life with. I was taken back to our time together, to how in love I'd thought we were.

We weren't, I realized now. It had been empty, shallow, forced on us by our parents and our expectations, but that didn't change that we'd had so many years together, that we had shared so many firsts.

"Hera..." he said, his eyes wide as if he couldn't quite believe it. Clearly, Moa had told him about me.

She moved her gaze between us, then excused herself and went out to the store just as my men had gone. It left Aaron and I alone together.

He stared at me as if he couldn't believe it, as if I'd come back from the dead somehow and he didn't know how to handle it.

I felt a bit like that as well. As it turned out, stepping back into a world that had forgotten about me, one that had kept moving despite my absence, was difficult.

My hand trembled as I wrote a single word, then held the pad out to him. "*Hello.*"

His gaze moved from the notepad to my throat, to the scar there. If everything else didn't explain how much things had changed, that did, right? "So you really can't talk at all, huh?"

I shook my head and wrote a response. "*I had my throat slit the night I changed. I'm a siren, which means I can hurt people with my voice, and the person who attacked me wanted me silenced.*"

"Shit," Aaron muttered and shook his head. "I shouldn't have left you alone, shouldn't have let you walk to your car by yourself." He rubbed his hand over the back of his neck, his voice full of regret. "I'm so damned sorry..."

"This isn't your fault," I wrote. *"You didn't do this to me. If I've learned one thing, it's that bad things happen, and we can only control what we do."*

Somehow, telling Aaron that soothed a strange part of myself. Releasing him from that guilt released me from some of my own anger.

I peered past him, though, toward the main room. *"So, you and Moa?"*

I'd moved on, but that didn't erase an ache inside me at how they'd moved on so quickly after I left, as if they'd filled that space between us. Had I been so unimportant to them?

Aaron sighed. "We aren't together."

I lifted my eyebrow, calling him a liar without having to write it down. I recalled calling Moa, the way he'd looked shocked, the way he'd avoided me. Clearly, they had something between them.

He shook his head and took a seat on one of the couches. "We aren't. You were gone, Hera, and we were heartbroken. No one else knew the truth about you, didn't know where you'd gone or what had happened because Larkwood had covered it all up, so it was just us."

"And you decided to screw to feel better?" As soon as I wrote that, my stomach churned. It wasn't fair to hold it against him, was it? Seeing as I had five men I was with, I didn't regret that Aaron and I were finished, that we had no future, yet an ache inside me at being so quickly replaced hurt. I was okay with where we were, but I couldn't shake the feeling that I hadn't been important to him, that he hadn't really given a damn about me. I could accept change, but I didn't like having to question my past.

At least Aaron had the decency to cringe at my question. "I'm sorry. I'm not going to defend it, but you were gone, and we were still here and hurting. We realized pretty fast that we weren't meant to be together, that this whole thing between us wasn't anything good. It was just us trying to find something familiar when we were heartbroken."

The door opened, and I turned to find Brax and Knox walking in. Knox didn't look me in the eye, but he hadn't since the fight at the church. Brax only glanced at me for a moment before turning his hard gaze on Aaron.

Aaron narrowed his eyes, clearly not caring for the men before him. "You know Hera?"

"Yeah, I do," Brax answered as he crossed his arms. It was strange how much more mature Brax appeared. Despite not being all that much older than Aaron, Brax looked like an adult. It was probably because of everything he'd gone through, everything he'd survived, but he made Aaron look like a teenager. He also offered no additional information.

"I'm Aaron."

And Brax sure as hell reacted to *that* name. He went deathly still, the blue of his eyes intense as he stared at the other man. "So you're the asshole who dropped her and fucked her best friend the moment she got sent away, huh?"

Aaron flinched at the accusation, but he couldn't deny it.

It was true. It had happened. Even if there were reasons, even if I could forgive Aaron for it, it *had* occurred exactly as Brax said.

Still, Aaron lifted his chin with that same haughtiness we had learned from birth due to our family and status. "What do you know about it?"

"I fucking watched her cry over you. I saw her whisper your name when she woke up only to realize you weren't there and you didn't give enough of a fuck about her to even try to help her." The lines of Brax's face shifted, a sure sign he neared the edge of his control, that he inched closer to do something he couldn't take back.

I put my hand on Brax's chest when he took a step forward, then shook my head. I didn't need him to defend me, to do anything to Aaron. We had been kids in a bad situation, both trying to deal with problems we shouldn't have had to.

Brax thinned his lips into a tense line, then stared at Aaron. "You're fucking lucky she's as nice as she is, or I'd make sure she was the last thing your worthless ass ever thought about."

With that, Brax turned and stormed out. Knox peered between Aaron and Brax, his expression less violent but no less angry. He bared his teeth in an expression that wasn't even close to a smile before following his brother.

Aaron's color had paled, his skin a white that said he'd taken the threat to heart. It was good, because too many people didn't realize just how serious Brax was, how willing to follow through. In our world, those kinds of threats weren't empty. "Seems like you moved on, too."

"*I spent a whole year alone. Of course I moved on.*"

He nodded. "I get it."

But did he? "*We weren't right for each other,*" I wrote. "*We were together because our parents told us we should be.*

116

Can you really say you loved me? That you would have chosen me if it had been up to you?"

He looked as if he might argue the point, but no words came. After a long moment, he let out a rough laugh. "I guess not. I think in the year you've been gone, I've learned a little, too. What's perfect on paper isn't always right for us."

That hit me, the truth of his words. Aaron and I *were* perfect in theory, both from important, well-connected families. A marriage between us would benefit both of us, but that didn't matter in the end. A marriage between us wouldn't make either of us happy. I wasn't sure why that hadn't ever occurred to me in my old life.

Maybe it was because happiness hadn't been a real thought of mine before. Larkwood had stolen everything from me, but I had rebuilt myself from the ground up. I didn't know what I wanted, but I knew what I didn't.

That changed everything.

Aaron wasn't a bad man, but he wasn't right for me, and I wasn't right for him. We both needed to find our own paths, and that fact allowed me to release those lingering entanglements, the what-ifs, the hurt from how things had gone between us.

"I'm not mad," I wrote. *"We were who we were, and we've both grown and changed. We aren't right to be together, but I'd still like to be friends."*

He stared at the words, as if taken back by the honesty there. After a moment, he offered me a sad smile. "Yeah, I'd like that, too. Why don't we get Moa back in here and find a good place for you to hide while we work out a plan?"

I nodded, grateful to move forward, to let go of our past and look forward instead. There were enough

problems ahead of me that I didn't need to wallow in
the past anymore.

Chapter Nine

Hera

I peered around the house, feeling totally out of sorts. The place was huge—far larger than was reasonable, considering our short stay—and that shocked me. In my old life, I'd have found this house unacceptable. The idea of staying somewhere without staff for the basic upkeep, the idea of living anywhere with such cheap furniture would have been a huge downgrade.

Now, though? After a year in Larkwood, this all struck me as unnecessary opulence. The house was a single-family home with five bedrooms, all on one level, and decorated with simple, usable pieces.

The idea of staying somewhere Aaron knew about made me uneasy, but he'd explained that the place was used as a short-term rental by a friend of his. Aaron paid his friend in cash and said he had a woman flying in, so he wanted to keep it off the books. It was as good an excuse as any other.

Kit and Deacon had left to buy food, both putting in contacts Moa had given them to hide their unique eyes. Since no enemies had survived our fight with the soldiers, no word should have gotten back to the Warden about them defecting, which meant they were safe for a while from having their faces on the news.

Brax and Wade checked out the property, figuring out escape routes from the house should we need them.

It left Knox and I inside, and he was still behaving oddly. Ever since the fight, he'd hardly looked at me, hadn't met my gaze, hadn't said more than a word or two to me and only when he couldn't get out of it.

It meant when I walked toward the kitchen and glanced into his room to find him sitting on his bed, his head in his hands, I hit my limit of ignoring it. I snapped to get his attention, then signed, *"What's wrong?"*

"Nothing." His voice came out rough, and in his words, pain and hunger hit me.

"You clearly aren't fine. Are you hungry?"

He let out a nearly feral sound, one that would have driven me backward if I didn't trust him so much. He stopped it as soon as it started, and nodded sharply once instead. "It's not your problem, though."

"Of course it is! If you won't feed from me, fine, I'm not going to force you, but you still have to feed."

He shook his head. "I don't want to go feed from some stranger. I don't want to betray you like that."

"It isn't a betrayal."

"Sure, it is. I'm tired of doing things I don't want. I'm over it."

"You can't just ignore this! I can't just watch you hurt yourself. It isn't fair to ask me to do that!" I set my hands on his cheeks, wanting him to really hear me.

He went to knock my hands away, but the action lifted his shirt a hair. Beneath the edge sat a massive dark spot. I didn't wait for permission, instead grasping the hem and pulling it up.

I hissed in a sharp breath at the sight. Black and blue covered his stomach, over his side, even his back. When had he gotten hurt? Was this just hunger?

I recalled the fight, the way he'd moved across the room with such ease, avoiding the hits.

Apparently not all of them...

I lifted my gaze to his, a question there.

He refused to look at me, and his words came out soft and unhappy. "I don't heal well when I haven't fed, and I haven't fed well in a long-damned time."

"You shouldn't have hidden this from me." I struggled to keep tears in, to not let him see how deep his words hurt me. He'd hidden something so significant, had kept his pain to himself, and for what?

How many times had he shouldered my pain? My problems? Yet he couldn't trust me to do the same for him.

"I'll go find someone for you," I signed, then went to pull away, to collect myself and talk to Brax. If anyone knew who he'd feed from, it was Brax.

Except, Knox caught my wrist and held me there. I couldn't turn around, couldn't look at him this time. He'd see everything in my face, and he didn't need to carry anymore guilt than he did. I didn't need to make this any harder on him than it already was.

"You saw my incubus," he whispered. "During the fight, you saw it. People see it as sexy, as seductive, but they don't see the thing it really is. It would happily kill anyone if it could only feed from them. It doesn't care about anything or anyone, just a beast, and the only way to keep it docile is to give it what it wants. Even Brax's other side cares about you, but not mine."

I met his gaze, wanting him to understand how I felt. I tugged my hand free so I could sign back. *"I'm not afraid of you or it. I love you, Knox. Please let me help you."*

"What if we change? What if you see that side of me and can't love me anymore? What if I change?"

I shook my head. *"Nothing will change. You said you become what your partner wants, but I want you, whoever that is. I don't care if you're rough or gentle or fast or slow or anything else. I just want you, whoever that is."*

He shuddered, a full-body tremble that made me realize just how tightly he held himself. Even still, his bright eyes bore into mine as if determining the truth. He must have figured it out, because one moment I looked down at him and the next, I stared up and into his green eyes just as he blocked out the world around me when his lips took mine.

And there was no mistaking that it wasn't just Knox kissing me — this was the beast he'd desperately kept away from me.

Knox

Moving *hurt*. Everything in me hurt, the ache in the middle of my body gnawing with each shift I made, the pain having grown since the fight.

It had only taken a few lucky shots to cause this, though I normally would have healed without problems. In fact, if I'd been properly fed, I might not have taken the hits in the first place. Hunger made me slow and sloppy.

Resisting since being with Hera had brought my energy to an all-time low, and it had meant that, instead of healing after the fight, my injuries had only worsened. I'd tried to hide them, hadn't wanted anyone to realize the problem. If any of them had known, they'd have made it into a big deal and pressured me to feed.

And yet, no matter how much I'd resisted, as it turned out, I couldn't win against Hera. Maybe we'd always been headed here, and I'd just dragged my feet, had just made it more difficult. Whatever the reason, I couldn't resist her anymore.

So I took her lips with all the aggression I felt, with the need inside me I couldn't ignore anymore. I gave in to it fully, and the rush of immediate power swirled through me.

It was a sure sign she felt the way I did, that she wanted this as much as I did. My incubus all but purred in response to the meal, to the power of her passion. I slid my hand up her side, dipping inside her shirt to feel her heated skin.

I'd touched her before, had felt the flawless expanse of her body, but that had been dulled. I'd had myself silenced from Wade's influence, but this time, I was whole.

I moved my lips from hers to her throat, to the place where her pulse thundered. I tasted it all, none of it lessened from Wade's powers. The scent of her skin, the sharp tang of her passion, the desire that spilled from her, it all clouded my head.

I felt aggressive and starving, wanting all her attention, all her focus. I wanted to feast on her until neither of us could move.

I nipped at her throat, then locked my lips on her shoulder, sucking hard until she gasped and dug her fingers into my back. I wanted to mark her, to leave her wearing love bites from me like a claim anyone could see.

My personality shifted, as I knew it would, as it always did, but I tried not to let it scare me. I wasn't some empty shell putting on a performance. Instead, I was rough with her because she wanted me to show her that I needed her, that I love her, that I felt every bit as ravenous as she did.

My incubus stretched out, feeding happily from her, and it only had her arching her back in my hold.

Waiting didn't seem possible. I moved my lips down her body, pulling away only long enough to strip her clothes off. My hands were rough and demanding, not giving a damn if I tore the fabric away as long as I could have her.

And Hera didn't fight me. In fact, her hands matched my frenzy, pulling my shirt up and over my head, pausing only for a moment at the sight of the still dark bruise.

"It'll heal," I assured her before dragging the tip of my tongue over her bottom lip. I didn't want to lose a moment of this to worry or regret.

She nodded, leaning in to press a shockingly gentle kiss to my side where an especially dark area of the bruising sat. The touch reached far deeper than the injury or the physical. It was as if she somehow managed to get deep enough to soothe old wounds of mine, the marks left behind from years of being nothing but a body to others, nothing but an orgasm dispenser.

Hera was different. She'd gotten me off with no thoughts of herself, as a way to prove to me that she cared about me, not what I could give her. In fact, her being here now, her wanting to feed me even after I'd warned her, proved the same thing.

So I shucked my pants, disposing of the troublesome fabric until we pressed against each other without anything between our heated skin. I was on her in a moment, unable to hold back any longer.

I bent, taking her pebbled nipple between my lips before raking my teeth over the taut nub. The taste of her passion blew anything else I'd had away. My incubus agreed, the beast quiet and sated on her desire. Normally it roared in my head, demanding more, driving me to go further, to take more, but not this time. It was as though each little bit it tasted from Hera fed it in a way nothing had before.

It was like going from empty calories to a nutritious meal. *Why?*

My brain refused to do the mental gymnastics to work that out at the moment, which was fine by me. I didn't want to miss a single moment of this due to pointless distraction.

I moved down her body, leaving kisses in my wake, until I grabbed her legs and slung them over my shoulders. I didn't try to do this in any special way, didn't think about anything but what I needed — to drown in her. The first touch of my lips to her wet cunt made me groan, and I feasted on her. I slid my tongue up her folds until I rubbed against her hard little clit, her hips shifting as if she wanted both more and less at the same time.

I wouldn't let her escape, though. She'd agreed to this, she'd given herself to me, surrendered to me, so I used my hands on her hips to hold her still for me. She tasted like freedom, like an offer for a life where I could do whatever I pleased, and I gorged myself on her and that promise.

She had her mouth open, and I missed that I couldn't hear her, that her sweet little moans didn't fill the room. I still feasted on her as if I could somehow draw those sounds out if I only tried hard enough.

It didn't take long for her to tumble into her first release, and the power that came with it astounded me. It was sweet in a strange way, and bottomless in the amount. Too often, sex provided a rush of power, made me strong for a short while, but that was it. It always faded too fast.

Hera was different. I could have drowned in it all and never reached the bottom. Why? What made her different?

I swiped my tongue up her cunt one more time before moving up her body, basking in the way she shivered, in how she arched sharply when I brushed against her hard nipples. Every part of her was so sensitive that even the lightest touch sent her into overdrive, and that was exactly how I wanted her. I didn't want her to think straight, to consider anything other than me and this moment.

My incubus spread out through me farther, taking over more and more, but it didn't shove me aside. The sensation was strange and new, as if we moved together instead of against each other.

Usually, I resisted his influence. I hated the feeling of feeding and losing control, so I tried to avoid it. My incubus then roused, taking over, devouring no matter what I wanted or how I felt. It made me powerless against the need.

This time, however, was different. I didn't experience that sickness, didn't feel controlled by my incubus. Maybe it was because I didn't fight for the first time, because I fully sank into that need, both of us in agreement over our goal.

Which was Hera.

I dragged my tongue along the seam of her lips as I caught her thigh and pulled her leg around my hip. The warmth of her pussy seared me, made me desperate to sink into her, and I didn't waste a moment questioning it or doubting either of us. Instead, I plunged into her waiting body and let her cunt wrap tightly around my cock.

The sensation astounded me. It was so much more than just physical, than the actual place where we connected. Sure, that was great, the snugness of her pussy, the way she squeezed more around me with each wave as her body recovered from her last orgasm. She writhed beneath me, and her heel dug into my back as she used her leg to pull me closer.

And I gave her everything I had. I braced my weight on one elbow, using that hand behind her neck to hold her still as I took her lips in a consuming kiss. Her breath was rough and ragged against my lips, but she only clung tighter to me.

I sank as far as possible into her heat, then withdrew and took her hard. That shifting inside myself, the one that read what she needed and became that, used to frighten me. I used to hate it, to feel as if I were losing myself in those moments, but I didn't feel like that with Hera.

I *wanted* to be what Hera needed in that moment. If she'd had a difficult day, I wanted to be the soft place for her. I wanted to kiss her gently, to spend hours worshipping at the altar of her supple body. When she was in a different mood, I wanted to be that for her too. I craved to hold her down, to overwhelm her with passion and aggression and prove just how much I needed her.

It meant when I was rough now, when I was demanding and fucked her with hard, deep thrusts, when I knew that was exactly what she needed right then, I finally understood and accepted it.

"I love you," I whispered against her lips, wanting to make sure she believed it. I'd craved her before, but it wasn't like this.

I needed her — all of her. I needed her by my side, in my life, supporting me. I needed her touch and her taste and her passion. I needed her humor, the way she made me smile, her bravery. Now, I realized something else — my incubus needed her, too. It fed in a way it never had before, feasting off her like a meal it would never finish with. I didn't even feel that old need to keep going, to drag more from a person, or the fear I might kill them from it.

Instead, it seemed my incubus was careful, as if it cherished her just as I did.

Hera put her hands on my cheeks, forcing my eyes to hers. Her lips moved and she mouthed, *"I love you, too,"* in return.

With that, I lost my composure. I pressed my forehead to hers as I gave up resisting, as I let myself fall over that edge with her again. She came hard, and whether it was due to me or my incubus, I didn't give a damn. If she enjoyed it, what did it matter?

For the first time, I really got it. I wanted her — every part of her — and I would do whatever I could to keep her happy and safe and fulfilled. So if my incubus was a part of that? If it could bring her pleasure and offer her protection?

Well, it seemed like my other side and I could get along just fine.

Chapter Ten

Hera

Walking up to my old house kicked me hard. Somehow, it stung more than seeing Aaron, even more than having my parents reject me.

I think it was because I'd grown up in this house, because most of the memories of my life had occurred within these walls. More than anything else, this place felt like my childhood, like the physical representation of my past.

"I don't sense anyone inside," Kit said from beside me. I'd brought only Kit with me on this errand, since having only one person would make this stop faster and safer.

"I don't hear anyone either," I signed. *"Moa said they aren't supposed to be home for another two days, so they'd give the staff that time off."*

There was a party in another few days, one my parents were expected to attend. It was the sort of thing

I would have gone to as well, where they'd have trotted me out like some trophy and made me talk to people I didn't know, people who didn't give a damn about me beyond my name. Just thinking about how they continued to live their life as if I wasn't gone made me close my hands into tight fists.

Kit nodded as we walked toward the entrance. Cameras would catch our approach, but unless the alarms went off, no one would monitor the footage. And what did I care if later they realized I'd come? I'd be long gone by then.

We'd already watched the house for over an hour, checking for any sign of surveillance or trap. Between my hearing and Kit's predatory sense, we could have identified anyone near the place, but nothing had moved. We just had to stay on our toes so we could bolt if that changed.

We went up to the porch, the massive front doors both reassuring and intimidating. It was a strange juxtaposition between who I'd been in the past and who I was now. Before, I'd have skipped into this house because it had been my home. Now, though? Now it felt strange, like some long-dead corpse.

Funny, since I was the only thing that had changed in the last year. This was the same door, the same landscaping, the same house.

I breathed in deeply before punching in a code. It flashed green and the lock clicked open.

"They didn't change your code?" Kit asked.

"They probably did. It isn't hard to guess my mother's code, though. She always hated to remember passwords, despite my father lecturing her, so she always uses our first dog's birthday."

Kit set a hand on my shoulder and squeezed without saying anything. Why would he say something? It just was what it was. We couldn't do anything about it. If I let every reminder of what I'd lost get to me, I'd never get a damned thing done.

So I walked into the house and closed the door behind me. I punched the same code into the keypad inside to deactivate all the security measures inside.

When I turned away from it, I froze. The house looked exactly the same. Worse, right there, on the opposite wall, hung a huge painting.

I still remembered posing for it, back when I'd been thirteen and my mother had forced me into an uncomfortable dress just so we could look like the family she'd wanted to portray. A stylist had come and curled my hair, doing my makeup to cover a blemish on my cheek, one my mother had made a big deal to the photographer about editing it out in the final product.

Along with the gray in her hair or any lines in her face that injections hadn't fixed.

I sighed as I stared for a minute, lost in the past, in that day. I'd hated doing it, but I'd done it. I hadn't complained when the dress had been too tight, when my feet had hurt, when my mother's cutting words had nearly drawn blood.

And staring at the girl there, I didn't think I knew her anymore. If I went through that now, I wouldn't stand there, silent.

Funny, given I couldn't actually speak, but I wasn't the same push over I had been before. I wasn't nearly so worried about looking a certain way, about being liked anymore.

I shook my head and pointed up the stairs. Kit and I didn't need to stare at an old painting. We were here for a reason—to pick up a few things that I wouldn't get another chance to grab. We had to run, but that didn't mean I couldn't try to take a tiny piece of my past with me.

Kit peered around the house as we went. "It's hard to believe you grew up like this."

"How did you grow up?"

"I honestly don't recall much. Memories get difficult to retain as more time passes for shades who don't age. Our brains simply aren't made to recall so much information, so while the memories are there, they are difficult to thread together and access or recall. I know I wasn't born privileged, that my family struggled, but that it was also a happy family."

"Then you were better off than I was."

"That painting showed a family who was happy."

"That's the thing about pictures and paintings—they show what you want them to. You just need the right clothes, the right artist, and it can look like anything. My parents were never home, always too busy for me, and I was just their legacy. I spent more time around my nannies than I ever did with them."

Kit nodded as he walked beside me up the stairs, following my pace. He didn't even call me on how slowly I moved. "Things aren't always what they seem, and that goes both ways. Sometimes people can care but show it in the worst ways."

"Sounds like an excuse."

"Perhaps," Kit admitted. "But we are all imperfect. I mean, I cared for you well before I told you properly. I thought it was better and safer to keep a distance, to not show my true feelings, but I still had them."

His words drew a frown from me as I considered it. It was easy to think of my parents as villains—and them abandoning me after I changed sold that fact—I couldn't deny that they were imperfect people.

Kit grasped my hand, entwining his fingers with mine in a comforting hold. "You don't need to know right now. Things like this take time to work through, to figure out, and no matter what the truth, no matter what decision you come to, you aren't alone." He squeezed softly at our clasped hands, and I squeezed back.

Not being on my own was the only reason I'd made it this far.

Kit

It was strange to think the woman I knew, the one I loved, had grown up like this. If I didn't know her, I would have hated her immediately upon seeing this.

The house was nothing short of a mansion, with marble floors and expensive artwork lining the walls. The ostentatious and nearly life-sized painting drove home that she hadn't grown up as most people did.

Yet, somehow, she'd remained kind. Despite having everything given to her, despite how she'd grown up wanting for nothing, she'd avoided turning cold and cynical. She'd retained her sweetness, her innocence, her caring nature. That alone proved just how special she really was.

She paused at a door, then opened it after a deep breath. The inside told me immediately where we were.

Her bedroom.

It lacked the awkwardness that going into a woman's room normally had. As an adult, there was always this undercurrent of sexual tension when in another's private space. Even with people who lacked any real attraction, societal rules meant being around a bed created a question between them.

That wasn't the case here, probably because it didn't feel like *her* bed. It didn't remind me of the woman I knew at all. Awards sat on the bookshelf, along with pictures in expensive silver frames. The images had her and others—including her old boyfriend and Moa. They were smiling in them, with Hera dressed entirely differently. She had heavy makeup on, and her hair was always perfectly styled. She wore clothing that appeared both trendy and expensive, though not edgy. Instead, they made her look classy, and she reminded me of the painting of her mother, or the many times I'd seen her mother on the television while discussing anti-shade legislation.

"This all feels so weird." Hera's hands moved, but I got the feeling she wasn't talking to me.

Still, I answered. "I'm sure it is. Still, it's not a bad idea to stop. You can get whatever it is you want to bring with you."

"I don't have a lot I'd want to take," she admitted. *"None of this stuff even feels like my things, you know? Like, it all feels like it belongs to someone I don't know."*

Strange, since that was how I'd felt as well. The girl portrayed in this room was not the one who had come to Larkwood. Perhaps that was the point, though. Larkwood changed people. This was the girl Hera had been before that, before circumstance had transformed her just as much as becoming a shade had.

She went to her desk and pulled open one of the drawers. She reached toward the back, bending down to do so, until a click said she'd found what she wanted. She withdrew something — a book of some sort.

"What's that?"

She handed it to me without answering.

I took that move as permission, so I flipped open the leather-bound book. A diary? Or perhaps a diary-scrapbook hybrid would describe it better. Articles and images were glued to some pages, with scribbled words beside them. Some had pictures with friends — not the staged ones in the frames, but candid ones. Dates, names, memories, it all was written down in colored ink on the pages.

I looked up at her, not quite understanding the relevance or importance of the book.

"The pictures in this room are ones my mom chose. She had them edited before they could be put up, because they needed to show what she wanted. That journal is the history I wrote. It was how I remembered the events, what I wanted to say but couldn't ever bring myself to. If my mom ever found it, she'd have destroyed it, so I kept it hidden. I couldn't imagine leaving without it, because eventually she'll go through this all, and if she found it, she'd probably burn it to save her false little story." Hera took the journal from my hands and cradled it against her chest.

She didn't meet my gaze, as if afraid to see I'd found it stupid.

She really didn't trust me, did she?

I went to reach for her when something hit me *hard.* It wasn't a physical blow, but it felt like a high-pitched sound I couldn't ignore, something that reached into me and set every nerve inside me on edge.

I cringed and pressed my hands to my head, trying to block it out. Except, it quieted again, allowing me to blink.

I was on the ground, and above me? Hera. I twisted, realizing my head was in her lap and her fingers ran through my hair, her worried eyes staring down at me.

As I came back to myself, I sat up, my head aching, the feeling odd. I so rarely experienced pain, and this was for sure pain.

Before I explained anything to her—how was I supposed to explain something I didn't yet understand myself?—I thought back to the feeling just before I'd passed out.

Source.

It took a moment to identify it, but that was exactly what it was. It was as if a huge tear had opened, pouring source through the room. The massive influx had overloaded my synapsis and essentially forced a shut down.

But what the hell could have done that? I'd lived for a long time without ever experiencing something like that.

I hopped to my feet, a bit dizzy but unwilling to let that stop me. Anything that could bring me down like this I couldn't ignore.

Now that I knew what I was looking for, I closed my eyes to sense it. Source left a lingering feel, like ripples in water. I moved forward, following that sensation, until my foot struck something. I opened my eyes to find myself right in front of her bed. On the nightstand sat the item that had caught my attention—a lamp with a moon at the top.

"Where did you get this?" I asked as I picked it up, pulling the plug from the wall.

"It was a gift from a work acquaintance of my mom's."

"When did you get it?"

Her lips tipped down, and I got the sense that she had to think about it. It meant she must have gotten it a while before, something that made me even more uneasy.

Finally, she nodded. *"About a year before I changed."*

That made sense. The way she'd turned into a shade, her high source levels, the time in Medical when the Warden had implied Hera hadn't changed naturally — it all fit together.

"We need to go see Deacon."

"Why?"

I held up the lamp. "Because I'm pretty sure this turned you into a shade."

* * * *

Wade

Deacon carefully examined the lamp Kit had brought in. It didn't strike me as anything odd, but that didn't mean much.

As an elder, Kit could sense things the rest of us couldn't.

Hera had seemed unsettled upon returning, but that was to be expected. She'd revisited her old home. I had no idea what I'd do in that situation. It made me sit beside her and press my covered arm against hers, trying to reassure her just by being close by.

Deacon grasped the top of the lamp and twisted, the wood cracking easily beneath his strength. The pieces split, and Deacon tossed the base of the lamp away. After that, he pulled apart the wood that surrounded the top, where the moon was.

When it gave way, he had something that looked nothing like the lamp. It had a large crystal in the center, but the crystal didn't appear like anything I'd seen before. It was a deep purple, and the insides moved as if alive.

I peered closer to realize it didn't swirl exactly. Instead, it was as if something inside it shifted around, staring back.

"It looks weird," I said, "but how can you be sure it's anything? People are all into New Age healing now. I heard doctors had to tell women that crystals should not be *inserted* anywhere."

Kit went to answer, but before he could, his answer became unnecessary. A wave of power left the object, something like pure source that I immediately identified.

Kit collapsed, and I moved without thinking. I grabbed the item from Deacon, wrapping my hands around the oddly warm crystal.

The moment I did, a wave of source rushed into me. It felt like holding six Kits, and the power astounded and overwhelmed me. Still, the moment I touched it, Kit blinked slowly and sat up. It meant it had worked, allowing me to absorb that source rather than him getting affected by it.

He shook his head in a hard jerk, then exhaled in a loud rush. He turned his gaze toward me. "That is extremely unpleasant. Are you okay?"

I grit my teeth together but nodded. The sensation was hard to put into words, sort of like a brain freeze after eating too much ice cream. It didn't feel good, but I still kept at it anyway. "It's not the best feeling, but it shouldn't hurt me."

Shouldn't being a very iffy thing.

Kit nodded and locked his focus on Deacon, as if trying to hurry for my benefit. "She received it as a gift from a friend of her mother's. Have you seen anything like this before? It was kept by her bedside."

Deacon offered a single quick nod. "They used them in the North Tower. They were a hell of a lot different back then, but I wouldn't forget a crystal that looks like that."

"What is it?"

He sighed. "I'm no scientist, and the ones there didn't like to talk to us much. They kept one in one of the central rooms, but it wasn't like this. It was six-feet-tall and took up almost a whole wall. They'd bring us in and make us do some of our lessons in there. I'm pretty sure the purpose was to expose us to source rifts and see if they could force a change."

"That makes sense," I said, thankful when the crystal stopped emitting the power. It seemed to come and go in waves, though I wasn't sure how often they happened. "They've been trying to make shades for a while. If they can figure out how to make one, they can figure out a way to unmake one."

Hera hadn't added to the conversation, her gaze locked on the crystal.

It wasn't hard to guess her thoughts there.

This crystal had changed her entire life. It had altered her course, had turned her into a shade and stolen everything from her. While becoming a shade wasn't easy for anyone, it was normally just bad luck. It was nothing more than the universe deciding to screw over a person.

It was the difference between losing someone to a horrible accident and losing them to a well-planned-out murder. One couldn't have been avoided, but the other could have, which made it harder to come to terms with.

"So I really was changed on purpose?" She signed. *"The Warden did this to me?"*

Deacon answered, his voice soft. "Yeah. No other academy has as much research as Larkwood, and this is the exact method they were working on. Clearly, they made a lot of progress since I last saw it, but between what you overheard from the Warden in Medical and this? Yeah, I'd say she had that lamp put into your room. It explains your high source numbers and late changing."

Hera stared at her hands, and I could almost see her questions. Turning into a shade hadn't just changed where she lived—it had been the catalyst that had stolen even her ability to speak. She'd lost Aaron, her family and her future. It had all happened because of the Warden.

That wasn't the sort of thing a person could easily shake off.

I wanted to wrap an arm around her shoulders, to pull her against me, but I knew better. I needed to keep my hands on the crystal, which left comforting her to someone else.

And the one to step up to the plate? Knox.

At least that means they've worked their shit out.

In fact, now that I thought about it, Knox looked a lot better. After the previous fight, he'd been in one hell of a mood and had moved slower. He'd been a fool to think no one would notice the way he'd walked slower or the way he favored his left side. Clearly, he'd taken a hit or two during the fight that hadn't healed.

And when he pulled her against his side without any flinching, I had a feeling he'd fed from her.

Why did that make me so happy?

Maybe because I'd watched them struggle, because I'd had a front-row seat to how terrified of his other side he was. He'd helped me through my insecurities, yet I'd had to sit back while he'd struggled with his own.

Which meant the sight of the two of them having come to some understanding made me feel as if I'd found solid ground as well. It made us, as a group, stronger. Upon escaping Larkwood, one thing I'd discovered was just how much we needed one another.

We'd gone from a random rag-tag collection of strangers to a group, to a — somewhat — cohesive team who all moved toward a common goal. It meant as we settled into our roles, as we worked out the relationships between us all, we grew.

"What does that change?" Kit asked.

Knox looked back, his eyes hard. "Excuse me?"

"We already suspected she wasn't changed naturally, so what does knowing it for sure change? Does it alter our plans at all? Does it change what we need to do?"

"You really want to be so blunt?" Knox asked, his voice taking on a dangerous edge.

"Why not?" Kit stared back, his expression blank as if often was, as though none of this mattered.

Of course, I'd seen the real him, the one who had tried to stop me just before the escape. He'd been panicked then, even if he didn't show it like others.

Knox narrowed his green eyes to slits, and I got the feeling that if Hera wasn't there, they'd have had a serious issue between them.

Kit sighed, then added on, as if wanting to resolve the situation, "I mean that she is what she is. How she got there, why it happened, those don't change where she is now. She still needs to leave—she still needs to hide. Getting lost in the whys will only drag her down and tie her to the past. It will do nothing beneficial for her."

Hera took a deep breath, then moved her hands to answer. *"He's right. I'm not happy about this, but it is what it is. We have to focus on what we have to do, on moving forward."*

"So what's next?" Brax asked.

"Moa said she'd have the next step worked out in the next couple days," I said.

Hera shook her head. *"I have something I need to do first."*

And boy did that not sound good. "What do you have to do?" I asked, sure I wasn't about to like it.

She took a deep breath, then faced me. *"When we leave here, we aren't coming back, right? I need to see my parents before I go."*

Just like I thought. A bad fucking idea…

Hours later, the bed dipped behind me, and a warm body curled around me. Sure, I knew it was Hera. I recognized the curves of her body, the scent of her skin, but that smart-ass part of me couldn't help but respond with some snark.

"Oh, Deacon, so you're finally giving into this sexual tension between us?"

A sharp, quick pain in my side said she'd reacted with a jab of her fingers before wrapping her arms around me.

Because I was in bed—and wearing all of nothing—she touched my skin directly. It meant I soaked in her powers, savoring the sensation, the way it filled me so gently. She sighed, her warm breath spilling across the back of my neck.

She didn't try to have a conversation, as if she only needed my touch right then.

So I held her arm where it was wrapped around me, keeping her against me. "Don't go," I asked, whispering into the darkness, sure she'd known what I meant.

She'd already told us her plan, about some rich, political party her parents were supposed to attend when they got back into town. No one had said a word back as she'd laid it all out for us, explained why it was a good plan, until the silence had gotten to us all. In the end, nothing had gotten decided, and we'd all retreated to our own rooms rather than argue.

She pressed her forehead against my back, tightening her arms around me.

"Going to a party isn't a good idea. Going to the house was bad enough, but actually seeing your parents? At least at the house, you could tell if anyone was close enough to grab you, if anyone was watching, but you can't do that at a party. You can't tell who in a huge crowd might be working for the Warden. Even if the Warden isn't there, what if your parents call her as soon as they see you?"

I wasn't sure why I asked her these things, why I tried to have a conversation when she couldn't respond. I just couldn't not tell her my fears.

"We got out of Larkwood, we risked everything to get here, and you're going to put yourself right back into the line of fire?" I held her tighter and closed my eyes. "I don't want to lose you, Hera. I can't."

She tugged softly until I shifted to lie on my back. She moved over me, sliding her leg across to straddle me. She had on a nightgown that rucked up, and the warmth of her body told me she had nothing on under it. The thin fabric of my boxers did little to separate us.

Still, I tried to ignore the sudden and insistent demands of my body as I stared up at her dimly lit face. Her weight settled against me as she sat up, teasing my hard cock.

"Don't do anything that might take you away from me," I all but pleaded.

Even without the light I could make out her hands moving. *"I can't leave without seeing them one more time. Would you really walk away without seeing your parents again if you could? If they were this close?"*

I set my hands on her thighs, wanting to touch her even if I couldn't deny what she'd said. If I was so near to my mother, I doubted I'd be able to ignore her even if I knew it wasn't safe.

"Is that what you really want for your future?"

"I don't know," she signed. *"I don't know where I'm headed or what I want or what we're striving for. I think about the future and…"* Her hands hung in the air as if she'd stalled. After a moment, she let out a slow breath. *"I can't think about a future, but I know I want to see them again before I lose the chance to. I don't want to regret not taking that chance, so trust me, please."*

"It's not a matter of trust. Wouldn't matter who it was—heading to a place the enemy expects you isn't smart."

"They won't expect it, because like you said, it's dumb."

"I feel like dumb is your specialty sometimes." I squeezed her thigh, holding her tightly as if that could keep her from going. "Take Kit with you."

She frowned, as if that didn't make any sense.

"He's more than capable of dealing with anything that could risk you and his face isn't on the news. Plus, he's got the sort of high-brow attitude that'll fit right in at a party like that. If you took Deacon, he'd just end up punching someone each time they made him feel dumb, which would be a lot. Kit can look like he fits in while also making sure you come back." I sighed, then looked right into her eyes. "And me suggesting you take Kit shows I'm trying here, right?"

Hera offered me a smile that melted me. It was the sort of look that reminded me I was in serious trouble with her. She rendered me helpless when she looked at me like that, when she made me want nothing more than to pull another smile like that from her.

"I don't think Bowen was right," I said, unable to help it. "Because I do trust you. If that's all it took to get me to not use my powers, don't you think I'd have seen it by now? I love you, Hera, and you mean more to me than anyone else. If it were really that easy, I'd know it by now."

She smiled again, but this time it held a sad edge. She called me a liar with that look, implied that even if I didn't understand it, even if I didn't know any better, she believed I held back with her.

She thought that if I only really trusted her, if I opened myself to her, I wouldn't use my power on her.

I couldn't imagine that, though. The idea of someone touching me with that sort of power, it made no sense to me.

She didn't make me say anything, though. Instead, she leaned down and took my lips in a painfully sweet kiss. When she swiped her tongue across my bottom lip, I parted for her, letting her in. She tasted of cinnamon, a holdover from her toothpaste, no doubt.

She dragged one hand down my bare chest and to the line of boxers, pausing for only a moment before reaching down and into them. She wrapped her small, warm hand around my cock, forcing a thin hiss from me. It felt amazing and I lifted my hips into her grasp.

She tilted her head to deepen the kiss, and I lost myself to her, to her touch, to what she offered me. I wondered how I'd been so nervous before, because I wasn't, now. Now, I only felt my need and her desire.

I wrapped my arm around her and flipped us, settling into the space between her thighs. It was strange how small she seemed when I did that, but I didn't give myself long to think about it.

Instead, I pushed my weight off her and reached down her lush body, slipping beneath the silky fabric of her nightgown to find nothing but hot wetness. "Fuck…" I groaned as I ran my fingers up her slit, then focused on that hard bundle of nerves. She arched up against me, reminding me of what I'd done when she'd touched me.

It seemed no matter how different we seemed, we were far more similar. I shifted my hand down and plunged two fingers into her heat, using the heel of my palm against her clit.

She planted one foot against the mattress and lifted her hips with a wanton plea.

"That desperate, huh?" I chuckled, ignoring how the break in my voice gave away how much I wanted this, too.

She bit down on my bottom lip, the sting driving me onward. The way her cunt gripped my fingers said she was more than ready to take me, that she didn't need any more time or effort.

And, hell, I didn't want to wait any longer, either.

I pulled away long enough to push down my boxers, stripping down to nothing so I could have her. I allowed myself a moment to stroke the head of my cock against her folds before sliding deep into her with a single hard thrust.

She released the kiss and exhaled hard, as if surprised.

I pulled myself back enough to look down into her eyes, wanting to check. "You okay?" My words came out breathless, balancing between lust and concern.

She met my gaze, and that hit me like a rough caress. Why was it that when I looked into her hazel eyes, when we were joined, when I was buried so deep inside her, I felt an impossibly deeper connection.?

It made it more than just sex, more than just bodies, sweat and mechanics.

She rolled her hips, and that gave me the confidence to keep going. I pulled back and plunged in deep, taking her roughly and quickly. If Hera had a problem with it, she showed no signs. Instead, she met each thrust of mine, lifting her hips against me, urging me to keep going.

So I did. Especially since I had no idea what would happen, what was coming. So I took her as if it was our last time, as if I'd never get another chance. I lost myself in her body, in the warmth of her, the softness of her skin, the curves of her breasts.

I'd never believed in happiness, not really. I'd thought it some fairy tale people told kids, but I'd lived my life knowing it didn't happen. Hera made me a believer. She made me think that those stories they told about some perfect life were actually possible.

I didn't chase my release, not right away. Instead, I focused on the way she moved, on the little signs she gave about what she enjoyed and what drove her crazy. It was in the clutch of her fingers, the lift of her hips, the way her breath sped.

She was so beautifully close, and the fact I'd done this to her made it all the better. It wasn't Knox, it wasn't anyone else, it was all *me*.

I didn't mind sharing her, but I couldn't deny the confidence I felt because of this moment. Then again, what I'd discovered was that when in the moment, when I let my partner's wants lead, when I stopped thinking and trying to prove anything and just spent time with them, things just worked.

In short? I'd spent too much time worrying, too much time questioning myself.

Now, though, with all my focus on Hera, on us, it just worked.

The sensual roll of her hips and her shiver said she neared her end, and I desperately wanted to watch her crash over that cliff, to watch her freefall into her release. She gasped, her fingers curling in so her nails dug into me just as she came.

Her pussy clamped down around me, the snugness staving off any hope I had of lasting longer. I gave in to the moment, the pressure of her cunt, the connection between us. A tightness rolled through my lower back, my body tensing just before I spilled into her, before I took her lips in a punishing kiss.

She was going to put herself in danger — again — and I was going to have to let her.

But that didn't change that I could enjoy her for right now, that I could take her for a time and pretend it could last forever.

We might have escaped Larkwood, but I knew better than to think all our problems were over.

Chapter Eleven

Kit

The sight of Hera in a fancy party dress shook me. I'd seen her in the Larkwood attire of sweats, I'd seen images of her in her house wearing high-end casual, I'd even seen her in the sundress when I'd first found her after the escape.

None of those had been *this* though. It was the first time I'd seen her all dolled up, when I was forced to recognize just how out of my league she would have been if we'd met outside of Larkwood.

Her hair was pulled up, with curled tendrils hanging down to frame her face. She had subtle makeup on, the kind that looked simple but no doubt took an abundance of time to achieve. She wore a long black dress with lace over her chest that covered the scar at her throat while staying open in the back.

She lifted her hands in a *'what gives?'* gesture, and it made me realize I still stared at her as we got out of the car.

To be fair, it was the first time I'd really seen all her outfit.

I'd already been waiting in the car when she'd gotten in, but somehow, on the sidewalk outside of the mansion where the event was to be held, under the soft glow of the strings of lights, it all seemed so much more romantic.

She wasn't the girl I'd met at Larkwood, but neither was she the pawn she'd been in this world. She'd grown, and for the first time, I truly saw her as she was — as an equal.

"Sorry," I said, not bothering to hide my smile or the slight shyness at having been caught ogling her like a boy who first spots their prom date. "I've never seen you dressed up like this. I suppose you stunned me."

She didn't respond at first, then grinned as if pleased by the praise. *"You dress up well, too,"* she signed.

It made me laugh softly and glance down at the tux I wore. "Sometimes the wardens have liked to trot me out and show me off like a pet. This isn't the first time I've dressed up. Besides, men's fashions don't change so much over time, so this is surprisingly familiar to me."

She shifted her gaze from me toward the front door of the party. Music floated out from the building, beckoning us in, and I held the invitation I'd gotten from Aaron in my pocket. He'd gotten it easily, since his family had been invited. While neither he nor Moa had approved of Hera's plan, neither had they been willing to try to stop her.

I held my hand out to Hera, who hesitated. I got the sense it was less that she didn't want to touch me and more that the entire situation was odd. We felt so normal right now, like any couple, which we had never been.

Still, after that slight delay, she took my hand. I wrapped my fingers around her wrist and tugged her closer, allowing myself a quick kiss to her soft red lips, before sliding her arm through the crook of mine to escort her past the front doors and into the party.

Security stopped us, showing an amazing level of politeness, probably because they had no way of knowing who attending could seriously screw up their life and who couldn't. When I handed over the invitation Aaron had gotten us, the security nodded and welcomed us in under the fake names we'd given.

Mr. and Mrs. Harris Lester.

Sure, that wasn't really my name, but something deep inside me reacted possessively when someone referred to Hera as my wife. I'd never considered myself a man who cared about such things—I'd never wanted a claim like that, not even on Jasmine. I'd loved her, but she'd been her own person. Something about Hera made me more wild, more possessive.

I led her into the party, past the front doors. No one looked at us too closely, at least not out of suspicion. Hera turned quite a few heads all on her own, though none acted as if they recognized her.

Then again, she didn't hold herself as she had before. It was funny how much just a year could make a person's entire aura so different as to render them nearly unrecognizable. She held her head high not because of unearned arrogance but now because she knew her own power.

When a server paused in front of us, I took two wine glasses from the tray and handed one to Hera. At her lifted eyebrow, I smiled. "I am able to drink, though I have no need to consume food or water. Alcohol has no effect on me, however." She peered down at the glass, so I went on. "We look more in place if we have glasses. You may drink that one, but I wouldn't suggest any more than that. You must keep your wits about you."

She nodded, then subtly shifted her gaze around the room. I wondered just how many of the people here she recognized. It was strange because I'd bet it was most of them. This was the world Hera had grown up in, the people she had known. None of them recognized her now, but she'd fitted in so well here not so long ago. Much of my past escaped me, the years growing dimmer until I could hardly recall the early years. Still, I tried to put myself in that place, thought about how I'd feel if I found myself thrust back into the life I'd had before, if the world remained the same while I'd changed.

I had no idea how I would react, which meant I had to give all the credit to Hera for keeping it together as well as she did.

"Do you see them?"

She nodded, then brought her glass to her lips and flicked her gaze behind me. I took the hint and sipped my wine as I turned to glance over my shoulder.

Hera's parents looked as if they could have stepped right out of that painting from her house. It was quite astounding, really. Despite the passing years since then, they hadn't aged or changed a bit. Her mother's hair was the same shade and no new lines showed in her face. They even wore nearly identical forced smiles.

"We should wander around a bit before we approach them," I said. "It's better to survey everything and make sure there isn't anyone else here we need to worry about."

A moment of disappointment said Hera didn't like the idea of not immediately going there, but she nodded quickly. She was smart enough to understand the wisdom of my suggestion.

Once again, she tucked her arm in the crook of mine, and I savored the closeness, the way she fit against me. In fact, it gave me a moment to even think about it as if this could have really been us, as though we were just another happy couple enjoying a party.

I let myself have that, partly because it sold our story better. As we moved through the crowded party, I caught pieces of each conversation. Most were vapid, pointless topics. Stock markets and good help and what the best private school was in the area. They talked about their children's French lessons and violin recitals, and who had gotten an acceptance letter from what prestigious university that their Daddy had made a donation to and who had rebels headed abroad for a year.

"Do I know you?" The voice made me stop short, turning to find an older woman staring hard at me.

I flashed her the brightest smile I could manage. "I'm not sure, but I feel as if I would have remembered you had we met before."

The woman seemed to melt at my practiced words. It was funny, as I was sure given the amount of jewels she had covering her, she was hardly new to flattery. Still, she reacted to my words as if they hit her better.

She'd hardly noted Hera, and when she finally did, her expression had hints of jealousy. I doubted she expected anything between her and I, but she likely still viewed a younger woman as a rival. "How lovely you two look together," she said, words dripping with condescension.

Hera smiled but it matched the woman's, with the same barely concealed threat. It made me realize how easily Hera navigated this world. If she had offered an honest smile, it wouldn't have fit. It would have labeled her as easy prey. Instead, she matched the woman's level of aggression. It made it clear she wouldn't be walked on and that she belonged in this arena.

I matched my expression to hers and spoke to the woman. "Please, excuse us, we still have quite a few people to greet. I'm sure you understand how these things are."

The woman nodded. "Of course. It was wonderful speaking to you both. I hope our paths cross again." With that, she took her leave.

I leaned closer to Hera and lowered my voice so only she could hear. "Those are some impressive claws you have. Dare I say, if I wasn't already madly in love with you, I certainly would be now."

Pink colored her cheeks, and she jerked her gaze away. It made me remove my arm from hers and drag my fingers up her bare back, teasing the tempting skin there. "It is a pity we have a task ahead. While you look enchanting in that gown, I am quite certain you would look even better out of it."

Her full lips parted as though she couldn't draw in enough air, a sure sign that my words landed.

And the temptation to do as I claimed surprised me. I was normally clear-headed to a fault, more than willing to put aside any momentary desires to achieve my goals. Why was it that right now, I struggled to focus? The thought of pulling her into a side room, of stripping her out of her dress, hit me hard.

I pulled her against me, swaying slightly, appearing like any other couple in love, the sort who were still early enough in our relationship to struggle with self-control. I let my lips brush her ear as I leaned in close. I knew I didn't need to be so close—her hearing was phenomenal, after all—but I wanted this to feel intimate.

"I didn't get the chance to see you well last time. I was so ravenous for you I didn't savor as I should have. I intend to remedy that." As I whispered, I stroked my thumb against her back, rewarded with a shiver. "Rest assured, the next time I get you alone, I will spend all the time exploring every last inch of you. It is a time I find myself thankful for my not needing sleep. I can spend as much time as I wish devoted to my exploration." I said the words to tease her, but somehow, they turned me on just as much.

She trembled in my arms, and it made me want to keep her there forever, to swear that nothing would ever cause her harm again.

That wasn't possible, of course, not even for me, but I still felt an undeniable need to promise it.

At least until a throat clearing to our side reminded me of where we were.

Which was in the middle of a party with people who would throw her back into Larkwood in a heartbeat if they got the slightest chance to do so.

"Unfortunately, that will have to wait," I said as I moved away from her, but kept my hand on her back to guide her. "For now, it's time to see who we came to see."

Hera nodded, appearing shaken by either my words or the task ahead of us. Whatever it was, I used my hand on her to pull her closer to my side.

I couldn't protect her from everything, but I'd damn well protect her from what I could.

Hera

Who is this man and what did he do with Kit? I couldn't stop the thought from hitting me when Kit had whispered those filthy promises into my ear.

The man I'd grown close to over my year at Larkwood had been careful and steady. I'd seen no signs of desire from him. Then, I'd glimpsed that passion beneath his carefully cultivated surface when he'd seen me after the escape, but that had been quick and wild.

This seemed another side of his, one where he was teasing and tempting.

And I liked every side of his. They all pulled me in in a different way, all spoke to a different side of myself.

Except, his words reminded me we hadn't come to flirt and play footsie.

I peered across the room to watch my parents say goodbye to someone, their smiles forced and tense. It seemed they were as easy for me to read as they had been before. After that parting, my parents went back toward one of the private rooms. No doubt, they'd grown tired and wanted a moment to collect themselves, and they were important enough to have access to the VIP rooms there.

I nodded that direction, and Kit nodded back, telling me he understood my point.

We went up the stairs they had, following their path to the door. Before opening, I paused just outside, straining to listen for any sign of an ambush.

I wouldn't put it past my parents to work with the Warden in order to trick me, even if I hated that thought.

I shook my head. No signs of anyone else.

The handle didn't turn, so I stepped aside and gestured at it. Kit wrapped his hand around it and twisted. To anyone looking, it would seem he'd simply opened the door. He showed no outward signs of using much force, yet the lock snapped open.

As soon as it did, he pushed the door and held it open for me, allowing me to walk in first.

And for the first time since they'd thrown me away, I stood face-to-face with my parents...

Chapter Twelve

Hera

"Hera..." My mother's voice came out soft and full of so much pain.

Well, at least she knew who I was. I didn't know how I'd feel if my own mother hadn't recognized me anymore.

I opened my mouth to respond, but no sounds escaped. I dropped my gaze, ashamed for the first time in a long-damned time. What was it about parents that could make a person feel like a little kid?

The gentle touch of Kit's hand at my lower back gave me courage. Somehow, having him by my side helped. I glanced his way and he nodded, knowing my question already.

"I couldn't leave without seeing you both again."

Kit translated for me, keeping his voice without inflection and without adding any extra words or thoughts. It helped me feel that my true meaning was getting through.

My mother moved her gaze between Kit and me, an obvious question there.

I didn't bother to answer her. At this point, she didn't deserve any answers about my life. She'd lost that privilege.

When I showed no signs of giving in, her eyes widened. It was probably the first time I'd really stood up to her. Still, it prompted her to answer. "I thought you were still gone."

By *gone* she meant locked up in Larkwood. What a ridiculous way to phrase that, to water it down. *Gone* pretended I had been at a spa or on vacation instead of imprisoned and tortured.

"I decided I didn't want to die there, so I escaped. Don't worry, I'm not here to cause you problems. I just couldn't leave without seeing you both one more time."

My father frowned as Kit translated my words. He stared at me, his eyes so familiar that they hurt. When Kit finished, my father walked closer to me. He reached out, but Kit moved faster, wrapping his large hand around my father's wrist, a warning on his face.

I set my hand on Kit's hand to tell him it was fine, that I wasn't afraid.

My parents were terrible people, clearly, but I didn't believe either had the guts to hurt me outright. They'd never even spanked me as a child, probably because neither had cared enough to do it.

Kit didn't release my father right away, narrowing his eyes for a moment as he stared him down. "Your daughter is a lot more understanding than I am. I would suggest you remember that before choosing to do anything unwise."

My father didn't wilt, staring back. "And who are you?"

"Who I am matters far less than what." He shifted the hand that held my father's wrist, the bones twisting to take on his wendigo form.

My father jerked away, and he let him do so. Kit took a step backward, as though happy enough to have made his point that he didn't feel the need to hover so close.

My father gulped, then reached out again, much more slowly. He touched the lace neckline of my gown and pulled it down slightly, just enough to see the scar at my throat. His expression softened. "I saw it on the video before," he said softly, "but that was different. It was easier to think you weren't my daughter anymore."

"She's the same person," Kit said. "No matter what the government wants to tell people, the truth is that shades retain their old personalities. I've seen many changed over my life, and they're all different, because people are all different."

"But I've seen how dangerous they are," my mother said.

I was taken back to the werewolf I'd seen with her, when I'd been younger, recalling how scary the situation had been. *They show us what they want us to see. The truth is that the right drugs, the right treatment, the right subject and anyone can seem dangerous. It doesn't take much to drug up and torture a werewolf until they turn feral, then show it off and say, 'look, they're all monsters!'*

Both of my parents seemed to listen as Kit translated. Whether they believed me, whether it sank in or not, that I had no idea. It would likely take time, assuming they ever really understood. A part of me hated I even cared if they believed or understood me. It shouldn't matter, not after all they'd done.

"You never would have spoken to us like this before," my mother said. "You don't seem like the same girl."

"That's because I spent a year locked away. Do you have any idea what life is like there? I was completely alone. They took away all my freedom, experimented on me, drugged me. I was attacked by guards and by other shades. That will change anyone. It made me realize that if I had one life, if I could only do this once, I was going to stop worrying about what other people thought, about what they wanted from me. It wasn't turning into a shade that changed me – it was getting imprisoned at Larkwood."

"The Warden said—"

Kit cut my father off before he could get the rest of whatever he planned to say out. "The Warden is at fault for her changing in the first place."

"What?" My father's voice held surprise and honest disbelief. Clearly, he had no idea of the Warden's plans. Not that I ever really thought they'd had a part of it— my turning into a shade didn't benefit them at all, and they did little that couldn't help them.

Kit continued. "We found a lamp on the nightstand in her room with a crystal inside. The crystal creates small, concentrated tears that release high levels of source. That is the reason Hera changed and why her levels of source are far higher than anything we've seen before. She was an experiment—nothing more."

My mother shook her head. "I've known Anna for years. She'd never do something like that."

Hearing the Warden's real name felt strange to me. She was always 'the Warden' at Larkwood, with no one uttering her actual name, as if it were a spell that might risk drawing her attention. Hearing it now almost humanized her.

"She's gotten a lot of extra favors from you to keep me out of sight, hasn't she? That's probably why she never mentioned to you that I escaped, because she wants to keep getting things from you. The well dries up for her without me."

My mother pressed her lips together, a clear sign she accepted at least some of what I said. Then again, my parents might have been shitty parents, but they were very intelligent. When presented with obvious information, they wouldn't ignore them just because they didn't like them, especially if that information made it clear they were being used or taken advantage of.

"I don't know about all this," my father said with a conflicted expression. "But I'm glad you came."

Something struck me, a sound that pulled at me even if I wasn't sure why. It made me close my eyes and filter through all that background noise, the sounds that rested on the peripherals of my senses. I identified and abandoned conversation after conversation—a couple having an affair, a woman calling her nanny to check on her kids, the waitstaff complaining about the rude party guests.

Then I found it. "Have you seen her? Her hair might be different."

"Not yet. I studied the men's faces, too, so if any of them are here, I'll know."

My blood ran cold at that, at the realization that they could only mean me. It meant Larkwood had guards here looking for me.

I turned my gaze to Kit, my eyes wide. The way he tensed said he read my expression correctly.

"It seems our meet and greet is over. Larkwood guards are here." He offered my parents a hard look. "I'd say if you ever cared about her at all, you should not mention having seen her, but I don't honestly believe that would make a difference to either of you. Instead, I will say something that will likely strike deeper for you. If either of you value your own lives and future, do not cause her any additional trouble."

Kit's tone left no room for misunderstanding his meaning. It was a threat—plain and simple.

My parents nodded, offering him a startled look. Their life had people who threatened more subtly, who could destroy a person's reputation and legacy, but not ones who would attack a person physically.

"No matter what you believe about me, I loved my daughter," my father said.

The use of loved past tense spoke volumes, didn't it?

He didn't move closer, locked in some sort of battle of wills with Kit.

My mother, meanwhile, stared at me. I sighed, once again disappointed. It was hard to admit, but I'd secretly wanted them to give a damn. I'd wanted to stand before them and have them realize what a huge mistake they'd made. I'd dreamed of them telling me that they were sorry, that they'd been wrong, that they understood now and wouldn't send me away again.

I didn't get any of that, though.

I struggled to hide my disappointment in how they'd failed me yet again.

I let out a slow breath, then turned to walk out.

A hand wrapped around my arm, and I turned ready to see what Kit wanted, only to find it wasn't him. It was my mother. She pulled me into a tight hug, one that felt nothing like what I'd experienced from her before.

Normally hugs with my parents felt like a show. They rarely happened unless others were around, unless they were expected and furthered the lie of a happy family. This was nothing like that. Instead, my mother clutched me tightly, her fingers digging into my back, holding onto me as if afraid to let go.

I returned her hug, unable to help it, and I had no idea how long I basked in the unexpected affection. Eventually, Kit's voice broke the spell, his tone all apology. "Hera, we need to get going."

My mother pulled away, her eyes red, but even still, she said nothing. She didn't apologize, didn't tell me we'd figure things out.

Then again, what I'd gotten was already more than I ever had expected.

I nodded at my parents as my own goodbye before following Kit. All of this would be for nothing if I got caught here.

I took his hand, and he pulled me behind him, his gaze hard as he studied the room. His focus was unparalleled, and it reminded me just how capable he truly was. He guided me along the back wall of the upstairs, then toward a door near the south end. "There are a set of stairs near the back that lead out to the courtyard. We can scale the back wall once we're there." He didn't look back at me, so I squeezed his hand in agreement.

We went through the door he indicated after he opened it with another twist of his hand that resulted in the crack of a lock.

When he pulled the door open, we froze.

On the other side of that door stood the one person I really didn't want to see.

The Warden.

I took a step backward.

She smiled, her calm and collected expression making it seem that she'd planned this all.

Maybe she had. She'd proven herself remarkably calculated, and I wouldn't put anything past her.

"Ms. Weston," she said. "My advisors didn't believe you would come here, that I was wasting my time, but after I saw the footage of you visiting your parents' home, I knew you would come here. It was the look on your face, this wishful, wanting expression. I saw it from you before, back in Larkwood, and it made me have the camera feed at your parents' house monitored — people who look like that don't just walk away. No matter how smart or powerful a person is, sentimentality tends to get them in the end."

Kit tucked me behind him and spread his arms wide in threat.

The Warden glanced at him. "You, however, have surprised me. I had assumed as a wendigo, you'd have easily outmatched a siren. Wendigos are known for their ability to bend any being to their will, and yet it seems this one little siren managed to do that to you. How pathetic. Where is Deacon?"

"Breathing, last I checked, but the gorge I threw him into was a rather long way. I can't guarantee he still is."

The Warden shook her head. "What a pity. He was a rather useful tool. Still, I thought you a better tactician than this. Are you truly willing to put this woman's life above that of your daughter?"

I didn't need to look at Kit to feel tension that ran through him. Her question had haunted me as well.

Yet, when Kit spoke, he did so without any hesitation. "I know you lied to me about my daughter all these years. Why would I trust anything you say?"

The Warden turned her gaze to me for a moment. "So you found out the truth and told him? You truly are troublesome, you know that? Fine, yes, I've had your daughter all along. That should make you more willing to heel rather than less, though. I have a very useful chess piece."

"A wendigo isn't a chess piece. That has been one of your mistakes, to think we are. If my daughter is anything like me, you won't be able to control her for long, no matter what you do. We are creatures not suited for captivity."

I thought back to the girl I'd met, and he was right. It was one of Larkwood's biggest issues. They thought they could control us all, but that wasn't how things worked. They weren't as strong as they thought.

"I won't let you take Hera," Kit said. "Between the two of us, you won't be able to do this quietly. Are you prepared for the collateral damage that will occur here, the political backlash?"

The Warden grinned. "Rest assured, I have no plans to turn this into a conflict if I can avoid it."

I moved slightly out to look at her more clearly, to read her expression. My hands moved, and Kit glanced my way so he could translate. *"Why not?"*

"I like to hedge my bets and determine the best course based on the current circumstances. I've seen too many people fail because they let themselves follow things to an unfavorable conclusion, usually based on their own arrogance. I'm not so foolish. You've proven yourself more troublesome than I ever would have expected from a spoiled rich girl. I picked you because not only would your parents be useful, but I expected you to be easily controlled."

"So what are you going to do?"

"I will offer you a deal," the Warden said. When I didn't respond, she crossed her arms, her back straight. "I know when to cut my losses. You were useful because of your parents. I believe I can still salvage some that, but keeping you under control is far too difficult a task. Not to mention, if I caused a scene here, it would harm my case. So I propose something that will help us both. You turn around and run, just as you plan. Run away with your friends and do not return to this country. Go live your life out in whatever hole you wish. Just ensure I don't hear a word about you. In exchange, I won't come looking. I'll tell your parents I captured you again, and everyone will move on."

"Move on? You turned me into a shade, ruined my life, and you think we can just pretend none of this happened?"

"What I think is that you can have a life again. It may not be the same life you had before, but you still can have one. Isn't that what you want? Isn't that why you did all this? My having anything to do with how you ended up here doesn't change where you go from here."

Her words drove my temper up and made me want to use that power she'd forced into me, made me want to throw her against the opposite wall. She turned me into this — she should get a real taste of what it meant.

Kit set his hand on mine, which made me realize I'd drawn it into a fist. The touch helped cool my temper.

This wasn't just about me. Doing anything to her now would turn this into an all-out fight, and that wouldn't help anyone. Not only could innocents get hurt, but the odds of escaping it weren't great. I couldn't throw everything away for nothing. I needed to bide my time.

So I drew in a deep breath then exhaled slowly. *"What if I don't accept your offer?"*

Her smile held no concern, as if she already knew I'd do as she'd planned, that I'd fall into her trap. "Then I will have you picked up and brought back to Larkwood. I will drug you to the point that you never cause a problem for me again. I will recapture your friends and have them sent to the North Tower. I am fully capable of ending this the way I want it to end. I'd just prefer to do it with the least risk possible." She nodded behind me, which made me turn to find a number of men dressed nicely, their hard gazes locked on me, telling me they were from Larkwood.

She moved past Kit and me as if she had no fear of us. "It's up to you, Ms. Weston. Do you want to die in Larkwood, or do you want your freedom?" She peered over her shoulder, her lips curled into a confident grin. "I trust you'll make the right choice and be very happy for the rest of your life."

She offered me everything I wanted—freedom, safety, a chance at a real life. To get me through those horrible days in Larkwood, I had focused on my one goal, on escaping, on surviving. Now the Warden gave me exactly what I'd wanted, but now that it was so close, could I really accept it?

Running away because I didn't have another option felt like survival, but having that door held open for me made me hesitate. Could I really leave knowing everything I now knew? After seeing what the world was really like, could I still turn my back on it all?

I'd chased my own survival so far, unwilling to admit that I was part of a community, that I was a shade, that their plight was mine. The Warden was offering me a chance to not have to look over my shoulder anymore, but it meant turning my back on everything that I'd learned, on the horrors I'd seen, the people I'd watched suffer.

I never thought I'd hesitate, yet here I stood, frozen.

The Warden was holding open a door for me, a chance at a future, everything I thought I wanted...but I didn't know if I was the sort of girl who could walk through it anymore.

* * * *

Brax

"The Warden is just letting us go?" I struggled to accept and make sense of it.

The Warden wasn't the sort of woman to just give up, especially after we'd embarrassed her by escaping. Was this some sort of trick? Was she trying to get us to let our guards down?

That didn't make much sense. It would be far easier to hit us unaware.

"So it seems," Kit answered. "I told her I'd probably killed Deacon, so she believes he is still loyal if he lives."

Deacon snorted, as if he didn't care for the lie. Then again, I got that. I didn't like the idea of Kit being able to take me out, or someone else believing it so easily.

Whether or not it was true, well, that I wasn't sure of. If it were a fair fight, I believed I could take Kit, but the problem with fighting a man like Kit was that if he could steal a person's free will, there was no real fight.

It was like fighting Hera. If she could speak, if a scream could take out an enemy before they ever got a chance to get close, what hope was there?

"Could it be a trick?" Wade asked, voicing my own concern.

Deacon shook his head. "I doubt it. I've worked under the Warden for a while, and it wouldn't make any sense to offer that only to trick us. It makes more sense for her offer to be real. If Hera leaves, the Warden can use her name to get favors without risking another riot. She'd probably finally realized just how dangerous Hera is, not just because of her powers but because she's got an impressive ability to get people to work together — even people who are normally enemies. The Warden hasn't ever faced that before."

"Doesn't that mean it'd be better to get rid of her?" Knox asked.

Deacon peered at Hera, as if in apology for the conversation. "Not really. Sure, it'd be better if Hera was at Larkwood, but since she isn't, it changes the risk and reward. The less dangerous option is to just let her go. She's trusting that Hera wants to stay out of there enough that she'll happily take her up on the offer."

"So we're taking that choice, right?" I asked when no one spoke.

It was the obvious one.

Except... everyone remained silent.

Hera stared at the floor rather than at me.

"This is what we wanted. This was our plan. We escaped because we wanted away from Larkwood. We wanted to be free. The Warden is offering it up to us and you're hesitating?" My temper slipped, my jaws aching from my fangs dropping.

"This changes things," Wade said, ever the bleeding heart. "We need to think about our next step."

"What next step? If we don't take her up on the choice, we'll end up right back where we started. That's all we've got. Options A and B."

No one responded, neither to argue with me nor agree. Everyone knew I was right, but no one wanted to be the bad guy who said, 'it's not my job to save everyone else.'

Berserkers were used to being the bad guys, though. I was accustomed to being the brute, the killer, the dangerous one. If everyone wanted to blame me for being smart, for doing what was right, that was fine. So long as it protected Hera, I'd take that hit.

"I'll be the asshole. We are *leaving*. I don't care who is still at Larkwood, I don't give a fuck about how other shades are getting treated here. That's not our problem. We aren't saviors, we aren't fighting the system and we sure as fuck aren't going to risk getting locked back up because we want to play hero. I'm leaving tomorrow and I'm taking Hera with me. Anyone with a speck of smarts will go, too."

With that, I rose and stormed out, slamming the door hard enough to crack the wood.

I went to my room, then paced back and forth. Each time I thought I might have calmed myself, the thought of Hera ending up back in Larkwood drove my rage right up again. It was as if she had not only the key for easing my anger but could dial it the other direction as well.

How long I paced, I wasn't sure, but soon enough, the door of my room opened.

Only two people would dare approach me in this mood—Hera or Knox.

A glance toward the door told me exactly which it was, though.

"You shouldn't be around me right now," I told Hera. The last thing I wanted was to risk her with my temper as precarious as it was. I didn't believe I'd ever hurt her physically, but I didn't want to say something I'd regret or worse, frighten her.

She shook her head as she shut the cracked door, closing us in. *"I'm not afraid of you,"* she signed, her back against the door.

And boy did that make me want to prove her wrong. Maybe it was because I still felt challenged, but I found myself moving closer until I crowded her, wanting to see her recoil, wanting to remind myself that no matter what I did, I'd always be the untrusted one, the scary one. My entire worth rested in losing my control.

But she didn't rise to the occasion. She stared up and into my eyes as if we were having a calm conversation rather than what was happening.

I brought my hands up and slammed them against the door, caging her in. And maybe it was pathetic, but I liked it. I enjoyed having her like this, wanted to push her, to trap her.

And Hera reacted without a single sign of panic. Even though I was sure I looked every bit the monster I felt like, dancing on the edge of losing myself entirely, she didn't even flinch.

"I won't lose you," I swore to her, my voice a rough, desperate growl. "Not after everything we've survived, not now. I don't care what anyone says, I won't let it happen—I can't."

She reached up and set her hands on my cheeks. I could have laughed at the way I flinched. Even though my entire point had been to get that reaction from her, I'd been the one to blink first.

Figures, doesn't it? She's always been tougher than I am.

She stared into my eyes, and she didn't need to say a word for me to get her point. She wanted to go back.

"Why?" I asked, dropping the play, not bothering to hide the quaking fear in my voice. "Why aren't you jumping at the chance to run? This is what we wanted all along."

She sighed softly, then pulled me closer and brushed her lips against mine. Funny that after how well we knew each other, after the time together, I could read her without her having to say a thing.

Worse, her kiss eased my berserker. No matter how badly I wanted to be angry, she sucked it right out of me. She broke the kiss and looked at me, a question in those soft hazel eyes of hers.

Would I follow? Despite my fears, my misgivings, would I trust her? Would I help her...

I let out a rough breath before resting my forehead against hers, still caging her in between the door and my body. A part of me wanted to figure this out right now, to go head-to-head until she gave in and saw things my way. I wanted to have her explain to me just what the hell she was thinking so I could tell her how wrong she was. Rather than that, however, I whispered the truth, the thing beneath all the churning rage inside me. "I can't survive without you, Hera. Remember that whatever you choose to do, you're gambling with more than just your own life." I let the rest of my anger leave me and sagged against her. Then she kissed me, the touch gentle and sweet and a whole different sort of tension grew inside me.

No matter what I'd said before, I couldn't force her to do as I wanted, but she'd understand how strongly I felt about her soon. I'd make the point and burn away my fears and anger with her body.

Maybe, after a few hours together, I wouldn't feel so damned out of control.

* * * *

Hera

As it turned out, letting a berserker take out his anger on a person would leave them sore and tired. Sure enough, the aches and pains in my body said he'd worked out a lot of aggression.

And I'd enjoyed every last moment of it. Brax could be surly and difficult and passionate, but he could turn that same intensity on me.

We'd spent hours in bed together, teasing and tasting every inch of each other, reminding me of one of the many reasons I loved him.

However, it meant when we'd finished, after we'd both showered and redressed, we found ourselves back in the living space with the rest of our group. I stood before the rest of them, having taken some of that time resting with Brax afterward to explore how I really felt.

I hadn't been able to sleep, instead staring at the ceiling as the past year replayed in my head over and over again. I saw the shades in Larkwood, the ones frightened and abused and alone. I thought about Wade getting sent there so young, about how many had died leaving behind nothing but names in files. I remembered Bowen trying so hard to keep his group alive and the squalor they lived in. It all swirled together in my head, the reality of the world and the people who I was leaving behind.

And for what? For what future? No matter how many times since my life had gotten fucked over I tried, I hadn't been able to picture an actual future for myself. Even when I wanted nothing more than to escape, I had no clear idea of what that would actually look like.

And I finally understood why. I finally figured out why no future came to me, why, no matter how much I wanted to be with the men I loved, I couldn't answer what I wanted after this was over.

And *no one* would like that answer.

I knew what I had to do, but I couldn't do it alone, and I owed these men so much...

They had to make their own choices.

"*I can't leave,*" I signed, met with a chorus of grumbles that said none of them loved the idea.

Not that it shocked me. These men were nothing if not protective.

Still, I pressed on, needing them to understand what I finally had figured out. "*You've all trusted me and done more than I have any right to ask of you. We made it out of Larkwood together. I'm only alive because of you all.*" I paused for a moment, then got to the hardest part. "*When we left, all I could see was myself, was what I'd lost. I didn't really think about shades — I don't think I even really thought of myself as one. Since then, I've seen what life is like for shades. I've finally seen that life outside of Larkwood isn't much better than life inside it. I can't go and live some happy life and pretend I don't know how many are still here suffering. I don't think I can spend the next forty years of my life closing my eyes at night and knowing I did nothing, that I didn't even try to do something.*"

"You can't think you can fix that for the whole world," Knox said, his voice unfailingly kind. He used the same tone a person used when breaking bad news to a child.

"Maybe not, but I can't just do nothing, either. I've seen how big of an influence Larkwood and the Warden have. They have power over politicians and legislation that hurts all shades. They tell the story they want and the public believes it, because they don't know any better. If we could just take out Larkwood, it would change so much. If we could make people see the truth, we could make a difference."

Deacon crossed his arms and shook his head. "You managed to about burn down half of Larkwood and it only took a week for it to look like it had never happened. That proves attacking Larkwood doesn't work."

"Larkwood has the power it does because of the story it tells. We've got to stop letting it control the narrative. We've got to take that back and tell the truth. People go along with Larkwood. They pay whatever the Warden wants because she tells them we're dangerous and they need her to keep them safe. What if we got the truth out?"

"And how do you expect that to work?" Brax asked. "Plenty of bleeding hearts have tried to expose the truth and change how the public views shades. This isn't a new idea, so why do you think you can do it any better?"

I peered at the door just as it opened and two people walked in.

Moa and Aaron waved awkwardly.

"You've got to be kidding me," Brax muttered.

"I've worked at helping shades for years," Moa said. "I've seen what they went through and realized I couldn't just do nothing. I've helped a lot, but no matter how hard I work, the problem remains. I want to do something that actually helps. Something that stops this at the source."

Aaron tucked his hands into his jacket pockets, rocking his weight forward, to his heels, then back again. "You've got no reason to trust me, but after Hera got taken away, I had time to think. I don't want to be the person my parents want me to be anymore. The world turns out to be bigger than I thought, so I pursued journalism instead of business, and this story? It's one that matters."

Aaron's words surprised me. They lacked any arrogance, any of that bullshit savior-complex thing that was so common in men from his history. He didn't want to save people—he wanted to help in whatever way he could.

I nodded at them both, my own thank you for two people who were willing to risk themselves in a fight that wasn't their own.

"I'm going back to Larkwood to finish this, but I don't expect any of you to come with me. If you don't want to, if you're done, I won't blame you. You've all suffered, and you deserve the freedom we fought so hard for. I'm going to go with Aaron and Moa for right now, because it isn't fair to ask you right now. I can't put you on the spot. What I'm going to do is more likely to get us killed than it is to work, but I still have to try. So, I want you to have time to think, to really consider what future you want. Larkwood stole so much from us all and I can't do the same thing. Only you can decide what you want."

It felt nearly impossible to finish the statement. They needed this, and it was the right thing, but it didn't make it any easier. I wanted them by my side. I didn't know if I could do this on my own. I needed their support and their presence in my life.

But I'd do right by them no matter what.

"If you want to help, meet me here in two nights." I set a card with the address where I'd be on the table.

I didn't look at the men again, unable to stomach seeing them and still walking away. Somehow, that was scarier than facing Larkwood. Instead, I went outside with Aaron and Moa and tried to hide just how much it hurt.

Chapter Thirteen

Hera

I put my feet on the coffee table as I leaned back, trying to look comfortable despite the situation.

"How long has it been?" Moa set a mug of hot cocoa on the table beside me.

"Feels like forever." Aaron sat in the recliner, slouching down the way he'd always done when not in view of his overly strict mother.

I took the writing pad and scribbled down my response. *"It's only been a year..."*

Moa blew out a slow breath before she took a seat beside me, her own drink cupped in her palms. "Is that all? God, it feels like so much longer. I thought we'd all head off to college and nothing else would ever change." She looked toward me, but her gaze landed on my throat before jerking away as if not wanting to make me uncomfortable.

I smirked before writing. *"It's fine. I'm not that sensitive about it. You don't get to be sensitive about stuff like this in Larkwood."*

Her cheeks flushed, but she nodded and allowed herself to really stare at the scar. "I just can't believe it. It feels like a story that happened to someone else, like it couldn't all be real. Larkwood, you, the work I've done. It all feels like so much."

Her words struck me as oddly naïve, and it made me want to laugh. Maybe it was because of all I'd suffered, but too much didn't mean anything to me anymore. I'd watched others killed, saw them imprisoned, had suffered so much pain myself that it all felt very real to me.

It wasn't like I could blame her for that, though. She'd done what she could with what she had. If anything, I should have been happy that she didn't have a frame of reference that would let her understand the reality of life as a shade. It took me back to what felt like so long ago, when we'd walked around the day I'd been attacked.

The three of us had picked out those necklaces, worried about our future, and Moa had lectured me about that young werewolf we'd seen. I'd shaken my head as I'd accepted that her history hadn't allowed her to understand the truth.

Funny how things changed yet stayed the same. This time I felt the same, about her history blinding her, but she'd been right before where I'd been wrong.

"Do you think they'll come?" Aaron asked.

"Yes." I wrote without hesitation.

Aaron took a sip of his drink, his eyes locked on me. He didn't say anything directly, but that look sure meant something, didn't it?

Moa must have picked up the strained tension between us, because she laughed the way she always had when she was playing nice. "What will you do when we succeed?"

That question hit me hard, made me consider a future. The idea of winning felt so far away, so impossible. What sort of future could I have after all this?

I wanted to say I planned to buy some farm and live off the grid and spend my days with backyard chickens and a vegetable garden. That was the right answer, wasn't it? The one everyone gave after so much trauma.

I couldn't even picture such a thing.

"I want to be happy," I admitted. *"I've spent my whole life living up to other people's expectations. I did what my parents wanted me to because I thought that was right. I thought it was the path I was supposed to take."*

"But not anymore?" Moa asked.

I shook my head. *"When I saw my parents, I realized they were doing what they thought they had to. The world is full of people doing what they think they should, and they hide behind that when they do terrible things. I did it, too. I ignored reality because I thought that had nothing to do with me. Now, I'm done living by other's rules."*

Moa let out a long sigh. "That sounds great, but not many people can do that. They can't just decide to live their life differently."

"Didn't you? Bowen sending us to you says you've been making your own choices."

Moa offered a soft smile. "I guess. I just couldn't sit back and do nothing. I couldn't start a revolution or attack Larkwood or do anything for you, but I figured if nothing else, I could maybe help a couple shades find freedom."

The way she spoke, so unaware of how much she'd done, what she'd risked, made me really look at my friend.

I'd been so angry before between what had happened with Aaron and generally wanting someone to blame. I'd wanted to hate Moa because she'd gotten to keep living her life, because she hadn't had her life torn apart like mine, but hearing her speak made me recognize how little she saw her own accomplishments.

"Do you know how scary life is when you're alone and on the run? I didn't know what I was going to do, how I was going to get out of the country, who I could trust. I ran into trouble where Bowen was when a group of men attacked a child. I saw the way humans looked at me, the way the guards saw me, the way Medical at Larkwood used me like a toy without caring about me at all. I came out of the hell of Larkwood to find the outside world no less dangerous, no less willing to destroy me for no reason. You being there, you risking yourself knowing what Larkwood would do if they found you, it was a light in a very dark tunnel for me. Don't think for a moment that what you do doesn't matter."

I tore the page from the writing pad and handed it over to her, wanting her to keep it, to read it again and again until it stuck.

Moa read the words slowly, tracing them with her finger. Her eyes reddened, a sure sign I'd gotten to her. Then again, I fully understood how it felt to think I wasn't doing enough, to think I wasn't living up to what I could, and that was a very heavy burden to bear for long.

She folded the paper and tucked it into her pocket as though precious, then gave me a smile. "Thank you—I needed to read that, I think. It's hard to fight when I don't know if I'm doing anything, when I feel like I'm not making progress or a difference. It's hard to offer help but then not know if it mattered at all, if the shades got away."

"Even if they were caught later, I can tell you that having someone willing to help, having someone look at me like I'm not a monster, that makes a difference."

Moa blinked slowly, then glanced up at the ceiling as if to stop herself from crying.

I gave her privacy by turning my gaze to Aaron to take the attention off her. *"So, journalism, huh? I can't imagine your dad was happy when you told him."*

I pictured Aaron's dad, the stern-looking man who rarely smiled at me when I'd come over.

Aaron shrugged. "He wasn't happy at first, but he got over it pretty fast. He told me that he wanted me happy, and if I really thought journalism would make me happy, he'd support me."

I tried to picture my own parents reacting to me in such a way, but I couldn't. They weren't the type to accept something they didn't like. In fact, they'd left me in hell just so I didn't risk denting their precious reputation.

"I'm glad he accepted it," I wrote, trying to ignore the pain.

Moa glanced between us, then stood. "I better get some sleep. Tomorrow's going to get here early, and I haven't had enough respect for mornings lately." She excused herself quickly, leaving me and Aaron alone.

Somehow, it was both less and more awkward than the last time. Maybe it was because I'd had time to calm down, to prepare myself to deal with him. We had a better feeling of where we were, but that didn't erase the years we'd had together.

"I really did love you," Aaron whispered. "You said I didn't, and maybe I didn't love you the way you wanted, but I did love you."

"*I know,*" I answered even if it wasn't a question. "*I loved you, too.*"

He snorted softly. "No, you didn't. Don't look at me like that. It isn't an attack. At first, when I saw you with those men, I didn't understand. Sure, it was my own fault that you didn't wait for me—I didn't wait for you—but that didn't change that it hurt me. I looked at you and I didn't understand why you never looked at me like you look at them."

I sighed because I couldn't deny it. No matter how much I wanted to, I couldn't stop myself from admitting he was right. I hadn't felt about him the way I should have, the way I tried to.

Or, hell, maybe I hadn't ever tried hard enough.

"I'm not judging you, Hera. Life happened the way it happened. I like to think sometimes that it could have been different, that if you hadn't changed, if you hadn't gotten taken away, maybe we would have grown together, you know? Maybe we could have found what everyone else thought we could have."

"*No, we wouldn't have,*" I wrote. "*I think sometimes people work or they don't, and you and me? We didn't work.*"

Aaron lifted one of his eyebrows, no doubt thrown by my argument. I'd never been the type to argue with him. Normally, I'd given in, accepting his choices, playing the part everyone expected me to. I wasn't that same girl anymore, though. "Why not? What was wrong with me that you don't think we could have fallen in love for real?"

I thought about it, then answered, writing slowly. "*Because you never saw me. It wasn't your fault—I never saw myself. I didn't know who I was, so how could we ever be close or honest if we were both hiding?"*

He read the words over slowly then let out a soft laugh. "You know, you've gotten pretty smart over the last year. I can't say I fully understand, but don't get me wrong—I don't have any hard feelings. I pushed you away, I made my mistakes, and I take the blame for what happened. I still think we would have been happy, that I could have been a man you could have loved, but I screwed it up. I'll still do whatever it takes to help you, to do the right thing now."

He pushed himself up and out of his chair. "I should get some sleep, too. Tomorrow's going to get here early, and I don't know how much sleep we'll be getting pretty soon." He went to pass me, to head toward the bedroom he'd taken.

I grasped his wrist, pulling him to a stop. He peered down into my eyes, and the familiarity of the moment hit me hard.

I didn't love him, but that didn't erase our bond. It didn't erase the years we'd spent together. Time and circumstance changed things, but that didn't mean I could just forget everything and pretend it hadn't happened.

He gave me a kind smile, one that reminded me of when we'd been younger, before the problems of dating and romance had colored our relationship, when we'd just been friends. "You should sleep soon, too. I have a feel that you're going to have the hardest time of any of us." He twisted his arm so he could clasp his hand around mine and squeeze reassuringly.

So I let him go and took a moment there, in the living room alone, to sip my hot chocolate and think about what was coming. My entire life collided together. My past, my present, my future, it all sat around me to keep me company.

I didn't know what would happen, didn't know if success was even possible, but I knew we had to try.

We would lose plenty if we fought, but if we turned around and ran, we'd lose everything.

And I had far too much that mattered to me now to let it go.

* * * *

The cool breeze moved my hair, making it tease the nape of my neck as I waited.

It was time. I've given the men their choice, had left them to it, and now I had to simply wait and see.

Aaron and Moa sat beside me on the porch in the front yard. The time we'd spent here had soothed a part of me I hadn't even realized was so wounded. While in Larkwood, I'd found love. What I hadn't made were friends, and it wasn't until I spent time with Aaron and Moa again that I remembered how much I needed that. They made me feel grounded and content and whole in a way that the men I loved couldn't. It reminded me that I needed more than just romantic bonds in my life.

They'd come outside with me to wait no doubt because despite the confidence I'd tried to have, I still couldn't help but worry. What if they didn't come? What if I never saw them again? What if I was alone again?

Still, I tried to play that off, to look in control and unconcerned. The way I peeled at the label of the water bottle in my hand showed my nerves.

"They'll come," Moa said, but I heard her doubts loud and clear.

I shrugged in response.

"They can't *not* come," Aaron added on. "I saw how they looked at you—no way they'll no-show."

Their certainty didn't make me feel any better. It seemed like when a parent told a kid that the only reason they were picked on was because the bully is jealous. It sounded great, but it was rarely true.

I wanted the men I loved to show up, but I understood if they didn't.

"If they don't come," Aaron asked, his voice low and careful as though he hadn't wanted to upset me. "What are you going to do?"

"Nothing changes," I wrote. *"I still have to go back. I'll do it alone if I have to."*

"Not alone," Moa said, reaching over to place her hand on mine. "You're not alone anymore, Hera, no matter what happens."

Aaron stretched across the table to set his hand on top of Moa and mine, making us feel like the team we'd been before. "We're here. Even if they don't show, that won't change."

And that helped. After thinking they'd both abandoned me, this connection to my past helped center me, helped me tell myself that no matter what, I had this handled. I could adjust and adapt and I would go after what I wanted no matter what others did.

"Take your hand off my mate before I remove it for you."

That threat, all but snarled out in a rough and angry voice, melted me in a way that was damned near embarrassing. Though, not as embarrassing as just how fast Aaron tore his hand away.

I turned to find Brax standing there, his eyes bright and angry, the jealousy there obvious.

And with him?

Everyone.

Deacon stood beside Brax, his purple eyes appearing no happier about Aaron touching me than Brax had. Then again, those two tended to be more jealous. Wade smirked as though amused by the annoyance of the other two. Knox ignored Aaron entirely, his eyes locked on me, a hunger there that said his incubus hadn't had its fill of me. Lastly, Kit stood near the back, tall enough for me to catch his black eyes past the others. His lips tipped up on one side, as if to laugh at me doubting any of them.

And I didn't care if I had an audience. I didn't care if Moa and Aaron could see, if it was awkward, if I should have been embarrassed.

I'd really worried they'd think twice, that they'd decide it wasn't worth it to come, that they'd abandon me. Even if I wouldn't have blamed them or been angry about it, it would have hurt.

So seeing them felt like sitting on a raft in the middle of the ocean only to finally glimpse land.

My body moved with little thought on my side. I headed right for them, like I was pretty sure I'd always do.

I paused when I got to them, uncertainty taking hold. *"You came,"* I signed.

Wade snorted. "Of course we came. I faced down an angry *dryad* for you. Knox there banged you *with me present,* Kit and Deacon broke out of Larkwood and betrayed the Warden to follow you and Brax turns into his less-friendly half whenever you're in danger. After all that, you really doubted we'd stick with you now?"

Yeah, I really had... Except that sounded so pathetic, I kept the thought to myself.

"You really are trouble," Deacon muttered before catching my wrist and pulling me against him. He tilted my head up and took my lips in an aggressive kiss that seemed to tell me everything while also mocking me for doubting him.

My cheeks heated when he finally broke the kiss. Even though we'd all settled into some sort of understanding between us, that didn't mean it was easy, didn't mean I was comfortable putting those relationships on display.

The scraping of the chairs against the porch made me turn to find Moa and Aaron standing, looking slightly awkward.

Moa spoke first. "Tomorrow's the day. Let's plan to meet in the morning to solidify the plans."

"You're leaving?" I signed, so used to using ASL that I forgot Moa and Aaron couldn't understand. Thankfully, Deacon translated for me.

Moa nodded. "Yeah. I figure you all deserve a bit of privacy before tomorrow."

She left the rest unsaid. None of us knew what would happen tomorrow, if we could win, if any of us would survive. She gave us the evening alone to make up for that, to allow us some time for just us.

Aaron nodded, quiet, and followed Moa out of the house. The two of them had more than enough money and ability to find somewhere else to stay for the night, so I let them go with a silent thank you.

Of course, as soon as their car pulled away, it reminded me that I was now alone with the men I loved.

Talk about awkward…

Trying to erase that, or at least ignore it, I waved the men into the house after me. A quick tour let them know the general layout, showed them where the rooms were, the bathrooms, the kitchen. The fridge was full of easy food — we'd stopped by the store to ensure we had enough to feed everyone if they did show.

When I reached the end, when we all stood in the living room, I turned back toward the men and froze.

I wasn't sure I'd ever felt quite so outnumbered, when I questioned my sanity about this relationship, about pursuing *five* men — no, not men, but shades.

The confidence I'd had talking to Aaron and Moa floated away.

Because now, looking at them, I wondered just what the hell I'd been thinking.

And worse?

A deep, simmering heat inside me as I faced them all said no matter how stupid, I wasn't about to back down.

Chapter Fourteen

Deacon

I couldn't stop staring at Hera.

She'd given us a tour, had made sure we had everything we needed, but none of that changed the tension between us all.

And there sure as hell was tension.

This undercurrent ran, sparking from person to person, and it increased each time we found ourselves faced with that troublesome siren.

And now, Hera fresh from a shower, smelling of the soap she'd used, a sheen on her damp skin, it grew even more.

A deep sound echoed in the room and for a moment, I thought I was growling. I tried to stop it before I realized…it wasn't me.

Instead, Brax had let out the sound.

Hera froze by the bathroom door, like prey who had just realized she was surrounded by large and scary beasts who were *extremely* hungry. She widened her dark eyes, going entirely still.

What, did she think movement would make it worse?

It probably would… I thought about how we'd react if she ran, how much fun chasing her would be. Hell, we'd been chasing her for the past year, hadn't we? Each in our own way, each at our own speed. Maybe we had herded her into this trap all along.

Hera gulped, then grasped the neckline of her robe tightly as if it were some sort of armor instead of a flimsy piece of fabric. She moved her gaze from one to another of us.

Was she wondering what to do?

I could almost see the questions on her face. We had one night only. Who would she spend it with? How could she possibly make a choice like that?

And her answer? She let go of her robe to sign. *"I guess I'll go to sleep."*

I nearly snorted at her words, at her decision. I knew her well enough to read her easily, to know her thought process. It had me speaking up despite how I normally let others do it. "Really? Might be our last night, and you're just going to go to bed alone?"

She whipped her gaze to mine as if surprised to be called out so directly. *"What else am I supposed to do?"*

"Well, I know I sure as fuck don't want to miss out on what might be our last night."

She shifted her weight from foot to foot, the discomfort obvious. *"I can't choose,"* she signed.

"No one's asking you to," Knox said.

"I knew you liked me." Wade smirked then winked at Knox. I knew the two of them had slept with Hera together, but the comment made me wonder if Wade was just being an asshole as usual or if there was actually something between the two of them.

Before I had to wonder long, though, Brax interrupted. "I'm fine with it."

Which was one hell of a statement. Out of any of us, Brax was by far the most possessive, the most jealous. If even he was agreeing, well, hell might have just frozen over.

Hera furrowed her eyebrows, then looked over at Kit in question.

Kit let out a soft laugh. "I am far too old to worry about things like jealousy. I wouldn't give up a night with you, no matter what the circumstance."

Which meant we were all on the same page.

Well, almost all of us.

Knox walked up to Hera, ignoring the way she backed up until she pressed against the closed bathroom door, caged in by Knox's larger body. He set his hand on the door beside her but didn't touch her. "You know what we want, Hera, but it's up to you. None of us would force you into anything you aren't comfortable with. So, do you want this?"

"What is this?" Hera asked.

Knox grinned, and an increase in the pheromones he let out drew a groan from every single person in the room. "*This* means that all six of us will spend the night together. Enough of dancing around the uncomfortable, of trying to hide things, of pretending things are different than they are. Tomorrow will change everything one way or another. Tomorrow, we make a last stand and win or lose, things won't stay the same. I'll be damned if I give up a moment with you before that." He leaned in closer until all Hera would be able to see was Knox's face. "Tell us yes, and we'll spend all damned night showing you exactly how we feel."

I held my breath, surprised to find just how invested I was. I'd slept with Hera plenty of times, but something about this felt different. It felt strange, like putting everything out in the open, like embracing the truth, and I really wanted that.

I wasn't stupid enough to think tomorrow would go off without a hitch. We couldn't achieve what we wanted without sacrifice. It meant tonight was our last chance, and I didn't want to miss any of it. I wouldn't push Hera, wouldn't force her into it, but I closed my hands into tight fists as I waited for her answer.

It felt like it took forever, but Hera brushed her lips against Knox's in a barely-there-kiss before she looked past him, at us, and nodded.

And *boy* was that all the foreplay I needed…

* * * *

Knox

Wondering if there was actually a bed large enough for six people was the sort of question I never figured I'd have to think about—yet here I was.

If we survived this all, maybe we'd have to look into one of those huge family beds, ones that would give us the space to actually stretch out.

And somehow, the idea of that didn't bother me as I would have expected. Even just a few weeks ago, the thought of seeing anyone else touching Hera might have set me off.

What had changed?

Maybe I'd finally realized that what I thought I wanted or needed wasn't always the truth. I needed Hera, and even if I hated to admit it, I was pretty sure I needed the others, too.

They were annoying sometimes, troublesome always, but they'd become part of my life so quickly that I couldn't imagine not seeing them anymore, not having them at my back.

Still, I rewarded Hera with a passionate kiss, trying to tell her how proud I was of her bravery. She could have said no, could have run away, but she didn't.

No, not Hera. If anyone was brave enough to stand before the five of us, it was her.

When we broke apart, she gulped and bit softly at her bottom lip. The questions in her eyes were obvious and beyond adorable.

How will this go?

She was nervous, which I couldn't blame her. Not that many girls, especially from her background, had ever considered having sex with five men at the same time. It wasn't like she had some how-to guide to explain how that worked. Any smart woman would hesitate.

I dragged my thumb across her soft bottom lip and for once, my incubus didn't bother me. Even as I felt it inside me and its need for her, I didn't try to hide or restrain it. It felt as ravenous for her as I was, and since I'd let it have her, since that time I'd given up resisting, it hadn't cared to care about anyone else. It seemed that siren had even hypnotized and beguiled my incubus.

"You don't need to be afraid," I whispered to her. "No one here would ever hurt you."

She nodded, so quick to accept my words, to trust us. It humbled me, reminded me again just why I'd fallen so hard for her.

I grasped her hand in mine, astounded by how small it felt, how fragile, then tugged her into the living room. While I preferred beds, we couldn't all fit in any of the ones here.

Wade seemed to get the point, because he grabbed cushions from the couches while Deacon and Brax shoved the furniture out of the way. It only took a few moments to clear the center of the living room, and the pillows Wade had thrown down made it look rather welcoming.

Or so I thought until Brax frowned. "I don't like this."

Hera hesitated, looking toward him. I could *feel* her worries, her fear that she'd make one of us feel bad, that we wouldn't feel as important as the other. It was a lot for anyone to juggle.

Except, Brax snorted. "You deserve a hell of a lot more than getting fucked on the floor," he muttered.

Which was about the last thing I expected to hear from my brother. Who would have figured him for a romantic? It was enough to get a chuckle from me, one he returned with a glare.

Hera's anxiety evaporated beneath a smile as she moved past me and to Brax. She didn't touch him, but her hands moved as she signed. *"I don't care about that. Where we are doesn't matter to me. It never has. All I care about is that you're here."*

Except Brax didn't look all that ready to accept her opinion. "The problem is that you don't understand what you deserve. You don't ask for enough from other people."

"Are you turning me down then?" She asked that like a challenge.

And Brax had never been one to back down, so he caught her with an arm behind her and pulled her against him. She gasped, but he didn't release her, didn't apologize. Instead, he stared down at her as if to make sure she understood him perfectly. "You should know me better than that, songbird. I'm not about to turn you down. If you'll have me, I'm here."

The words meant so much more than I'd bet Hera realized. After Brax had spent so long looking after me, after giving up so much, he was offering himself happily to Hera. That meant everything.

Hera wrapped her arms around Brax and went up to her toes, letting him lean down to kiss her. The kiss said everything the two of them were horrible at saying. It was deep, full of feeling, and Hera grasped Brax as if afraid he'd slip away.

Not that Brax seemed willing to passively accept it. He kissed her back, returning every ounce of passion she'd given to him. He reached between them, sliding his hands between their bodies, only to grasp the edges of her robe and pull it apart.

If Hera cared, if she was self-conscious, she didn't show it. She didn't fight him as he moved the fabric down her arms. It fluttered to the ground, forgotten, and gave me a view of her naked back.

And I couldn't ever forget or ignore that view. Her skin was still the same sun-kissed hue, even though she didn't get a lot of sun. Darker spots — both freckles and moles — dotted her and made me want to kiss each one, to count them all and commit them to memory.

And why the hell not do it?

I leaned in and pressed my lips to one mark on her shoulder blade, rewarded by her shivering at the contact.

Brax broke the kiss to look at me, and a smirk of mine made him roll his eyes.

It didn't matter what happened, we'd always be brothers, always trying to show each other up. It seemed this was no different.

I ran my hand along her softness, teasing where her waist dipped in then the delicious curve of her ass. Hera had a body that deserved worship, and I had no problem devoting myself to it and to her.

I dropped to my knees behind her, offering one quick bite to her left ass cheek that I hoped would leave a mark.

And Brax took that chance to turn her, to face her toward me, putting me eye-level to her stomach. I offered more kisses there, making my way down over her smooth mound as I slid my hands up her shapely thighs. Each part of her excited me more, made my mouth salivate for a taste.

And I didn't think there was any damned reason not to let myself have it.

I used my fingers to spread her open, to pull the hood of her clit out of the way, then swiped my tongue along that sensitive bundle ruthlessly.

Hera jerked backward, but a wrapped arm by Brax kept her still. He pressed his lips to her ear, then whispered so softly I almost couldn't hear above her harsh breathing. "Stay still and let him."

Hera shivered—no, it was more than that, it was like a full-body tremor. Even so, she seemed to try to obey even as each muscle twitched.

I took advantage of the situation and latched onto her clit, ignoring how sensitive she must have been, how overwhelming it must have felt. If tonight was the last time, I'd damn well make sure I pulled every last sensation I could from her, until I drowned us both in pleasure.

Hera set her hand on the back of my head, as if to push me away, but someone else caught her wrist.

I expected it to be Brax, but when I glanced up, it was Deacon. He held her wrist gently but firmly, as it if were precious to him. The look was strange on Deacon's face, like something I wasn't meant to see.

It was one of the things about tonight that both terrified and reassured me. Seeing the others with Hera felt like a glimpse into their private worlds, into parts of them that they never showed anyone else.

And I was no different, was I? While the others knew about my incubus, about the need and hunger inside me, only Wade knew about how focused that need was on Hera. Doing this wasn't just about Hera accepting us, but us accepting each other.

Deacon brought Hera's wrist up and pressed a chaste kiss to her pulse, then dragged his tongue across her skin in a way that was *far* less chaste. In fact, despite me touching her in a far filthier way, something about the slow touch of Deacon's tongue, the way his gaze locked with hers, damn near made *me* blush.

And it certainly excited me, so I got back to work. I used my free hand to press between her thighs, to make her spread her legs for me, to open for me, then sank two of my fingers into her waiting cunt.

She squeezed around me, but I gave her no time to think or consider anything. Instead, I curled my fingers forward, searching her reactions, finding the perfect place as my lips sucked relentlessly on her clit.

I wanted to give her everything, to let her get entirely lost to pleasure, to the moment, to *us*.

So I used my extensive knowledge and skills, bringing it all to the forefront, letting my incubus feast and drive everyone else into the same frenzy that locked me.

We had a long night ahead of us, but I planned to get it started the right way, to drag the first orgasm of the night from Hera's sexy body.

Sure enough, she shattered, unable to resist my touch for long. Her lips parted on a silent cry, her back arching forward, her eyes shut tight as each muscle of hers tensed. It reminded me yet again of just how much I loved this brave, smart, infuriatingly stubborn woman.

I pressed a kiss to her clit after pulling my fingers free of her clenching, wet pussy, smiling when she relaxed as if thinking we were finished.

"Oh, songbird," I whispered to her, letting my warm breath tease her oversensitive body. "That's the first of the night, but *far* from the last. Let's hope you can keep up."

Kit

Sitting back and watching Hera lost to pleasure was one of the sexiest things I'd ever seen. Sure, she felt amazing when I touched her, when I stroked over all that soft, sweat-soaked skin, but this had a charm all its own as well.

I hadn't been kidding when I'd said I was too old to worry about jealousy. I knew exactly how long and empty life could be, had suffered loss due to it, so I didn't mind people finding comfort where they could.

It meant that seeing Hera pinned between Brax and Knox excited me in a different way than touching her, but in a no less impactful way. Her cheeks were red, the flush and the want in her eyes showing how badly she needed our touch.

She truly was astounding, wasn't she? How many women could stand on their own here, could face so many powerful shades without backing down? Not just here, either. She planned to face the Warden, to face the full might of Larkwood even though she had the chance to run to safety.

She prioritized the wellbeing of others over her own, and that drew me like nothing else.

She rested heavily against Brax as if her legs had weakened so much that she couldn't hold herself up anymore. Brax's strong arm wrapped around her, holding her against him, keeping her upright.

I let out a low groan at the sight, a desire to stroke myself surprising me. I thought I was beyond such things, beyond needing another in such an instinctual and powerful way.

Apparently not...

Hera opened her eyes and looked at me as if she could feel my need. Maybe she could because of our bond. Hera had managed to always do things differently, to never quite fit the rules and mold I had grown accustomed to. I would be arrogant to think I could predict her or her abilities anymore.

She ran her tongue across her bottom lip, the tease nearly enough to cause me to rise, to go over and take her into my arms, to bury myself inside her heat and feel warm for once.

Except, as it turned out, I didn't need to do that. She moved toward me, no doubt feeling the same draw I did. Brax released her, though after her first step, she stumbled. It seemed her body was still thrown out of balance after her orgasm, and something about that excited me all the more.

I caught her easily, letting her fall against me on the couch, pulling her into my lap. She straddled me as if it were the most natural thing in the world, as if she knew exactly where she belonged.

And her being entirely naked while I still wore clothes created an imbalance I hated to admit enjoying. She probably felt my reaction, being in my lap and all, so admitting it wasn't all that necessary.

Her lips found mine, the kiss quick and hungry, a sure sign she'd given up thinking or resisting or worrying. She acted on lust now, on the desires trapped inside her, and that was fine by me.

I ran my hands up her thighs, over her hips, to feel her waist. I teased her as I moved up farther, cupping her breasts, brushing the hard points of her nipples with my thumbs.

She arched and squirmed in my lap, causing her to grind against my erection.

I am tired of waiting.

I released her breast and reached between us, undoing my pants with an easy flick of my fingers. She fell against me when I raised my hips to work the fabric down enough to free myself, and I loved how small she felt against me, how she fit perfectly into my lap.

I allowed myself the pleasure of stroking my cock once, the moment of denial heightening my expectations. I'd taken her already, but I doubted I'd ever grow tired of this or her.

"Do you want me?" I asked.

She furrowed her brows as if my words made no sense.

I used a grip on her waist to hold her still, to rub the head of my cock against her without entering her. I kept what she wanted from her. "I need to know you want me," I whispered.

The confusion on her face drifted away, a sweetness replacing it as she understood. Her reading me so easily, her knowing my scars without me having to say them out loud humbled me, even more so because she gave a damn about them.

She protected those wounds as if they were her own.

That openness made me go on, let me utter the words I would have never admitted only a few months before. "I can force compliance, can turn anyone into my puppet, but I don't want that with you. I need you to want me, to choose me because you want to, not because I force you to."

Her expression softened into one so loving, it hurt. She sat up straight enough to draw her hands from me so she could sign. *"I want you,"* she told me, the words so simple.

She wanted me. She knew about me, what I was, what I could do, and she still accepted me.

It was more than I deserved and certainly more than I'd ever thought I'd find.

After answering me, she slid her hands over my shoulders and I regretted not stripping down entirely. Then again, this was only my first round. I'd make sure to feel her small hands all over me the next time.

For now, I rewarded her honesty by pulling down on her waist and sinking my cock into the tight grasp of her wet cunt. And just like before, it was more than I could have even wished for.

Coldness and an endless hunger had always filled me. The wendigo's ravenous appetite had always kept me frozen. Somehow, Hera warmed it. She warmed *me*.

She reached into that emptiness I had and took up space there. She filled it so I didn't feel hollow, and I didn't know such a thing was even possible.

Probably because I'd spent so damned long hiding the real me from Jasmine, keeping the truth from her. I hadn't wanted to face the fear in her eyes, hadn't wanted to risk her turning away from me.

Hera had never accepted that subterfuge from me. She hadn't been content to get the nice, edited version of me, the one I showed to most people. Instead, she'd wanted the truth.

Then she'd been strong enough to not turn away when she came face-to-face with it.

She moved her lips, and I easily read her silent words, her gentle reassurance. "*I love you. I want you. I'm not going anywhere.*"

I let myself believe every one of those promises as I used my grasp on her waist to make her rise, then sink back down, taking me deeper. The sight of her above me melted any resolve I might have had to resist her. With her position, she hid *nothing* from me.

I could see how my cock plunged deep inside her, the way her pussy stretched around my length, the glistening left behind on my length from her wetness. She was perfect, and each movement she made, each little shuddering gasp from her only proved it again.

A glance around reminded me we weren't alone. Knox sat back, a satisfied smirk on his lips telling me that his incubus enjoyed the show. Brax had his hand around his cock, stroking himself slowly as if edging himself to the sight of me sinking deep into Hera. Wade sat on the floor, his legs crossed, his lips parted as though he struggled to draw enough air. Deacon sat on one of the couches pressed against the wall, his purple eyes bright and the tension inside him showing how closely he held himself.

Then again, Deacon struck me as a rather jealous man. Perhaps it was because he wasn't a shade, so he hadn't learned to be grateful for what he could have. Instead, he wanted something all to himself.

The thought made my lips lift on one side, a challenge in my eyes that I offered to him.

And Deacon took me up on it, since he wasn't the type to back down.

He approached with sure steps, removing his shirt as he went. His body showed signs of a rough life, scars dotting his skin. Then again, that was what made him who he was, I guess. He'd lived enough to know what he wanted and how hard he'd press to get it.

He slid his fingers into Hera's hair and used the grip to turn her face toward him. He didn't wait, didn't ask, didn't let her realize who it was. Instead, he kissed her roughly, as though he could devour her with that touch and wipe away everything from her mind except his lips.

I used that chance to pull her down more roughly, to draw her attention back to me, to remind them both they weren't alone.

Maybe I can be jealous...

I let out a laugh at my own immaturity, though Deacon's groan said he didn't mind what I did or Hera's reaction.

So I gave up going slow and gripped Hera tighter, increasing the speed and power. She didn't ride me, not exactly, since I controlled her movements. Her rapid breathing and the tremble in her thighs said she had no problem with me using her almost like a toy.

Tingling in my body made me shiver, a tightness of my skin as I struggled with my own control. I wasn't human, and my wendigo shape was my true form. It was harder for me to hold onto my human form, to remain as I was, and Hera stripped each layer of that control away.

My fingers lengthened, the tips sharp, but I was careful to keep them from her. I didn't want to risk cutting her on accident or frightening her.

"I can't stop," I told Hera.

She broke from Deacon's kiss to look at me, a question there. However, when I gripped her tighter, when she felt the way my hands had changed, she seemed to understand.

This was it, the final point of no return.

If Hera could understand this, if she could accept me like this, then we had no more chasms of understanding to cross.

She swallowed hard but nodded. I'd love to say she didn't hesitate, that she had no worries in those brown eyes of hers, but that would be a lie.

Scared or not, she still said yes.

Which I appreciated, because if she'd said no, I had a feel I'd need to stop this, to leave her be. I had passed the point where I could stop the feelings inside me.

So I let go. I stopped trying to resist, trying to hold onto my form, and gave in to her, into this, into a future I never thought I'd get.

But could Hera actually accept the monster I was? Or would this all end with her running away?

Chapter Fifteen

Hera

I'd seen Kit's other form enough times that it didn't frighten me as it once had. It was just another part of him, one I understood. It wasn't even like Brax, where he felt like a different person, or at least a hidden part of the same person.

Kit was himself, no matter the form.

At least, I told myself that as the body beneath me shimmered, as it twisted and changed against me. The sensation was strange, the skin stretching, the limbs lengthening. Even still, he didn't pull away, didn't hide any of it from me.

After a moment, he sat there, his body foreign. He was far thinner in this form, but he lacked any softness. I struggled to read his eyes normally, given they were entirely black, but it was so much worse like this.

His head was a deer skull, with the tall antlers that reached up but no actual mouth. He stared at me, but I couldn't read him, couldn't tell what he was thinking.

We waited, locked into that staring contest. *He's waiting to see if I reject him.* I knew it easily, was sure that was his plan. He gave me the chance to pull away, to decide I didn't want that, to abandon this part of him.

And the more time I spent around him, the more I knew this was *him*. It wasn't another part of him — this was the real man. His other form was nothing but a pretty outfit he wore, just camouflage that let him move around the world without problems.

So what would I do? Would I do as he expected? Pull out of his lap and leave him alone with that bottomless hunger he had?

No. I knew without even considering that I couldn't. So instead, I set my hands on the sides of his face, the bone cold against my warm palms, ungiving in a way that was so different from human faces. I leaned in and pressed a gentle kiss to the front of the deer skull.

Kit shuddered as though the tension suddenly leeched away, had rushed out of him until he could hardly hold himself up. And as soon as that happened, his movements turned frighteningly rough. He jerked his hips up, thrusting into me so hard and deep that I opened my mouth as if I could cry out at the overwhelming sensation.

Sparks flew through my body, lighting me up from the inside, and Kit didn't slow.

Even though his eyes were pure black, I could tell he stared at me. The heavy weight of his gaze trapped me. He studied each reaction from me as he fucked me hard, as I could do nothing but accept him in all his terrifying, rough darkness.

A hand on my chin tipped my head backward, made me look up to find Deacon there. My forgetting him made my cheeks burn, but he offered me a kind, unbothered smile. He leaned down from above me, brushing his lips against mine, the kiss strange since he essentially kissed me upside down.

He supported the back on my head as his other hand moved down my chest, zeroing in on one of my nipples, closing around it with a tight grip that made me press more into his touch.

As quickly as it happened, however, he broke the kiss and lifted his head. He ran his fingers over my lips, a question there in his purple eyes.

I nodded.

What he was asking, I didn't know — I didn't care. I'd do what he wanted because I wanted it, too. I wanted to taste all of them, to lose myself in their need, in the strength of us all.

Deacon gave me one of those rare smiles he gifted only to me. He tilted me backward, and I trust him not to let me fall, trusted them both to keep me safe.

The change in position made Kit's cock rub against a different place inside me, and it also stretched me out between them, displaying everything.

Before I could ask what Deacon had in mind, before I could wonder long, I found Deacon's hard shaft so close to my lips I could dart my tongue out to touch him.

He'd leaned me back in Kit's lap, then lowered me until his cock rested just above me.

Somehow, kneeling felt different. The times I'd given a blow job, I'd always felt in control. I'd teased the man with my tongue and my mouth, and I'd done it at my own pace.

This felt *nothing* like that. Instead, I was entirely at their mercy. Kit fucked into me with impossibly deep thrusts, his hands locked around my waist to take me exactly as he wanted. Deacon had one hand on the back on my neck and head to support the position, and his other wrapped around his cock. He stroked the head along my lips as if applying gloss, his gaze locked on the sight.

A drop of precum escaped his dick and I captured it from my lip with my tongue.

He groaned deeply. "I said before that you're a cliff, that I know you're going to be the end of me, but fuck it. I don't give a damn. I want to fall over it with you. Will you let me go over it with you?"

I opened my mouth as though I could respond, but Deacon took the chance to press his hard length past my lips.

And I gave in immediately. I ran my tongue along the underneath of his hot cock, wanting to suck, to take him deeper, but Deacon didn't give me any room to do as I wanted.

Instead, he rocked his hips forward slowly, sliding deeper for a moment before retreating. It wasn't as rough as I'd have wanted, but maybe that was what it did for me. I could do nothing but accept the roughness of the two men, split between them and used as they wanted, driving me farther into that decedent haze.

And I dove in happily. I moved my hands to my own breasts, needing to sink deeper into the feeling.

As soon as I did, something soft and wet touched my nipple through my fingers. I couldn't see because of my position, with Deacon's body the only thing in my line of sight.

"See, you're too much for any one person," Knox said, his voice a sensual promise. As he spoke, his breath warmed my skin and blew over my wet nipple. "So needy and so wonderfully honest. I love that about you, you know? You try to do the right thing, you care about others, but you also don't lie about what you want." He laughed, then dragged his tongue over the peaked tip again. "And you want us, don't you? You're drowning in want, and you need us to take care of you, don't you?"

I nodded, the action causing Deacon to slide deeper into my mouth. I did need them, each of them. The move must have been enough for Deacon to start losing his control, because his thrusts turned quicker and rougher.

And I loved it. I adored how I didn't have to think or worry.

My life had turned into some crusade. I'd had my future committed to what felt like an impossible task, and everyone looked to *me* for answers. I wasn't even supposed to become a shade, and yet I'd somehow ended up leading a revolution to save them.

The weight hung heavily on my shoulders, too many questions and too many decisions for me to make on my own.

That was why I relaxed into their care, into their touch. I didn't *have* to think about it right now. I didn't have to be in charge, didn't have to think about what to do or how to act. Instead, I gave myself over to them, to their wants, and let my mind go blissfully blank.

"That's a good girl," Knox whispered against my heated flesh. "Just lie there and take it, hmm? I can taste how much you like it, how badly you need this, and it is *delicious*."

How could words that seemed so simple hit me so hard?

The reason didn't matter as I shook beneath the weight of their touches and words.

Kit let out a terrifying sound, and even without seeing him, I could feel the intensity of his gaze as his hips snapped harder. There was no question that I'd be sore tomorrow, and I didn't give a damn.

He plunged deep into me and held still, his thick cock spilling into me, his hands tight as if he wanted to ensure I would take every last drop of him.

Deacon groaned — *is he watching? Does the idea of Kit coming turn him on?* — then pulled back enough so that when he came, it pooled on my tongue. It allowed me to savor the taste.

Deacon withdrew from my mouth so he could meet my gaze. He didn't tell me to swallow, didn't order me to, and that made me want to more. His purple eyes locked on my throat when it moved as I did what he wanted — what we *both* wanted.

A softness entered his eyes, something strange in the heat of this moment.

Still, what pushed me over the edge was when Knox moved his lips from my nipple to my mouth, when he kissed me aggressively, licking into my mouth as if searching for a taste of the cum Deacon had left there. The idea of it made my body tense as I came.

Whether Knox managed to get a taste or not, I didn't know, but the heat in his green eyes when he pulled back made me shiver.

Clearly, my night was *far* from over.

Brax

People often joked that I had no patience, and right now, I had to agree. I didn't mind watching Hera with the others, but I craved the ability to touch her.

Sure, seeing Knox run his tongue over her nipple, and watching the way her lips had stretched around Deacon's cock and Kit sinking deep into her had turned me on. The dazed expression on her face, along with the filthy way she was positioned, made my cock ache with need.

Still, I wanted to touch her. I wanted to taste the sweat that glistened on her skin, to feel the way she trembled, especially since she couldn't moan or speak.

And I was well past willing to wait any longer.

I went over to her on the other side as Knox. Kit and Deacon only chuckled as I gathered her against me, ignoring the slight whimper as Kit's softening cock slid out of her. White rested on her thighs, some of his cum having leaked from her.

Why the hell did that excite me? I wasn't sure if I liked her marked in that way or if it was the knowledge that I'd mark her as well, as if I were washing away Kit's claim with my own.

All I knew for sure was that far too much of my blood was in my cock at the moment to think about any of it clearly and come to an answer.

Instead, I went with it, with instinct, with the desires that filled me, demanding I have her.

I pulled her into my lap, her back to my chest, as I sat on the floor. Her knees pressed against the ground on either side of me, and I leaned back to grasp my cock.

I gave her no chance to worry or think as I guided her down to take my length in a single thrust. I nipped her earlobe, then whispered to her, "You're so wet, but it's not just you, is it? I slid into you so easily because of Kit's cum."

She sucked in a quick breath and rose. I almost thought she'd pull away, but leave it to me to underestimate her even still. As soon as she lifted up, she sank back down hard, as if she needed to take me as deeply and roughly as she could.

And for some reason, I let her do it. I let her fuck herself on my cock, let her have me in whatever way she needed. Sure, a part of me loved to hold her down, to make her submit, but another part of me saw the benefit in letting her use me for her own pleasure.

It seemed if I were twisted for getting off on Kit having already fucked her, so was she.

Being perverted together is better than being perverted by myself, I guess.

She looked like a dream, someone so stunning that I struggled to believe she was real. She moved with such beautiful, intrinsic fluidity. She was, on one hand, fragile and broken and trapped. On the other, she was a predator—tough and dangerous and hungry. They were two sides of her, both real and both precious to me. I leaned in and bit down on her shoulder as if I could create a bond the way Kit had, as if I could ensure she carried something from me no matter what.

She shuddered hard at my bite, her drenched cunt squeezing around me. Had she come again? It seemed she'd hit a point where one ran into the next, where it was all so much that she couldn't tell.

She wasn't done, though, judging by the way she rode me, as rough as before, straining for something that remained just out of reach. Maybe she was outrunning tomorrow like the rest of us, trying to build a tiny place here between us where we didn't have to think about anything else.

I was happy to stay in that place with her forever.

"You know," Knox said, his voice drawing my attention to where he'd knelt in front of Hera, how he looked straight into her eyes. "Normally my incubus is happy to stay on the outskirts, to taste the passion of others without my own pleasure. I don't know what it is about you, but you make *me* crave you. My incubus is satisfied with whatever way it can taste your desire, but I'm not. It's not enough for me." Knox leaned down and dragged his tongue over her nipple even as she rode me.

And somehow, it was even more lewd that he did it without touching her anywhere else, without palming her breast, with his eyes locked on hers.

No, don't finish yet. I drew my hands into fists to hold off, unwilling to embarrass myself by coming already, unwilling to let the moment end.

I forced myself to calm down even as the tightness of Hera's pussy threatened to undo me.

Knox flashed me a smirk. No doubt he knew exactly how I felt and how close to my edge I remained and enjoyed teasing me over it.

Brothers never changed, did we?

Knox palmed Hera's breasts tightly, telling me he enjoyed that particular part of her. "I like these," he said before he moved his fingers back to take her nipples in a tight grasp. She moved forward to lessen the pull, but her shiver screamed her real opinion.

Knox rose to his feet when he let go of her, and Hera seemed to guess what he wanted. She dragged her tongue up his hard length, then pressed a kiss to the head.

Except Knox shook his head. "As much as I love your mouth, that's not what I'm after right now."

She furrowed her eyebrows, her motions slow as if she didn't understand.

Knox's smile widened before he bent enough to dance his fingers over the curve of her breast. "Let me be clearer, then. I'm going to put my cock here" — he moved his fingers up the valley between her breasts — "and you will push your pretty breasts together tightly. I want to fuck between them, then paint your sweet face in my cum."

His words had me baring my teeth with a snarl, a sting in my tongue saying they'd shifted to sharpened points.

Knox chuckled at my reaction even if he didn't look my way.

Which was fine by me. I enjoyed the friction as Hera rode me, the impossibly tight heat of her pussy, the way she twitched and squeezed down around me.

Knox didn't move as he stared at her, not demanding but not giving in, either. He wanted Hera to do as he said, to volunteer and give in to him. It took only a moment for her to do just that.

She brought her hands to the outside of her breasts, then waited. Knox had to crouch slightly, but he moved close enough to rest his cock right where he'd said he would. "Tighter," he growled out when Hera used her hands to squeeze herself around him. She obeyed, and Knox's eyes glowed a bright green, flickering between the man and the incubus, both clearly enamored with the woman before them.

He rocked his hips, gliding against her, testing the speed and angle. It didn't take long for him to quicken and to try to get more.

And Hera gave him everything. She let him set his pace, and instead of rising and falling as she rode me, she rolled her hips and ground down against me.

Fuck, it was everything I'd wanted. Hera's panting, her scent drowning the room, the promise of more — it made me sure I wouldn't last much longer.

I took the chance to just lose myself in it, in her, in the grasping snugness of her sweet cunt.

Knox must have felt my need, because he followed suit. No doubt the pleasure inside Hera and I drove him closer to his own release.

"You're the only person who makes me want to be touched like this," Knox admitted softly. His gaze was soft as he looked at Hera, which felt odd. He was fucking her breasts while she had my cock inside her. She'd already fucked two other men. We had an audience currently. That gentle look belonged in dim evenings in bed, moments of quiet romance, not here.

Yet, that was how he looked at her, as if she were precious and special and he cherished her.

I didn't look at her like that, didn't know how to offer that sort of thing, even if I felt the same way.

So I let Knox give her what I couldn't, forcing myself to stay still, to let her chase her own release because it would take me over that edge with her.

Knox reached down to take Hera's breasts in his large hands, moving to pinch her nipples tightly, to tug them as he kept the snugness around his cock. Hera gasped, and if she had a voice, I had no doubt she'd have screamed.

What a loss to not be able to hear that…

"Fuck," Knox muttered to himself before he let go of her and wrapped his hand around his cock. He stroked himself quickly, his hand moving so fast it was nearly a blur, showing just how badly he wanted her.

Hera closed her eyes, a reluctance there as if she didn't want to lose a moment of the sight. That signaled Knox, because he let out a nearly feral sound as he came, spilling onto her face, over the freckles on her cheeks, the pink of her lips, with some running down to drip off her chin.

The sight was unbearably filthy, especially when Hera's sweet little tongue slid across her bottom lip to take some of Knox's cum into her mouth. She came again, hard, and something about her having Knox's spend on her face, about her getting off on that, drove any hope to resist from me.

At the end of the day, I was only a man.

My release shuddered through me as I gave in to my desire to bite down on her shoulder again, to leave a deeper mark there in her skin as I added my own cum to Kit's, to Knox's, to Deacon's that she'd already swallowed.

As soon as I could breathe, as soon as the tension inside me relaxed, I kissed the bite mark I'd left, soothing it with my tongue.

I never wanted this moment to end.

Wade

God, I want to touch her so badly.

The thought kept running around in my head, making it impossible to focus on a damned other thing. Hera wore the scent and cum of the others, but I hadn't touched her yet.

Why not?

I looked down at my gloves and sighed.

That was why. Because I couldn't touch anyone without hurting them, without stealing from them. It didn't matter what Bowen had said — it just wasn't true.

Hera's hazel eyes met mine, and I offered her a strained smile.

She held a hand out to me, but I glanced down at my gloves again, hesitating.

Hera pulled away from Knox and Brax, moving between them, her body seeming heavy and exhausted as she crawled toward me. She reached out when she got to me, and I flinched just before her palm touched my cheek.

Immediately, I felt that rush of power, the pull from her to me, and it shamed me.

"I'm sorry," I muttered, because I had no idea what else to say.

Supposedly I could touch her and *not* do this. It was something in my own head that caused me to fear her, to fear everything around me and to strike first by draining anything I touched.

Shame ate at it, only made worse when that power slid inside me, pleasant and familiar.

Hera didn't give me a dirty look, though. She didn't seem to blame me, to hate me for my lack of control, for how I couldn't be with her without taking from her. Instead, she grasped the hem of my shirt and pulled it up and off me. She didn't try to take my gloves, didn't remove them or complain. Instead, she ran her own hands over the bare skin of my chest as if to prove that she didn't hate me.

But her accepting me didn't mean I liked it, didn't mean I accepted it.

It was why I'd kept my distance tonight, why I hadn't joined in. I'd had a place before because Knox had needed me to silence his other side. Now that he'd come to terms with it, though, now that he and his incubus seemed to be best buddies, it was just me on the outskirts. If I had been a part of this, I'd have only weakened them all.

I didn't add to this connection — I took from it.

Before I could worry about that, though, Hera helped to numb the pain inside me. She brushed her lips to mine before deepening the kiss, before telling me with that touch what she couldn't say with words.

And that helped remind me that no matter what else happened, I wanted her. Maybe it was selfishness that drove me, but I couldn't stop. Even without as much experience, I was helpless against her. I wrapped my arm around her waist and flipped her so she rested on the floor beneath me.

She gasped, breaking the kiss, so I pulled back to give her room to breathe. I dragged my tongue along her cheek, licking off some of the cum Knox had covered her with. In addition, wetness on my jeans reminded me of just how messy she was and how much I enjoyed it.

"You look good well-used," I whispered to her, and her blush at the compliment said she knew *exactly* what I meant.

She lifted her hips, rubbing shamelessly against me in a silent plea, one I was more than willing to give in to.

I leaned my weight on one arm while I reached for the button of my jeans with my other. I undid it, then shoved my jeans off, going as quickly as I could, not giving a damn about looking sexy while I did it. No, I wanted to slide into her and nothing else mattered.

As soon as I freed myself of my clothing, when the only thing I had on were my gloves, I settled into the cradle of her hips, her sexy thighs spread around me. It let me fall into the space there, my cock nestled against her drenched cunt.

I reached between us, fitting the head of my cock into the heated entrance of her pussy, pausing to stare at her until she looked up at me.

I wanted her eyes on me, to bask in the gentleness there, in the safe place that she created in a hostile, unyielding world.

And when she did, when she looked up at me, I went still. She reached inside me and silenced every ugly voice inside my head, all those horrible things I'd told myself over the years. She shut them all down until the world went quiet, all because of the way she wrapped her arms around my shoulders.

I sank into her slowly, pressing my cock into her heat with the utmost care. She was precious to me, and I wanted to treat her that way. So I rocked into her, advancing and withdrawing in small thrusts, chasing each little catch of her breath she let out.

"I love you," I whispered into her ear, pressed tight against her. "I trust you, and I'll do anything I can to keep you safe, to keep *this* safe." I meant more than just her and I, of course.

I meant everything she'd built, this family she'd created, this home that was made of the six of us. Six people who had no business around each other, who had no connection, and who she'd somehow bridged that gap for. She'd made us all better versions of ourselves, gave us hope when none of us had it in us to hope anymore.

That was the most impressive part, the thing about her that the Warden hadn't understood, that she'd underestimated. Hera was powerful, sure, but it wasn't that power that really made her truly dangerous.

Instead, it was her faith in others. It was her fearlessness in facing down the worst in others without blinking, in accepting them, in risking herself for her belief in them and their goodness.

Hera had no reason to trust any of us. We weren't good people, weren't brave and fearless like her, but she'd gone out on a limb and done it anyway.

She'd given us that gift, and that was where her power really came from. She made us want to be better, to want to earn the respect and trust she gave us so willingly.

I gave myself over to the moment, to the pleasure of her heated damp skin and her sharp gasping breaths. It was everything I wanted, and because I knew exactly how fast life could change, I refused to waste another moment of it.

I buried my face in her neck, breathing her in, trying to make her a part of me that I'd never lose, trying to imprint her on me so I kept her with me always.

Her nails dug into my back as she clung to me, her hips writhing in a desperate attempt to get more of me. That was one of the reasons I loved her so much, though, because she accepted me but couldn't ever get enough.

"Greedy girl," I whispered as I plunged into her harder, deeper, letting myself feel as possessive and needy as I wanted. I could be embarrassed later, could wish I'd played it safe and looked cool, but I didn't want that right now.

Right now, I wanted to give it my all, to take everything, so I did.

My muscles tensed, a tightness in my lower back telling me I was close. I didn't bother to try to resist, instead taking Hera harder, putting all my feelings into a kiss and into the way I roughly thrusted into her.

A groan escaped me, and Hera swallowed it down as I came, plunging in as deep as I could to ensure I marked her just as the others had. Hera writhed beneath me, her lithe body squirming as her hands both pushed me away and pulled me closer. Her body had to be in chaos, to the point where she wasn't sure if she needed more or less. Whatever it was, she tightened down on my cock, milking every last drop of cum from me, continuing to squeeze even after I'd finished. It made me hiss, the stimulation too much.

She shivered beneath me, too spent to even try to put on a show.

Boy, I understood that feeling, though. A part of me wanted to wrap my arms around her and just close my eyes, pretend the night would last forever.

Too soon, however, she shifted, making me sit up. She still had cum on her face and her hair stuck out wildly.

All that desire to sleep washed away under the look in her eyes, especially when I glance to the side to find four other sets of eyes locked on us.

It made me laugh and offer Hera a smirk. "Poor little siren isn't even *close* to done. You're in for a very long night."

Her cheeks flushed again, but she didn't shake her head.

Damn, I love this woman…

Chapter Sixteen

Hera

I tried to silence the panic inside me at being back here at Larkwood. I'd worked so hard to escape it, but here I was.

Not just Larkwood, but the North Tower — my own personal hell.

And worse, the silence in my head made me uncomfortable. Wade had taken my powers many times before, when I'd felt this silent emptiness inside me, but this was the first time it ever made me feel so vulnerable.

With our hands bound tightly together, I couldn't pull away and even properly sign. I'd gone from feeling free, from tasting what a real life could feel like, to being trapped and bound and silenced yet again.

Which meant when the Warden stared at me in the intake area of the North Tower, I gulped hard and tried to keep the fear from my expression.

Deacon's heavy hand grasped the nape of my neck, a touch I would have welcomed and savored any other time.

"I didn't expect to see you again," the Warden said, a laugh to her tone as if it amused her. Then again, with the way I stood there beside Wade, I wasn't much of a threat.

She moved her gaze from me to Deacon. "And I thought you were dead."

"I'm harder to kill than that."

"But you let Kit get the upper hand over you."

Deacon shrugged, somehow able to keep an entirely straight face. "That happened because *you* wanted him to come, so I trusted your judgment."

The Warden shook her head. "Perhaps I'm losing my touch being able to read people. I truly thought Kit would obey, and that our Ms. Weston here would accept my proposal and leave." She came closer and grabbed my chin, lifting my face until she could stare right into my eyes. "I find it frustrating that you continue to not react the way I expect. I've made a career out of reading people, out of understanding what they want and how to use that to get what I want. You, however, continue to fail meeting those expectations. Why is that?"

I didn't bother to try to respond. She didn't really care, either. This was nothing more than a fancy-sounding hissy fit.

She turned her gaze back to Deacon. "Where are the others?"

"Hera was on her way back here with only Wade when I caught up with her. It seems most of those idiots who followed her around weren't nearly as devoted as she thought."

The Warden let out a cruel laugh. "At least that doesn't surprise me." Her gaze moved to Wade. "And the fact that it was the touch-starved virgin who didn't abandon her makes sense as well. Should I worry about Kit showing up to reclaim his toy?"

Deacon shook his head and reached into the bag slung over his shoulder. He tossed a white antler onto the tile beside the Warden. The sight of it twisted my stomach. I recalled the crack when Deacon had snapped it free of Kit's other form, the subtle tic Kit's jaw gave, but the way he didn't show any signs of pain.

The Warden leaned down and picked it up, a chilling smile pulling across her lips. "I have dealt with Kit for as long as I've worked here. He has been a pain in my ass for thirty years. I believe I will keep this as a favored memento."

I swallowed down the bile that churned in my stomach at the idea of her mounting Kit's antler on the wall like some prize. I told myself that I'd finish this, reassured myself that this wasn't over, that I'd make her pay for her cruelty.

She met my gaze, going still. "You're not broken yet, are you? Even after everything, after breaking out, after thinking yourself some sort of savior, after one of your lovers dragged you back here, you still think you have a shot, don't you? You grew up spoiled, hearing how special you were, how much better than others you were, but do you want to know the truth?"

I really didn't, but I had a feeling she'd tell me anyway.

"You are distressingly average. The only things special about you were given to you. Your last name, your family's money, even your status as a Level 1 shade you didn't earn. Your escape was nothing more than men you spread your legs for showing off *their* skills, and guess what? None of that worked out for you."

She ran her fingers down my cheek in a touch that made my skin crawl. It felt almost like some twisted form of affection mixed with hatred.

"I made you into what you are, and no matter how much you struggle, no matter how hard you try, you'll never win against me. So, Hera, welcome back to Larkwood. The North Tower missed you."

* * * *

Knox

Boy, I never expected to be back here. The thought hit me so hard that I slowed my pace. It had taken so much to escape this place that walking up to it again felt insane.

I'd risked *everything* to get out. I'd planned to start my life again, to have some semblance of happiness with Hera, and yet that had all changed. I hadn't just gotten dragged back, either. Instead, I'd walked my ass right back here.

Now I waited outside a back door in the Level 1 area. *We're all idiots.*

And by *we all* I meant the seven of us huddling beside a door in the back of Level 1. Brax, Kit, Aaron, Moa, Bowen, Soshi and I waited for Deacon to open that door, to let us into the last place I wanted to be.

Sure, I trusted Hera. I'd agreed that this was the right choice—I still agreed with it. That didn't make it any easier.

At least Hera hadn't had to take the steps by herself. She'd had Deacon shoving her forward, had no way to back out. Instead, I had to tell my body to move even as every instinct inside me said *fuck this* to the entire idea.

The door opened, and I exhaled slowly when I met Deacon's purple eyes. That at least meant everything with Hera must have gone well.

Deacon stepped backward and waved us all in. The door led to a small back room, one not made for the number of people we packed inside. It left me with Brax pressed to my arm on the left and Aaron to my right.

Come to take down Larkwood and end up packed with a bunch of other guys.

I glanced to where Moa stood, with everyone nice enough to at least not crowd her as much. *Mostly guys, at least.*

"Everything go according to plan?" Kit asked.

Deacon nodded. "Hera and Wade were taken to the North Tower. The Warden took the bait and believes that I killed you."

Kit let out a snort that said he didn't think Deacon was capable of such a thing.

Deacon pushed a box to the center of the table. "These radios are already set to a channel not used by Larkwood. We can use them to communicate and make sure we're in the right place but keep the volume low so no one hears them."

I nodded before I reached in to take one, the others doing the same. It slid easily into the pocket of my sweats, small enough to not be noticeable.

Deacon pulled out a stack of access cards out next, taking them from his cargo pants. He handed them out, one at a time. "I've already programmed these. They should open everything."

"No one will notice that?" I asked.

"The next time a basic security check is run on the access card database these will come up as anomalies, but that won't be for another three days. If we haven't finished by then, we're all probably dead."

"You could have sugar-coated that," Aaron muttered as he tucked his access card into his sweats pocket.

"I don't hide things," Deacon answered, crossing his arms and standing straight. "We're all in this together, and that means we're relying on each other. You deserve to know the risk. While the shades know it—we've lived it—we've got two humans here who haven't faced this before. You both need to understand how this could go, because if you're not willing to take that risk, you need to leave before you take us down with you."

Aaron narrowed his eyes, a sure sign that while he'd been on his best behavior, he was far from some quiet doormat. It seemed he was willing to acquiesce to Hera, but not so willing to play second-fiddle with us.

Still, Moa was the one to actually respond, and the strength in her voice made the room go silent. "I know the risks."

"You say that, but I doubt someone like you understands it at all," Brax snapped, ever the charmer that he was.

Moa turned a hard look on Brax, not flinching from him or his words. "I left letters behind for my parents in case I don't come back. I updated my will and my advanced directives. Trust me—I know exactly how dangerous this is. In fact, I'm not a shade. I don't heal like you all do. I'm not as strong or as fast. I don't have any special skills to keep me safe. If this goes wrong, I'm well aware that my odds of making it out are worse than any of yours. So if you're trying to scare, if you're trying to prove some point, don't waste your breath. If I wasn't willing to see this through to the end, I wouldn't have come this far." She held her hand out toward Deacon and waited.

And again, I found myself impressed.

She'd ignored Brax's glare and faced down Deacon, as well, all while being a human girl who was barely an adult.

Deacon stared back for a long, tense moment before letting out what might have been a chuckle and setting a card in her palm. "Be careful," he said before releasing it. "It'd be a shame if you got killed."

Moa tucked her card in the pocket of her sweats, then nodded.

I laughed at the exchange, drawing all the eyes in the room. I shrugged and crossed my arms. "It'd be a bigger shame for us, because Hera probably wouldn't be too happy about it." I nodded toward Kit. "I suggest you keep her safe, because I'm not above throwing you under the bus if anything happens to her."

Kit shook his head as if he refused to rise to my barb. "Come on, Moa, we should get going. There is no point in wasting time here."

Moa nodded and followed Kit as if she had no worries about it at all. Again, she reminded him that she was tough. Not many shades, let alone humans, would willingly follow a wendigo.

With them gone, the room felt slightly less cramped.

Bowen glanced around, a frown on his features. "I expected something different," he said. At Deacon's look, he went on. "I've heard about Larkwood for a long time. I've dealt with shades who came from here, and I honestly never thought I'd see this place in person."

"It doesn't live up to your expectations?" I asked.

He shook his head. "Honestly? No. The way people talked, I expected to find some old dungeon with stone walls and a moat. A place with this much ugly history shouldn't look like a something between a low-end hotel and a boarding school. It's like Kit looking like a stuffy professor but being able to turn living things to ash."

I thought back to when I'd first arrived and found myself stuck here that first night. "Trust me, come here as a kid, when you're locked up alone, it feels like a dungeon." I recalled how tall the towers had seemed back then, how far each floor spanned, how the guards had looked like monsters.

"Does it still feel that way?"

I pressed my lips together as I considered it, then shook my head. "It's just a place." It took saying that for me to really accept it, for me to understand what had changed.

When I'd arrived, I'd felt frightened and alone. I'd had Brax — that made me luckier than most shades — but they'd ripped everything away from me. Larkwood had been a monster who had eaten my old life.

When had that changed?

Hera.

The answer was as obvious as it was embarrassing. Before her, I hadn't thought I had anything else. It had felt as if I'd been swallowed by a giant beast and was busy just trying to not die yet. Hera had made me realize that I could have a life, that Larkwood wasn't the insurmountable enemy I'd pegged it as.

Bowen lifted his eyebrow as if he could almost read my thoughts before he shook his head. "You put too much faith in one person. No matter how skilled or impressive they are, they aren't infallible."

"Maybe," I said. "Or maybe you just haven't found someone worth putting that much faith into."

Bowen nodded, though I got the sense he didn't really believe me. "Maybe," he said softly, then turned toward Brax. "We'd better get ourselves set up as well."

"Is everyone else in place?" Brax asked.

"They should be. The other levels will be easy to take control of, so I have little doubt that the shades who volunteered can handle it. We need to keep our focus here, on Level 1."

Trusting a bunch of strangers to handle a portion of our plan didn't thrill any of us but we had to focus our attention on the biggest threat—Level 1 and the North Tower. Bowen and Moa had called in favors, surprised to find many shades who wanted a piece of this place. We didn't want reinforcements to rush in from another area, which meant allowing others to take care of levels 2 through 4 while we faced down the most dangerous.

Brax met my gaze for a moment, so much resting in that one look without us saying a damn word. We'd spent most of our lives looking out for each other, ignoring everything beyond that, but here we were ready to risk ourselves.

I refused to consider that either of us would fall. I couldn't even picture a life without my twin. It seemed empty and impossible. Still, we'd committed, so I nodded at him, trying to tell him not to worry, that I'd be fine, that I didn't need him to take care of me anymore.

Brax nodded back, then followed Bowen and Soshi out of the small room.

It left only three of us still there.

Aaron, Deacon and I.

Deacon gave Aaron a look that said he didn't care for that man. Then again, Aaron had been Hera's first...everything. Still, that wasn't a fight to have here, and even Deacon could set aside his jealousy for the moment.

"Keep in touch," Deacon said, his tone rough. "If there are any changes or issues, make sure you let us know so we can adjust." With that, Deacon headed out to take care of his own tasks.

Aaron's gaze followed Deacon, his brows furrowed as if he wasn't sure how to deal with the man. Then again, that wasn't a shock. Deacon wasn't the easiest person to handle, even for me and I'd known him for a long time.

Of course, I wasn't human. I wasn't an ex-boyfriend here out of some sort of guilt? I waited to see if Aaron would give up. Moa hadn't, but that didn't mean Aaron wouldn't.

He drew his hands into fists and pulled his shoulders back, and for one moment, I saw what Hera had once seen in him. He nodded as if to answer a question no one had asked then turned back toward me. "Let's get going."

I didn't bother to hide my smirk. Maybe this was one reason Hera was who she was—she'd surrounded herself with people who had more strength than I'd have expected. Or maybe that was the other way around, maybe her courage had rubbed off on the others, had taught them how to stand tall even when facing the impossible.

"Yeah, let's go," I said as I slipped past Aaron and stepped out of the small office, into the hallway on the first floor.

After all this time, I was ready to really face Larkwood.

It can throw whatever it wants at me.

* * * *

Hera

"I'm sorry," Wade muttered, his voice strained and soft.

I sighed before I sat on the floor of the room we were placed in. The action forced Wade to sit as well since our hands were bound tightly together.

This place wasn't a cell, not a holding area like the others I'd seen in Larkwood. Then again, without my powers, they had no reason for much security. The empty space we were in appeared to be an old office. At least that meant it wouldn't have any real security and the North Tower didn't keep regular security cameras around to help keep their dirty secrets quiet.

Instead, I didn't recognize this area as I'd been taken in. Few people suggested it wasn't used often, so I doubted it was connected to any of the projects I knew about.

What exactly she planned to do with us, I didn't know, but it didn't much matter, either.

I didn't plan to wait around and find out.

Wade let out a long sigh, and when I turned toward him, the profile of his face made my chest ache.

I leaned closer and bumped him against my shoulder.

He curled his lips into a half-assed smile to reassure me. "Who would have thought there was a place worse than solitary, huh? Got to say, I give the North Tower two stars — rude staff, lack of amenities, but the room is clean, so there's that." His words came out with the same humor he always used but it didn't take my skills to hear beneath them.

Especially since I didn't currently have any powers, which was exactly the cause of Wade's poor mood and apology.

I signed with my single free hand. It was awkward, but I went slow to make sure Wade understood. *"It's fine."*

"No, it's not." Wade slouched forward, his shoulders hunched and his gaze on the floor in front of us. "You're relying on me, and I can't even do this."

"You will."

"How do you know that?"

I squeezed his hand, a silly response since our hands were bound together already. *"Because I know you."*

He let out a long sigh. "You've got way too much faith in people, you know that? This whole plan, everyone has such important parts, but me? I just have to get out of the way, and I can't even manage that." He went silent for a moment before adding, "Maybe I'm just not capable of it. Maybe I'm so screwed up that I can't trust anyone even if I know I should." He turned his gaze toward me, his face surprisingly serious. "And I do know that. You've never betrayed me, never given me any reason to not trust you, but maybe I'm so broken that it isn't possible."

"That's not true," I assured him. *"You were brought here as a kid, you lost everything, you've had to be suspicious of everyone. If that didn't leave some scars, then there would be something broken or wrong about you."*

Still, my words didn't seem to do anything to improve his mood. It was perfectly clear he wasn't listening to me at all.

So I tried another option. *"What will you do when this is all over?"*

The corners of his lips tipped down, as if he hadn't expected my question. Perhaps it was that suddenness that spurred him to answer instead of making a joke in return. "I don't know."

"Will you go home? Visit with your family?"

He hesitated for a long moment. "I'd want to visit them, but I wouldn't want to live there." I didn't have to ask before he gave me a strained smile. "Home isn't there anymore — it's with you."

My cheeks warmed and I looked away, hating that I felt like some child who blushed over getting my hopes up.

Wade went on, though. "Other than that, I think I'd like to help kids."

"That makes sense. You'd be good with kids. You have about the same maturity level."

He snorted. "I just know what it's like to turn into a shade early, how it feels to have everything in your life change and not know who or what you really are anymore. I wish I'd had someone who had been through that, who understood it when I was that age. So, when this is all over" — he paused as if he struggled to believe it would end, at least in the way we wanted it to — "I think I'd want to work with young shades, help them grow their confidence and accept what they are. I see Soshi and it makes me realize how important that is."

His response caught me off guard. Why though, I didn't know. Thinking about it, it made perfect sense, but somehow I hadn't expected his answer. Maybe it was because I was so used to Wade taking nothing seriously, because I'd grown accustomed to his teasing and light-hearted attitude that hearing him speak honestly made me go still.

"Pretty stupid, huh?" he asked with a hollow laugh, as if he wanted to lessen the discomfort of telling the truth.

I shook my head and caught his chin with my free hand, drawing his eyes to mine before I brushed my lips against his. The truth was that I could say nothing that would make a difference. The best I could do for him would be to accept him — all of him. So I kissed him to tell him that I supported him, that I believed in him, that what he wanted wasn't only possible, but I'd do whatever I could to make it happen.

Wade slid his hand to the nape of my neck and pulled me closer, deepening the kiss as if something inside him snapped.

With our hands bound together, it was awkward, and facing each other like this twisted my arm, but I didn't give a damn. Instead, I let myself picture the future he'd mentioned.

I almost smiled at the memory of Wade and Soshi, at the way he'd protected her, and it made it clear he'd excel at working with kids. I could see him making jokes that the kids would giggle about but the rest of us would glare over. I pictured the trouble they'd get into, but also the way that when one of the kids had a problem, they'd go to Wade, they'd trust in him. Most of all, I thought about how Deacon would get angry at the antics of the kids and how Wade would take the fall for whatever they'd done—especially since I had no doubt he'd be a part of it if not the mastermind.

It was a future worth fighting for, worth making happen.

Having the desire to get out of Larkwood, to escape the pain of our past, that was all well and good, but running away from something never proved as powerful as running *toward* something. The future Wade talked about was that something to go toward, something to make us push harder, to strive for.

He ran his tongue across my bottom lip, but that felt distant for some reason. I couldn't figure it out at first, until I winced at the way the overwhelmingly loud hum of an air conditioner scraped at my nerves.

Which made me freeze.

My powers…

I hadn't heard that before, which meant my powers had returned, right? I pulled back from Wade, whose expression didn't seem all that fond of it.

Still, I lifted my free hand along with the one trapped against his, then snapped. I used the sound wave and sent it toward our bound hands and was rewarded with the immediate release of the metal cuffs that had kept us against each other.

"I did it," Wade muttered, his eyes widened in amazement.

I nodded, then rose from the mattress, Wade following me even if his movements were stiff, as if he couldn't quite believe he'd managed it.

I went to the door and pressed my ear against it, closing my eyes to block out any stimulus other than the sounds outside. That hum remained, along with conversations from countless people. The conversations came from farther off — probably in offices on adjacent floors. Nothing seemed just outside the door. I also heard no other prisoners nearby, nothing that signaled we were housed in another project cellblock like I had been before.

I turned back toward Wade, glad to be able to sign normally again. *"It sounds clear,"* I explained. *"We've been here long enough. I think everyone should be in place."*

Wade nodded but didn't look convinced.

"It'll be fine," I assured him even if I didn't know that, even if I didn't really believe my own words.

"Right," he said with the same lie I'd told. "This is what we came back for, right? Let's do this."

I nodded and set my gaze on the door. They hadn't put me in a cell with a normal lock this time — probably because I'd proven that the electronics in those posed no issue for me. It meant they'd gone old school instead, with reinforced steel that could probably withstand an angry Brax.

I lifted my hands, ready to take the thing off its hinges when Wade wrapped his hands over mine and held me still. His eyes were soft but serious as he stared at me so hard, I wondered if he were trying to memorize my face or something…

Finally, he pulled me closer and kissed me so deeply, it felt like a goodbye. Then he pulled back and squeezed my hands. "That future I talked about doesn't mean a damned thing without you in it, so make sure you come back."

I found myself nodding, even when I didn't mean to. I couldn't make that promise — we didn't live in a world where I could know that was possible, where I could ensure that — but I knew I wanted to.

That had to be enough.

He released me and stepped backward to give me room. I took a deep breath, then snapped and slammed the sound wave into the door. Just as I'd hoped, the thing went flying, the screeching of metal against the concrete floors impossibly loud.

Neither of us waited for the dust to clear, though. We didn't have time for long goodbyes. Wade took off, headed for an elevator to make his way to the main tower while I surveyed the huge room I stood in, the high ceilings and glass windows that looked into labs on each wall.

This is as good a place as any for a last stand...

Chapter Seventeen

Kit

Moa made me exceedingly uncomfortable, though I wasn't entirely sure why.

It wasn't that she was human. Working as adjunct staff in Larkwood meant working closely with humans often enough. It wasn't as if they made me nervous — with the exception of a few, such as the Warden, they posed little danger to me.

Yet somehow Moa made me question myself. She made me watch each word and hesitant to take my eyes off her.

It was as if she posed a risk that I felt but didn't fully understand.

"Is this it?" Moa gestured at the closed door before us.

I nodded. "This entire floor is empty."

"Won't Larkwood notice people are here then?"

"Since there isn't anything dangerous here, they don't limit access to it. In addition, Deacon ensured the elevator sensors are in a testing loop for the next few hours, so it hasn't been recording anyone."

Moa pulled in a deep, slow breath.

"Nervous?"

She gave me a lopsided smile before nodding. "I've helped a lot of shades, but I haven't been around this many before."

"I can assure you that the ones you've already dealt with—by which I mean *us*—are the most intimidating. If you didn't wilt under Brax's glare, you can deal with the young, the old and the fragile here."

Still, Moa didn't move. She remained rooted in place, her gaze down. "How did Hera get so brave?"

"She had no other choice."

Moa looked up at me, as if my words surprised her.

I shrugged, trying to ignore the way the sweatshirt rubbed against my skin. I wasn't accustomed to the clothing Larkwood made shades wear since I'd been exempted from that requirement previously. It let us all blend in better, made us just another shade here, but that didn't mean I cared for it.

"Hera had two choices when she arrived here—adapt or die. I suspect most people would adapt in such a situation. Besides, are you truly so different? You risked your freedom and your life to help shades, and you were not forced into that position."

"But she doesn't even look afraid," Moa countered. "When she came to me with this plan, she didn't act like it scared her at all."

"It scares her," I admitted softly. Perhaps I shouldn't have told her anything, but it felt important, especially given how much Moa meant to Hera. "I have a bond with her, and it means I can understand her at times, that I can see deeper than what she wants others to see, that I can glimpse what she hides. Hera is terrified. She's afraid of failing, of losing people, of letting us down. She may hide it well, but do not think that she came here without any fears. In that way, I believe you two are more similar than you realize."

She didn't appear convinced but turned her attention toward the door. It made me realize finally why she made me nervous.

Moa had a connection to Hera outside of the one I had. Not in the same way she had a relationship with Brax or the others, but rather Moa knew a woman I didn't. Moa had grown up around Hera, had known her when she was just herself, before Larkwood and the world had twisted her. Moa knew her in a way I never would, knew a part of her that would be forever hidden from me.

And I didn't like that one bit. Perhaps it was my wendigo that made me feel so possessive, that wanted to own Hera entirely. I knew it, struggled against that need inside me, refused to give in to it, but that didn't change how it annoyed me.

We entered the large open conference room to find plenty of shades there, milling around, their conversations whispered.

The relief that hit me made me realize just how worried I'd been about if anyone would show at all. Telling a group of understandably suspicious shades to meet someone in a secret location under the noses of the guards would be a hard sell. For all they knew, it was nothing more than a trap.

Every set of eyes in the room swung our way when we walked in, and seeing me, the level of tension in the room rose.

This is not a wonderful start.

Not that it shocked me. I wasn't well-liked among the shades at Larkwood. Perhaps it would have been better for another to do this job, but I understood the reasons it had fallen to me. I was best able to protect Moa on my own, and I couldn't move as easily amongst the rest of Larkwood unnoticed. It was best for me to remain out of sight until I was needed.

"What are you doing here?" one of the shades asked. A glance that way told me the name.

Despite what so many thought, I knew the names of those who stayed in Level 1. They rarely had a desire to be around me, to spend any time actually conversing with me, beyond what was required, but I still valued the information and made it a point to commit it to memory. I could offer most of them little, but I would remember their names through my long life.

This shade was Honor, a twelve-year-old girl who had been there for almost a year. She'd been quiet for the most part, drawing little attention from the guards or staff. As a shifter—a shade who could take the form of any animal—she would normally be watched far more carefully, but her psychological tests on intake had shown her to be timid and of low risk.

"We gathered you here because we have a plan," I said, then nodded toward Moa. "This woman is involved with smuggling shades out of the country and out of harm's way."

"Are you planning some sort of escape?" another shade called out.

"That's crazy," came the response of another. A low level of anxiety ran through the shades in the room, murmuring as they whispered about how foolish such an idea would be. "You know what happened last time — how much we all suffered for nothing."

Before I could keep speaking, Moa stepped forward. "It isn't just about escaping." At Moa's voice, the whispers quieted. "I've helped a lot of shades, and a lot of them never made it. Even if I got them through where I was, if I passed them off to another person to help, they got caught. From doing this, I know that some shades who got away a decade before would get found and dragged back."

"So what's the point?" Honor asked, crossing her arms, not looking much like the pre-teen she should have been. "If it's so hopeless, why take the risk?"

"We aren't here to help you escape a broken system," Moa told them, her hands drawn into tight fists. "We're here to break the system. Instead of escaping Larkwood, our plan is to take it over."

And that garnered another wave of whispers.

Still, Moa didn't back down. She kept speaking, her voice gaining strength, her chin lifted. "The reason Larkwood has been able to keep control for so long is because no one tells humans the truth. They work together to hide it from us, to tell us stories to make us afraid of you."

"And what do you plan to do about that?"

Moa reached into the bag slung over her shoulder, pulled out the small camera and held it up. "I'm here to give you all the chance to tell your truth, for you to stop letting other people control your stories."

"What if the Warden sees this?" one of the older shades asked, her withered hand clutching a cane that she leaned against. "What happens to us when your big plan fails, and we pay the price? You'll run away and we will be left here to face the consequences."

Moa didn't answer right away, but at least that showed she took the time to actually consider it. "This is dangerous—I won't pretend like it isn't. I can't tell you what you should do, and anyone who wants to leave, can. You have to make that choice, to decide what it's worth to you. This floor will be locked down, so that when everything starts, you won't be in the line of fire. Even if you don't want to help us, you can stay here until it's over. The reality is that Larkwood *will* fall eventually, and you just have to decide whether you want to help it happen or not, whether you want to speak up or not."

The shades in the room looked between each other, the tension thick and overbearing.

What would they say?

A part of me wanted to speak up, to add to what Moa had said, but I knew better. Even though I'd thought I'd accepted my place in Larkwood, it didn't quite remove the sting. No matter how much I sacrificed and or how hard I tried, I'd never be looked at as anything but a threat.

The older woman peered around, and in her eyes I could see the years that had passed. I remembered when she'd arrived, when she'd been a young girl, so afraid of the world she'd been forced into. And in her eyes, I caught a glimpse of all the other's she'd known over the years, the one who never made it to her age, who Larkwood had crushed.

Finally, she nodded, her hand tightening around the handle of her cane. "Okay. I'll do it."

And, as if emboldened by her answer, other shades nodded in agreement.

Well, at least that's the first hurdle.

* * * *

Knox

I spread the papers out on the large metal table in the filing room, the words on each like a new reason for me to feel annoyed.

Or maybe that's just this asshole standing beside me.

Which wasn't fair, so I tried to push that thought away. It was the sort of thing Brax would think, not me.

If anyone understood how people had pasts, how sex and love existed in the world, it was me. I had a moment of thinking about all the people I'd had sex with, driven by the need of my incubus, and how unfair it would be for Hera to freak out over them all.

Yet here I was with a pointless, petty hatred for Aaron all because he'd taken so many of her firsts, because he owned a spot in her heart that would never go away.

It being over didn't change that they had been important to each other.

Aaron held a camera in his hand, taking pictures of the files as I placed them down. We moved from one to another, as quickly as possible, trying to gain as much information as possible.

We wouldn't have long to gather the information first, before everything really went to hell and we entered the second part of our plan.

Aaron made a soft sound in his throat, one that resembled choking. When I turned to look at his face, I found his eyes locked onto a paper.

Across the top of it—*Hera Weston*. I'd moved so quickly I hadn't read what was actually on the files. *Better to get copies of them all now and worry later about sorting out the information.*

I sighed and grabbed the paper, flipping it over. Aaron caught my hand to stop it.

"She wouldn't want you prying into her personal affairs," I said.

Still, Aaron stared at the paper without moving, as if struck by whatever he saw. "I know she was here, I know she suffered, but seeing her name on the files..."

"We don't have a lot of time. If you want to have a breakdown, do it while you take the pictures."

He stood up straight, then nodded and did as I said. However, the conversation didn't seem over since he spoke as he worked. "You don't like me, do you?"

"I don't have any reason to dislike you."

"Well, for someone with no reason, you sure manage it anyway."

That little bit of snark made me swing my gaze around to him and narrow my eyes. "Do we really need to have this conversation now? You don't think we have *anything* more important to focus on than bullshit jealous drama?"

"Learn to multitask," Aaron muttered, his focus on the pages as he took image after image. "Is it just because Hera and I were together?"

"Do you have any idea how much she hurt when you decided to sleep with her best friend? She got locked away in here, had everything stolen from her, then her wonderful, loving boyfriend didn't contact her and instead chose to fuck her best friend." I snorted softly. "Can't imagine why I might not like you."

At least Aaron had the decency to look ashamed. Not that that changed a damned thing. People embraced guilt because it enabled them to do whatever the hell they wanted, then sit back later and feel like they were a good person because at least they felt bad about it. It let people do horrible things and not change their behavior.

When Aaron did speak again, his voice was quiet and soft and lacking any amount of posturing. "I don't have an excuse for that, other than to say I had my future stolen that night, too. You seem to think the person who gets sent here is the only one who suffers. I had an entire future planned out with Hera. I loved her. I thought we'd spend our lives together. Hell, I already thought of her as my wife. Then I woke up and found out she was gone, that she was never coming back. It was like a death to me." His gaze darted around to the room we stood in. "Larkwood takes a whole lot more than you realize."

"If you're looking for pity, you're barking up the wrong tree. And if this whole *nice guy* thing you're trying to play here is about getting her back, don't think for a second that I'm about to let that happen without a fight. Also, I'm not above playing dirty."

"I'm not trying to get her back"

"So why are you really here?"

"Because I loved her!" Aaron threw his hands up as if unable to tolerate our back and forth anymore. After a moment, he took a deep breath and went on, his voice carefully controlled. "I won't pretend like I was the best boyfriend, but I did love her. Or..." He ran his fingers through his hair. "Maybe it's better to say I loved who I thought she was, who she pretended to be, who she thought she was. Maybe neither of us were honest enough to really love each other, but I cared for her, and I hurt her, and I want to make that right."

He didn't go back to scanning, instead turning to face me head on. "I know now that she had to force herself into a role, that she wasn't happy with me, that the life I had planned wasn't right for her. I never knew how strong she really was until I saw her again."

It took me back to the first day I met her, outside of that intro classroom. She'd been so afraid of the world, of us, of herself. It was strange to think that was the same woman I knew now, the one who faced down anything without so much as a flinch.

But it was, and I finally understood what Aaron was telling me.

Hera had always been this woman, but she'd hidden it because she'd tried to fit into a world that wanted her to shrink herself, to lessen herself for the comfort of others.

It made me look over at Aaron, at the sadness in his eyes.

"I didn't lose Hera. I know that now, realize she and I would have never been happy together long term. I see her with you, though, with the others, and it's so damn obvious that she and I weren't ever right for each other. I'm not here because I'm trying to get her back, but because I want to be as strong as she is for once. I want to do something good, to not just be some rich asshole who does what Daddy tells me to. I want to earn the trust she has in me. I want to be the man she thinks I can be."

The look in Aaron's eyes said he spoke the truth, that he hid nothing as he said those words. He bared himself to make me understand.

And it made me nod, accepting his truth. Hera and Aaron had a past. Nothing would ever change that. They'd both learned from each other, grown together and they'd helped each other become the people they were now — for better or worse.

The petty jealousy inside me dissipated at that realization.

Accepting someone meant accepting their past, and fuck knew I had enough ugliness in my own that I didn't want held against me.

"Thank you," I said softly, Aaron's responding look as surprised as I felt. "For coming here. I don't think I told you that, but thank you."

Aaron shrugged and went back to taking pictures. "I don't know if I'm much help compared to you all."

"You are," I said even though a part of me hated admitting it. "Having you and Moa here makes a difference to Hera. It tells her she's still the same person, that her life outside of this place isn't completely gone. In the end, that might be what gives her the strength to actually do this."

Aaron paused to meet my gaze, but instead of responding, he nodded and went back to work.

Which left us with the silence — less awkward than before — as we copied all the files we could.

Who would have figured Larkwood would bring people together?

* * * *

Wade

"Did you miss me?" I walked into the large central security office with a grin to find Deacon appearing *far* less amused.

"No," Deacon said without even a moment of hesitation.

"Words hurt, you know." I peered to the side to find a guard on the ground, his eyes closed and a dark mark on his throat. Still, the guard's chest rose and fell, showing Deacon hadn't killed the other man.

No matter how much Deacon liked to pretend to be some sort of heartless monster, he really was a softie, wasn't he?

I held my hand out as I took a seat in front of the computer. Deacon placed the external hard drive in my palm, which I quickly pushed the USB connecter into the slot at the front of the computer.

"Hera okay?" Deacon said in that quiet voice he used when he wanted to ask something but worried he shouldn't.

"Fine last I saw. We should hear something pretty soon."

Deacon nodded and crossed his arms, the action reminding me how much larger he really was. Yet, somehow, it didn't bother me the way it had before. There had been a time not that long ago when it would have annoyed me, when it would have made me uncomfortable.

Yet, that had changed. I saw Deacon as an ally, as someone I could rely on rather than competition I couldn't live up to. Large and broody was certainly *one* type of male, but I'd accepted that I wasn't that type and that was okay.

It felt like the first time I'd truly accepted myself—both the good and the bad—and it was all because I'd stopped running from it, stopped hiding it beneath jokes and keeping things casual. Instead, I'd bared myself — even the parts I didn't like much — and found acceptance for them.

Instead of getting lost in that, I went to work on the computer. There wasn't anywhere near enough space for everything, but I could get a lot of it transferred to the hard drive to smuggle out of Larkwood.

With any luck, we'd succeed on all fronts. So long as they didn't wipe the data, we could always come back for the rest of it later.

However, I didn't believe much in luck, which meant backing up what we could in case things went wrong was the smart play.

Larkwood had no cell reception, which meant the only way to get data out was to use the official network. Security was too good for that, so getting the drive physically out was the only immediate way to get anything we found to the world.

So I grabbed the most damning information — the videos in the discipline files. Why? Because they typically showed the punishments Larkwood put down and few things showed just how painful life here could be more than that.

The computer's fan grew louder, a sign it had to work to capacity, and it gave me a chance to turn and find Deacon standing behind me, his gaze on the guard.

"You sure you're up for this?" I asked.

He frowned as if he didn't understand my question.

I nodded at the guard. "Standing beside Hera is one thing — going up against people who were your colleagues is another. Are you sure you're ready to do that? That you want to actually have to face them down? Can you do what we need in order to win?"

"The guards were never my colleagues," Deacon said. "They were always very clear that I wasn't one of them, that I wasn't human, that I didn't belong. If you think we had some friendly relationship, rethink it. The guards here are far from my friends."

It wasn't just Deacon's words that hit me but his tone. As a guard, he'd always seemed unfeeling, as if he didn't give a damn about the world. That was a far cry from his tone right now, from the way he looked at me, from the pain in his words.

Maybe things were a lot less clear than they seemed to be, less easy to categorize. Deacon was a guard, but he was also a prisoner in his own way, just like us.

I went to respond, but the beep of the computer signaled it had finished. I unhooked the USB cord and slipped the drive into my backpack.

Deacon took his radio from his belt, the one tuned into the same channel as the others. "Videos transferred. Where is everyone?"

Kit answered first, his voice as careful as ever, as though this were just like any other day. "We have everyone secured and interviews done. As soon as I hear the alarms, I will head to the front."

"Got copies of most of the files," Knox said. "Headed to meeting point two."

"We're here and waiting," Brax answered, which meant everyone was where they needed to be.

"Guess that means it's time," I said as I rose from the chair. We'd planned, we'd suffered, we'd sacrificed, and it all came down to this.

One way or another, everything would change after tonight.

Chapter Eighteen

Hera

The North Tower was every bit as intimidating as it had been before. I'd have thought coming here again would make it feel less scary, as if since I'd survived it once, it no longer posed a threat.

The truth was a far cry from that.

This place was terrifying. Even alone as I was, in an area that didn't seem to get much traffic, every shadow reached for me. I'd lain low for as long as I could, to give Wade time to get to security before I made my move, before I drew the attention of the Warden.

Now it was time, though. The only good thing was that I seemed to have a skill causing a commotion and drawing the ire of Larkwood. It took one last deep breath to try to relax. This was it. Larkwood was a dragon and I was ready to kick it.

I clapped my hands and sent a wave of power at the pipe and sprinkler that ran along the ceiling. It broke, water pouring down into the room and setting off an alarm that would no doubt call every last guard here.

And I was ready for whatever they wanted to throw at me.

* * * *

Brax

Standing beside Bowen reminded me of just how weird the man was. He was what would be considered a low-level shade, but I'd gotten a glimpse of what he could actually do, so I knew better than to underestimate him.

"Everything's on track," he said as he leaned against the door frame, staring out into the yard.

"You don't need to sound so surprised."

Bowen let out a laugh and shrugged. "Of course I'm surprised. Who wouldn't be? This was an insane idea."

"Then why did you agree to help?"

He glanced to his side, to where Soshi sat, her back against the wall, her gaze up on the high walls.

"Never figured you'd bring a child to a fight like this," I said. "Before, you seemed overprotective, but then you drag her here to Larkwood?"

Bowen's gaze softened just a bit as he stared at her. The expression made him look so different. I didn't think he'd answer at first—didn't expect one, really, since we weren't friends—but to my surprise, he spoke. "She's going to outlive me, you know? I've been trying to keep her safe for a long time, but seeing Hera, seeing you all, seeing those soldiers break into our little haven, it all reminded me that Soshi is going to have to survive the world on her own one day."

"That's true of everyone. Don't know why that seems like a sudden revelation."

"That's because you don't have children." At my frown, he offered a tense smile. "She isn't mine, not biologically, but I've watched over her a long time. I consider her my child. I've tried to lock her up, to keep her away from danger, to teach her to defend herself, but eventually, it'll be all on her."

He tore his gaze from mine and stared up at the stars for a long moment. "I realized that perhaps the largest thing I could do was try to make sure the world she had to live in was a better one than what we have now. Protecting people isn't just about avoiding danger but teaching them that they can survive the danger." He let out a soft laugh. "Besides, with as stubborn as she is, she'd have just followed me if I'd left her behind. God save us from strong women, huh?"

I stared over at the young girl, as uncomfortable with her as I'd been the first time we'd met.

I wasn't the sort of man who dealt well with children. They tended to fear me, and I never knew what to say to them. They seemed to see right through me, and Soshi had been no different. The way she'd rushed into that fight, it wasn't that she hadn't known the dangers. No, in Soshi's young face had been far too much understanding of the risks. She'd done it because she saw the world in such a simple way, and she had the bravery to defend it.

Maybe that scared me the most about children... Losing them felt like a pain too deep to survive.

"You don't care for kids, do you?" Bowen asked.

"Who does?"

He laughed softly. "I do. I find the way they see the world refreshing. The rest of us, we get jaded, but not kids. They make surviving seem worth it."

"They're fragile," I said, my voice low. I'd meant it as a simple point, but the moment the words escaped, I knew it meant far more than I'd wanted it to.

And judging from the way Bowen lifted his eyebrow, he *knew* what I meant. "They can be," he admitted. "They're also more resilient in a lot of ways. Besides, not everything that is a risk is bad. I figured you understood that given how you follow that siren around."

Ouch. I swallowed hard at the way Bowen dug right to the point of the matter. "That's different," I muttered. "Hera can take care of herself."

"Maybe she can, but it's still a risk. The truth is that any connection we form is a risk. Maybe I understand it more because of what I am. My entire sense of self is wrapped up in those I serve, in those I take under my protection. Without them, what am I? What is my point if I have nothing and no one to protect?"

"Exactly," I snapped. "It's because of what you are. I'm not you, though. I don't need a bunch of useless burdens hanging off me to give me purpose."

Bowen lifted his hand and counted things off, lifting a finger with each one. "Siren. Meta. Wendigo. Incubus. Void. Seems like you've already got your share of people relying on you."

His words made me go still, especially when I couldn't argue it.

I'd worked so hard to go through life since coming to Larkwood without entanglements. My brother was more than enough to keep me up at night with worry.

I'd resisted every other attempt to draw myself into that sort of relationship with people.

And yet…here I was. I'd come back even knowing the dangers. I would throw myself into the line of fire to protect any of those people he'd listed.

Why?

Because I'm not alone anymore.

That was the easy answer, but the honest one also. After so many years of using my berserker as a way to keep others at a distance, after using my attitude and my threats to frighten off anyone else, I'd somehow found myself exactly where I'd never wanted.

And it left me back here at Larkwood, ready to face down every guard in this place in an impossible mission.

I let out a long breath, unhappy that I couldn't argue with Bowen's reasoning.

He laughed, his chuckle grating on my nerves. "It's not so bad, you know?"

"That's what people say to make themselves feel better."

"No, it's true. See, personal gain, the innate need inside living things to survive, those are powerful forces. The thing is, I've learned that they aren't the *most* powerful. I've seen it time and time again when helping shades. People will do a lot for themselves, for their own wellbeing, but they'll do far more to save those they love. You being here, willing to take on all of this, proves it. Caring about people, it's a double-edged sword, no doubt about it, but that doesn't change that there's some good there too."

I tore my gaze away, saved from the awkwardness of the conversation by an overly familiar voice. "Don't you all look cozy."

Knox's voice let me take a deeper breath. Even if I'd heard him over the radio, a part of me wouldn't believe he'd succeeded until I could actually see him. Beside him, Aaron stood, though surprisingly there seemed less tension between the two.

Had they worked something out?

I didn't bother asking. We had more important things to think about.

On their heels, the others arrived. Deacon and Wade came, a laptop in Wade's hands from security to let him counter some of the measures Larkwood might try. Kit and Moa came as well, meaning the more fragile shades were safe on the empty floor, barricaded in to help ensure they didn't get caught in the crossfire anywhere.

We were all together. It was strange, but something about seeing them all eased me.

We were getting ready to face the worst thing we ever had. This made our escape from Larkwood look like a child's game, like nothing more than kids playing around. This was for real, though. We couldn't back down, couldn't risk losing, not when so much rested on the line.

"Soshi," Bowen called, and the little girl hopped to her feet and rushed over.

Her expression held tension, even if she tried to bravely hide it. "Yeah?" she asked.

Bowen took the backpack from her, then held his hand out to Wade, Moa and Aaron. Wade gave him a hard drive while Moa and Aaron took out the SD cards from their cameras and replaced them with new cards from the backpack. Once the times were packed into the bag, Bowen handed it back.

Soshi's hand trembled as she took them and slid the bag over her shoulders. "That's it?"

Bowen nodded. "That's it. Do you remember where you're going?"

Soshi pointed in the direction of the town. The desert was vast, but we'd hidden supplies along the way so she could make the distance easily. She had a compass and knew how to read it, how to guide herself back to where friends of Bowen's waited. The idea of sending her on this mission, of leaving her on her own, made my chest ache.

Knowing that didn't change that it was the right choice, though. Soshi was young but she was tough. She could move quickly, and because of her skills, she could protect herself if she needed to. Her small size would let her escape notice more easily than others and no one knew her face or was looking for her.

Still, it didn't feel right.

Even with Bowen's words, with the realization that she would have a future for herself, that she'd have to survive this world on her own eventually, I hated that she had to be here, that she had to do any of this. She shouldn't have to face these dangers.

Which reminded me again why I'd kept my distance from anyone, especially children. The idea of losing them terrified me.

I swallowed and jerked my gaze away from her before I said something stupid.

"You be careful," Bowen said as he set his hand on her head to ruffle her hair, the affection clear. "Move fast, stay out of sight, and get these files to our contact."

Soshi curled her fingers around the straps of the bag, and it would take a blind man to not see the fear on her face. Still, she nodded. "I'll get it done," she promised before taking off toward the outer wall. We'd had the ability to set up this time, which meant it hadn't taken much to dig a small area out under the wall. Soshi wasn't large, so she could fit, and Deacon ensured the guard paths avoided the spot for the day.

We all watched Soshi go, like some beacon of hope for us. No, that wasn't entirely fair — she was despair as much as hope, a symbol of what we had to do, what we had to risk, to save us all.

Kit was the first to break the silence. He rolled his shoulders, his expression dark. "I guess this is my turn, isn't it?"

He didn't wait, didn't hesitate or look afraid. No, he seemed almost excited.

Then again, Kit had lived here longer than anyone else, had suffered longer and deeper than the rest of us. If anyone had a score to settle with Larkwood, it was him.

He walked forward, away from the wall where we stood, away from the hidden space we'd created for ourselves. His steps were slow and careful, without a speck of fear.

When he reached the center of the yard, outside of the front door, he rose to his full height, his body shimmering as he changed into his other form.

And again, I found myself grateful to not be pitted against him. My berserker was scary, but in a different way. I was fire and rage, but Kit? He was darkness incarnate, hunger made flesh. The thing that stood there looked like something that could devour the entire world.

And yet…he mattered to me. Just like the others, like Wade and his stupid jokes, Deacon and his shitty attitude, Knox and the way he tried to hide everything he hated about himself. They were as much a part of me as Hera, a found family that I'd never wanted but now cherished.

Kit stood there, one of the antlers on his head missing—his own sacrifice to the cause—and he held his hands out, the unnaturally long claws tipped with black nails. Never had his black eyes looked as fitting as right now. It almost felt as if he were source itself, like he was a glimpse of what had made us all.

He tilted his head backward, the moonlight making the bone of his face shine brightly, then let out a sound so dark and deep that it sent shivers right through me. The sound echoed out, no doubt drawing the attention of every guard in Larkwood.

Here we go…

* * * *

Hera

Somewhere along the way, seeing the Warden had stopped terrifying me so much.

Why was that?

She held as much power over me as she had before. If anything, she was more willing to harm me now, and I had a *lot* more to lose than I did when I first came.

Yet, as she walked in, the clicking of her heels loud even over the fighting, I found I didn't react to her as I once had. She was just a woman.

A twisted, broken woman, but not a monster.

Which meant I could win.

She walked into the room, and immediately, the other guards pulled back. The Warden showed no signs of fear as she moved between them and myself, as if she knew I wouldn't lash out at her.

Was that arrogance?

"You really are a problem," she said. "Each time I think I have you handled, each time I think I've managed to predict your moves, you do the unexpected."

I held my hands out as if to tell her I would get in her way every last time I needed to.

She laughed and waved the guards backward, telling them to leave us.

The action only set me on edge more, made me wonder just what she had up her sleeve. She wasn't the type to sacrifice herself, so what the hell was this?

Once alone, her behavior shifted, loosening, as if without the onlookers she could act more casually.

Was this the real woman?

"I wish you understood," she said. "Sometimes, I wish more people understood, really, but then I remember that it is my cross to bear. It is my task, and others don't need to be privy to it just to make me feel better."

She walked to a computer that sat on one wall of the large room, then clicked at the keyboard. A part of me wondered if I should stop her, if I should do something to try to ensure she wasn't doing something that would harm me.

Except, another part, a larger one, wanted to understand her. She didn't seem to be trying to trick me, so I let her type into the keyboard.

"Do you know where source comes from?"

My hands moved to sign a response, but I stopped myself and simply nodded instead.

"Most people know that much. It seeps through tears that exist between our reality and another, though few have any idea what sits on the other side of those tears."

Her words took me back to Kit and Lilianna, both of whom had mentioned being able to feel those tears, had both talked about what might exist on the other side.

The Warden hit another button and a large screen flickered on beside her, one mounted to the wall for presentations. On it sat a lab with a shimmering space hanging in the air. "Most tears are so small, only source leaks through. Exposure to this creates shades by charging humans on a basic level. There are larger tears, though, and through those, we've glimpsed that there are *things* on the other side."

"What sort of things?" I signed back.

I doubted she understood my words, but perhaps some things transcended language, because she answered. "There is a reason I've worked so hard to learn all I can about shades—you are the best chance we have at closing those tears and learning how to overcome what exists on the other side. Most people believe I hate shades, but that isn't true. You all are victims as much as we are, just unlucky individuals who were caught up in this outside of your choice. Still, once that happened, the only chance for survival for humans is to learn and use everything at our disposal."

I frowned as I listened to her, as the video on the screen continued, showing darkness moving inside that tear.

"This entire floor of the North Tower is devoted to studying those tears, to understanding them, to learning how to both open and close them."

I tapped my fingers against my chest.

She nodded. "Yes, this is where we discovered how to open the tears that turned you into what you are.

When we started, the crystals that created the tears were as large as rooms, but now they can be placed inside tiny orbs and set off on demand. You were not the first to be changed, though you were by far the most successful. Some bodies react to source well and others do not—you took to it well. Perhaps that was the big problem, that your body accepted and used it so well. Instead of turning into the tool I'd wanted you to be, you became dangerous."

She let out a soft laugh that sounded strange from her. "Tools are always a challenge. Make them too weak and they're useless—too strong and they may turn on you. You were made too strong."

I crossed my arms. If she wanted an apology, she could go fuck herself.

As if she read that on my face, she smiled. It made her look her age for once, as if she were far more tired than she let on. Still, she nodded at the video. "Out of all the projects in Larkwood, this is my passion. When I first came here, others didn't understand. They looked at me as if I were crazy, as if my ideas were too outlandish. They didn't understand, though, and because of that, they lack the stomach to do what needs to be done. They had no idea of the dangers. I know, however."

As she spoke, the shadows in that tear moved more, each one lumbering and terrifying. Nothing came through, nothing clear enough for me to identify, but it made it clear something existed on the other side.

"I know the truth, though, because I've seen it myself." She didn't look at me, instead staring at the video. "I was only ten when I found out what was really out there. My parents were nobodies. They ran a small restaurant and lived a simple life. I'd expected to follow them, to take over the restaurant someday, but life doesn't go the way we think. Perhaps in that, you and I are similar."

I didn't care for the idea of the Warden and I having anything in common, but I couldn't stop myself from admitting she had a point. I recalled how my life had changed entirely upon becoming a shade, how everything I'd expected happening disappeared in that one night.

If the Warden noticed my thoughts, she said nothing about it. She just went on with her story. "I don't know why the tear happened. Even after all these years, after everything I've learned, I don't know why it appeared there. Perhaps it was just bad luck, but one of the few large tears opened at our home one night. I was eating dinner with my parents when we heard a crack, loud enough for the dishes on the table to shake. My father rushed toward the sound, toward this shimmering space that hung in the middle of the room. As soon as he neared it, this hissing sound left the tear a moment before something came through."

She spoke with a flat voice, as if she felt nothing from the horrific story. "It was like nothing I had seen before. It was feral, animalistic, completely crazed. It made short work of my parents—I still remember the way they screamed and told me to run. I stood there and stared, too terrified to move. When it finished with my parents, it turned toward me. Blood covered it, all over its teeth, its claws, its entire body. It didn't charge me like it had with them. It approached me slowly, almost like it was toying with me. That was when I realized that what lives on the other side, the things there, they're evil. There is nothing good through those tears, and what leaks through, the source that warps our world, it's just a symptom of that evil."

A tremble ran through her, the only evidence that her story affected her, though she squeezed her hands into fists, and it disappeared as fast as it had happened.

I swallowed hard as I gazed at the shimmering in the video. While there had been whispers about things on the other side, it sounded as if that wasn't just rumors. While I didn't trust the Warden, the truth of her words rang through. It took me back to that flash I'd had from her, the sight of blood, her terrified screams.

They'd been from that night.

I gestured at her, my eyebrow lifted in question.

"Yes, I survived. The creatures that come through seem to be bound to the tears, and the tears never last long. Sometimes they'll slaughter and go back, sometimes they will take a person with them, but either way, they only remain here so long as the tear exists. As soon as it started to close, just as the thing got right in front of me, it was pulled backward. It swiped out, catching me with its claws, but it was taken back." She untucked her shirt and lifted it, showing a deep scar on her side that was purple rather than the normal white. "This is its mark. I can still feel it, through what separates our world from its. It stalks me, and this is how it knows where I am. I escaped it — not many do — and it has never forgotten me."

Suddenly, looking at her, I understood her a little better. I tried to imagine being stalked by something no one else believed existed for years. I pictured how that would change a person, how watching that thing kill my family while knowing it wanted me too might twist a person.

I couldn't forgive her, and it didn't excuse it, but I understood it better. Her obsession made more sense.

"I'm not looking for pity," the Warden said. "I just want you to understand what we are truly up against. I've spent my life knowing that hell is so close. We think it's far away, but it *isn't*. The veil between us and destruction is so thin and fragile. I've seen what's there, and if we don't do something, if we don't prepare ourselves, it will destroy us all. These tears? They're getting larger and more common. I am constantly cleaning up after them. They used to happen once a decade, then once a year, and now? There are tears weekly. If we can't find a way to defend ourselves, to stop this, the barrier will fall and we will *all* die. So you can look at me like I'm a monster. Maybe I am, but I'm the only one standing between us and the end."

Her words sounded pretty, like the sort of excuse a person gave to get themselves off the hook. I wasn't so quick to forgive and forget.

I walked over to the computer and typed into the keyboard, bringing up a small text window. *"It isn't about saving everyone – it's about saving yourself."*

She pressed her lips together. "I've wondered that before, but the reality is that my survival is the same as the world's survival. If I can figure this out, my future will be entwined with the rest of the world's. There is no difference."

"Of course there is. You're looking out for yourself, and you don't care who else you hurt."

"You get to say that because you haven't seen what I have. If you did, you'd understand that we can't always do things the right way here. We can't take the high road. We have to do whatever we have to or it's all over. No one is above that. I will torture and kill every shade alive, I will conduct whatever experiments need to happen on any human and I will run down anything that stands in my way. I will *not* let this world fall because I'm too soft, because I won't make the hard choices. If I have to be a villain to save us all, I'll do it."

I shook my head before typing out another response. *"If that's what it takes to save us, we aren't any better than what you're afraid of, and we don't deserve to survive. If we become that, we aren't worth saving."*

The Warden let out a sigh as if my words weren't unexpected. "You're young and naïve still. I wonder, if we'd met another way, if you'd understood back then, would things be different? If you could have grown up more first, if you'd known what we were up against from the start, would things have changed? Who knows — perhaps we could have worked together. You've proven yourself troublesome, which tells me you could also be useful. I've said it before, but it would be a shame to destroy you. You could have been one of our greatest weapons."

I didn't respond because there wasn't anything to say back. My job was to keep her busy, to keep the guards in the North Tower busy, to cause a problem big enough to give the others time and space to move around.

The Warden sighed, and she actually sounded sad for a moment. "I could just kill you here, but that feels like an odd loss, so I have one more offer for you. I could make you human."

I frowned, her offer so unexpected that I couldn't comprehend it at first.

"You know what the Corrander project was, but you haven't dealt with Lazarus. Aren't you curious about it? Lazarus, the man brought back from the dead — a fitting name if I do say so myself." She smiled as if at some private joke. "It's finished. It's difficult to produce, so we haven't made much of it, but I'll offer it to you. You can have your old life back and pretend as if this last year never happened."

My knees nearly buckled when reality hit me, at the idea that I could go back. If I said yes, this would all be over. I could return to my life, to the future I'd had planned, to the ease and comforts I'd grown up with.

I pictured eating dinner with my parents again, sitting and laughing with my friends, living free in the world without the fears I'd suffered through the last year. I could be normal.

But…as soon as I considered that, the picture drifted away.

I wasn't the girl anymore. It wasn't just the source in my blood or the scar on my throat that had changed — I'd changed as a person. I'd experienced the best and worst of people, had survived so much, that the idea of going back to that empty, pointless life was impossible.

It was like pouring a glass of water onto the sidewalk then trying to put it all back again. The water wouldn't ever be the same, and it couldn't go back to how it had been no matter how hard a person tried.

That was me.

Beyond the fact that I'd found things worth having — the men who I loved — I couldn't pretend my world hadn't been irrevocably altered, that *I* hadn't changed. It wasn't about what was forced on me anymore, about what I had to endure because I didn't have the choice.

Instead, as I stood there, I got to choose the path I wanted to take.

And somehow, that made it all the easier. I shook my head.

She sighed softly. "I think I expected that answer. I could do it anyway, but what would be the point? You've proven already what a problem you can be, so if you won't accept my offer and go back to your perfect little life, then you'll die here."

"Warden?" came a voice over the radio. The Warden walked back to the doorway and reached out until a radio was placed in her hand.

"Yes?"

"We have a problem back at the main tower."

"What sort of problem?"

"Kit, the wendigo—he's here."

"What do you mean *here*?"

A chilling scream echoed through the radio, as if caught from somewhere around the person speaking. "I mean he is standing out front."

The Warden turned back to look at me, her face pulled into tense lines. "It's just one shade. Deal with it."

"Do you want us to try to retake him?"

"No. All restrictions on lethal force are lifted. I've grown tired of this—it ends now."

I took a step forward at her words, at the fear that swamped me, but stopped when the guards pointed their guns in my direction. They hadn't had any luck with me yet, but it only took one bullet getting by to end this.

Except, the Warden shook her head. "You all, go reinforce the main tower. If Kit is here, I have a feeling we might just see a few other familiar faces."

"What about her?" The guard gestured my way.

The Warden offered a chilling smile that made my stomach sink. "I believe the Corrander soldiers can handle her. It really is a pity that things had to go this way. If you only understood what was really out there, I think you could have made all the difference. I would have much rather had you as an ally than as an enemy."

With that, she left, the guards also backing out. I went toward the door, but stopped as soon as someone else walked in.

Gerald, the dragon shifter, the 'toy' Lilianna had under her control. Not just him, though. One after another came in, the same vacant looks on their faces that said they couldn't be talked to or reasoned with.

I'd survived them last time by dumb luck, by being in a place where I could take down the bridge. Here, though? In their territory, in a large lab with no exits, I didn't stand a chance.

Which meant the best I could do was try to hold them off long enough to give the others a chance.

Please let that be enough.

Chapter Nineteen

Deacon

This fight wasn't for the weak.

No fights were, really, but when I slammed my body against one of the guards, I was reminded that this was especially true tonight. The guards had taken off their gloves, meaning the Warden had finished playing games.

Instead of tranqs or other non-lethal options, the guards had moved to real bullets. Thankfully, Bowen had already proven his worth. It had only taken a moment for him to use his powers to put up a shield that stopped the guards from using their guns. They could still pass through it, but it stopped anything that moved too quickly — meaning bullets.

Not that it discouraged them. They'd simply moved over to blades, which I didn't mind a bit.

And I was far from the only one.

Kit moved through the battlefield like a lion, taking down anything that ventured too close. Of course, he wasn't the target of most of the guards.

They probably didn't want to risk being the idiot who drew his focus.

If they went up against one of the rest of us, they might just survive it. I didn't try to kill, though I would if I had to. It was the same with the others. Kit, however, was entirely lethal. Turning someone into ash wasn't the sort of thing a person came back from.

A pain in my arm made me let out a rough, low noise. A glance down showed blood, and to my side? A young-looking guard whose hands trembled around the knife clutched in his hand.

His eyes held all sorts of 'what the fuck did I just do?'

It was why I responded with a closed fist sucker punch to his jaw. It put him down — I doubted he'd get back up after that. He was too young to lose his life over a fight that wasn't even his.

I knew how it worked here — they recruited young guards with nowhere else to go, people who the military didn't want, people without options. They isolated them and indoctrinated them. Enough time at a place like this would twist them into the sadistic people they eventually became.

At least this guard still seemed to have some of his humanity left.

Still, more and more enemies poured into the yard. Not just normal guards, either. The black uniforms of the North Tower showed up, which made my heart speed.

What did that mean for Hera? Was she okay? She'd been drawing their focus to split their response, but what did it mean that they were here?

I forced my thoughts away from that. I couldn't do a damn thing about it anyway, so why split my focus? The Warden probably wanted to ensure this got put down, which was why she sent North Tower guards here.

That made it clear how hopelessly outnumbered we were. No one else had shown up, no Larkwood residents ready to fight beside us. Hell, during the escape, they'd been just as quick to turn on others of their kind instead of joining with them.

"This isn't looking good," Wade said through the radio, a slight tremor to his voice. He'd taken a spot near the wall, mostly hidden from view. It let him keep an eye on the situation while also handling any security measures that came up. He could slow down guards by locking doors or end alarms if notice got put where we didn't want it. It was for the best, since he wasn't all that useful against human enemies. Alongside him, he had Aaron and Moa. The last thing I wanted was for the humans to get caught up in this bloodbath.

"There's too many of them," Knox said, panting hard into the radio. It reminded me that while Knox was far from helpless, he wasn't made for full-scale drawn-out battles like this.

"Giving up already?" Bowen asked into the radio. "I wouldn't have come all this way if I'd realized you all surrendered so easily."

"No one is surrendering," I snapped back. "But it's suicide to pretend like things are different then they are. You can't deal with a situation if you don't even acknowledge it."

Someone charged me, a blade in his hand. When he got close enough, I quickly wrapped my hand around his throat, stopping his forward momentum. A flick of my arm tossed him to the side as if he weighed nothing.

A crash behind me made me turn to find another guard, a knife in his hand as well, on the ground.

I peered across the way toward a smirking Bowen, telling me he'd used one of his shields to stop the man.

I lifted my lip in a snarl back. If he expected a thank you, he'd be disappointed.

Still, Wade's words rang true. Across the field, we were starting to lag.

Well, most of us. Kit seemed even more powerful than he'd been at the start, as if each person he turned to dust strengthened him. Then again, he had used the term *consume* when talking about it.

I didn't care for the idea that he ate them like snacks, but if it helped us, I could look the other way.

Bowen helped to isolate the guards, to throw them back when too many converged at once. It let us not get overwhelmed despite how outnumbered we were. Still, a war of attrition never went well, and we had far fewer people. It was only a matter of time before we lost.

It had started to appear hopeless. I felt like we'd all been too cavalier before, too assured of our plan, too quick to assume we could handle it all.

Still, Soshi had the files, which meant even if we fell, it wasn't over, not yet. We might die, but our mission might still work.

Kit let out another of those dark sounds before he shot his clawed hand out at a guard, raking the sharp talons across the man's throat. Wouldn't it be funny if after all of this, Kit was the only one to survive?

Somehow, I couldn't imagine him falling. No matter what was thrown our way, nothing touched him.

Then again, in some ways, he was the opposite of Larkwood, like some dark twin. Larkwood had stood here for so long, and he'd been here for it all. He'd seen those who had suffered, outlived the guards and the shades and the wardens over the years.

Wouldn't it be oddly fitting if at the end of it, only him and this damned building stood?

My distraction cost me, and something slammed against my side. I went down, struggling with the other person. They were well trained and strong, and a burning in my side said they had a knife they didn't mind using.

Still, I threw them off me, giving me space.

The guard rolled, and I stilled as I recognized him. I recognized all the guards — other than the North Tower ones — but this one I'd spoken to quite often. I'd trained this one, in fact.

"You traitor!" he yelled at me, his fingers clutching the handle of the blade which had my blood on it.

"Being a traitor to something evil isn't such a bad thing," I threw back.

He laughed, the sound hollow and strained. It showed how much the fight had taken out of him already. "What did you think would happen? You'd show up here with your little shade friends and that would be the end of it? You know how hard we all work, how prepared we are, and you thought you could come in here with some rag-tag team and come out on top?"

As he spoke, his words hit me as almost embarrassingly true.

I'd known how many guards there were, how they trained for just this sort of thing, but in my arrogance, I thought we could overcome it. We'd succeeded time and time again, and I'd assumed we would again. The way we lagged said that wasn't true, screamed that they were gaining the upper hand.

"I'd rather die here with these people than live the rest of my life with you all," I spat.

"Well, at least that's something we can agree on. The Warden said we can use lethal force — seems she's done with these stupid games, with letting you all do whatever the hell you want. And when this is over? After we put down this little rebellion of yours? Oh, I have a feeling the other shades here are going to get a wakeup call about just how good they had it before."

His words brought the truth home.

As much as I'd framed this as our fight, it wasn't just ours. No matter how hard we worked, we couldn't do it on our own, and we wouldn't suffer the consequences alone.

Instead, I hit the button on my radio. "Wade, patch Kit into the PA system."

"What?" Wade's voice made it so I could almost see his sarcastic expression. "I love a good serenade as much as the next guy, but is this really the time?"

"Yeah, it really is. You said it yourself, this isn't going well. We need help."

Silence crackled back through the radio at first.

"We can't ask the other shades to jump into this," Knox said. "They'll just get killed along with us."

"It's their fight too," I countered. "If we lose, they pay the price, too. It should be their choice. If they want a future, they need to step up and help create it."

"Even if we ask, they won't come," Wade said finally. "In case you've forgotten, they mostly hate us. Calling them is only going to add more enemies to this fight."

"Well, I'm not sure it can go a lot worse than it is right now," I shouted as I dodged the guard, who it seemed wasn't willing to just wait for my conversation to end any longer.

"Why me?" Kit asked, his voice making me turn to realize he'd somehow ended up right behind me. I stared up into his black eyes, the moon illuminating the bone of his face. "People don't trust me. I am not the one to rally troops."

"You're the only one who can," I told him.

When the guard came at us again, Kit reached out and wrapped his clawed hand around the man's face, smothering the sounds of his screams as he turned to dust.

I ignored the rolling of my stomach as I went on. "You've been here from the start. If anyone knows what this place is, it's you. You're the only person who can talk to them."

He opened his hand, nothing left of the guard but the ash that caught on the breeze and spread out like some funeral service. He nodded after a moment.

"Okay, do it," I said into the radio.

A few moments later, Wade's voice came back through, but not just from the radio. Instead, it spilled out over the PA systems of Larkwood, echoing through the buildings and over the yards of all four levels. "You're up, Kit. Good luck."

I held the radio out as I hit the button, waiting for Kit to speak.

Whether we survived or not rested on Kit's ability to convince a bunch of selfish, frightened shades to risk their lives for a chance at something better.

Kit

I didn't understand.

Then again, how often had I done things when I didn't fully understand? I did what I thought was right even if I couldn't connect with or feel the underlying emotions that led to it. This was one of those times.

Deacon and Wade seemed sure I could help, that there was some magical set of words I could string together that would cause the shades of Larkwood to come to their senses and fight. That meant I'd give it a try, even if I doubted it was true.

Out of everyone here, I was the least trusted, the least connected to the others, yet somehow this task ended up in my lap.

The world seemed to drift away as I stared at the radio Deacon held out. The fighting silenced, as if we stood in our own little bubble, untouched by the rest of it.

What should I say? How should I explain to shades that what happened here *mattered*.

It wasn't the shades here that I thought about, though. Even if I needed to talk to them, another person came to mind, one who I couldn't even picture as I'd never seen her face.

Lilianna. My daughter. She was there, in the North Tower, and this fight was as much for her as any other. According to what I'd heard from Hera, the Warden had twisted Lilianna, had raised her to do Larkwood's bidding. Lilianna hadn't known anything else, hadn't gotten to find out a world existed outside of what the Warden had told her.

I took a deep breath, then spoke, trying to offer words that were true, no matter how they hurt me. "I am Kit Porter and I have been at Larkwood longer than anyone else, back since it first opened. Most of you know me, have interacted with me, and written me off as your enemy. I can't blame you for that—my behavior hasn't always been easy to understand, and I certainly have never explained myself before."

Someone rushed us, but Bowen placed a barrier that the guard reflected off. It let me focus on what I would say rather than the people around.

"I've watched so many shades come here, watched as they withered and eventually died in these walls. I've seen the strong and the weak and the brave and the cowardly and they all end up the same way."

As I spoke, the memories of so many faces filtered through, all those who had lived and died here, the ones so few would ever remember. "Those people, they're just names in a file now. No matter who they were, that's all that's left because Larkwood took everything else away. I know you're afraid. I know you're weighing the risks. I know that Larkwood seems overwhelming, that it feels like this dragon that can't possibly be brought down. That's not true, though. It's strong—there's no way to deny that—but it is only as strong as it is because it keeps us fighting amongst ourselves. Do you know how much time the Warden dedicates to sowing division? Setting us up to hate one another so we don't pay attention to what she does? Larkwood is a pit we are all in, but instead of working together to escape it, we just keep thinking we need to destroy one another to become boss of the pit. I've watched this cycle for as long as Larkwood has stood, and I've realized that that cycle is *exactly* why it still stands."

I thought about Hera, about Lilianna, about Jasmine who had been murdered just to tear apart any connection shades within Larkwood had.

"We are stronger together. If we want to make changes—real ones, not the empty promises that Larkwood force feeds us to keep us distracted—we need to work together and stop allowing fear to rule us. All of us—Hera, Brax, Knox, Wade, Deacon and myself—we were given the chance to leave. The Warden offered us our freedom if we simply went and stopped causing problems. We came back anyway. We decided that we couldn't leave you all still locked here, not even if it costs us our own lives. So we're here, fighting for you whether you want us to or not, whether you thank us or not, whether you helped us or attacked us. The only question is…what will you do? What future do you want? Who do you think the real enemy is?"

A nod from me had Deacon releasing his finger from the radio, the announcement system going silent.

It felt like a final push, like an impossible hope that we had to rely on because we had nothing else. If we failed, if they didn't accept what I had to say, if they stayed quiet and out of this fight, we would fail.

Eventually, we would tire and the guards would win.

I turned to look out at the fight, at the way even Brax had lost his energy, to the blood on him from his own body as well. Knox still moved quickly, his speed astounding, but while he didn't have many wounds on him, his movements had slowed. Deacon breathed hard, blood dripping down his arm and from a wound on his side.

We were losing. Eventually, we would be overwhelmed.

All was lost.

If I was destined to fall here, if this was the end, I had a few more things to say. I reached out and took the radio, managing to press the button despite the elongated fingers and claws.

"Lilianna," I said, my voice soft, drawing the gazes of everyone else outside. The fight seemed to slow as if they hadn't expected me to say anything else. Or perhaps it was the tone when I spoke that caused them to stop. "I'm sorry. I didn't know about you, but if I had, I would not have allowed you to suffer alone for so long. You must be brave and do not give up. No matter how dark things seem, you have to keep going. Your mother would be proud of you, and I am sorry that neither of us got the chance to see who you will become."

I took a deep breath, then spoke once more. I could feel Hera, knew she lived, though in a place like Larkwood, that didn't mean much. "Thank you, Hera. No matter how this ends, no matter what happens, you changed everything for me, and I will never regret our time together for a single moment."

I released the button and tossed the radio back to Deacon. If this was our last stand, if we were going to go down here, we would go down fighting.

Larkwood might get the last word, but we would make them bleed for it.

I turned toward the fight, my back to Larkwood, staring out at the guards, at the shades who had become family, and I pulled my shoulders back.

A sound from behind me made me frown, but I didn't get the chance to even look before bodies rushed past me. It took a moment to identify them.

Shades.

They were all from Level 1, people I had taught, who I had helped negotiate for, who I had worried for even if no one knew it. They didn't stop next to me, didn't hesitate for a moment before throwing themselves into the fray.

All I could do was stare. What I had said mattered, it had changed things, and now we had a chance...

I shook off the surprise and rushed forward, taking my own advice and refusing to give up.

Chapter Twenty

Hera

I yanked back, but nothing helped. The strong hands that held my arms wouldn't relent. I'd thrown everything I had into the fight, but as it turned out, facing off directly against the Corrander soldiers was a hopeless battle.

I still fought it, though. If I didn't, if I surrendered, these soldiers would head off to the fight, and I couldn't let that happen. I needed to keep them here, focused on me, for as long as possible to give Kit and the others the best chance.

And yet that didn't last that long. It hadn't taken much before their numbers and power overwhelmed me, before the first lucky hit to my cheek had knocked me down and allowed them to close the distance.

They shoved me to my knees, my shoulders aching from the way they held my arms.

What was worse was the emptiness in their eyes. I never thought hatred would make me feel better, but it did. If I was going to die, I sure as hell wanted the person killing me to feel something, to care.

To be murdered by an empty shell felt like a hollow death.

"My name is Kit Porter." Kit's voice made me jerk my gaze up toward a speaker in the corner of the room.

He spoke to the residents of Larkwood, to the shades themselves. It wasn't hard to hear it for the rallying cry it was, and it told me their fight wasn't going well.

If it were, they wouldn't need to appeal to others, to beg for backup.

I also doubted it would work. The shades of Larkwood had suffered so much, I doubted they trusted anyone enough to go head-to-head with the Warden and her guards.

Still, I couldn't blame him for trying. When someone had no good options, bad ones started to look promising.

After a pause, Kit spoke again, this time to Lilianna. His words made my eyes sting, and I could only hope she heard. No matter what happened, no matter if we failed, she still had a future, a chance. Him sending her a message at the very least eased me. She deserved to have at least that much from her father.

In the end, he thanked me as well. It sapped my energy, made me give up and hang against the strong hands. I wanted to respond, to thank him as well, to thank them all.

I wanted to tell them all how much they'd changed me, how much they mattered to me.

Wade had taught me that life goes on, that a person can keep moving, can even smile at the worst of times.

Brax taught me that even the toughest of people need others around, that isolating oneself isn't really protection. Knox taught me that a person has to accept themselves, that they can't live a life where they hate themselves. Deacon taught me that even people who don't fit in can make a life and a family for themselves. And Kit? He taught me that we all do things we wish we didn't have to, that we all face choices that seem impossible, and that all we can do is move forward and decide where we go from there.

I had gone from a spoiled rich girl who knew nothing of the world, who feared and hated everything different, to someone I was proud of. I wasn't perfect, but I tried now. I didn't let fear rule me and I was grateful for that.

Which meant I wasn't sorry for coming back. I didn't regret standing up against the Warden or risking my life or fighting. Even if we didn't win, we might have planted the seeds of change. If the files Soshi had got to where they were going, it could be the spark that took down Larkwood.

If that happened, if what we did today finished this all, then I'd accept my own death without complaint.

Though I did wish I could see *them* once more.

One of the soldiers crouched down in front of me, his eyes empty and flat. He lifted his hand, which had vicious claws tipping each finger. I didn't flinch away, staring right back at him. If this was the end, I wouldn't cower.

His hand swung forward, and I braced myself for the pain.

"Stop." The single word seemed to freeze time itself. The soldier's hand hung mid-air, as if unable to ignore the order.

Lilianna didn't fit in with the room at all. She wore another sundress that made her seem young and innocent, yet she walked between the frightening soldiers as if she had no worries.

Though, she probably didn't. Judging from the reaction of the one holding me, I'd bet she had nothing to fear from them.

"Let her go," Lilianna said.

Immediately, I collapsed to the floor, the hands that held me releasing me. It was then I realized just how much my head hurt, how difficult the fights so far had been. It was as if all the adrenaline inside me had seeped away, leaving me an empty mess.

Still, Lilianna knelt in front of me. She said nothing, waiting until I lifted my gaze to hers. When I did, she tilted her head. "I heard Kit. He doesn't sound as I expected him to, but that could have been the speakers. He mentioned my mother. Did you know her?"

I shook my head.

"I don't remember her. Kit does, though, and I can hear it in his voice that losing her hurt. It doesn't hurt me—I didn't know her—but I feel a strange heaviness at his pain. If my toys killed you, he would be sad. I don't want him to be sad, not over something I could have stopped."

I nodded, then forced myself to my feet. I gestured at the door, then pointed at the soldiers.

She shook her head. "No. I was listening when the Warden gave you the chance to become human again. I truly thought you'd accept it. Most shades want nothing more than to become human again, to regain their old life. You gave that up." She reached out and set her hands on my cheeks.

The world shifted, a familiar feeling now. I found myself in that old darkness, the same place I'd been before when I'd spoken to her.

"Please, help," I immediately begged. "If Kit asked for help, they need it."

Lilianna sighed and stared off into the darkness. "I can't."

"Why not?"

"Because I watched you pick your path. I watched you choose who you wanted to be, and it makes me question what I've done to my toys. I've taken that ability from them. I've lived my entire life here, with no choices, and yet I turned around and did that to others." She shook her head, pain drenching her words. "I will pull my toys from the fight, send them back to their cells. What happens will fall to you, to the others, because I cannot ask my toys to take any other lives. Kit said my mother would be proud of me, that he wished he could see who I would become. It makes me think for the first time who that might be, and I don't think I want to be a person who would force others to kill. I hope you succeed — I hope you all survive."

She paused, then stared straight at me. "Kit thanked you for changing him, but to me, change is rarely good. Change is different, and that difference doesn't always make a person better. You changed him, you changed Larkwood, and I suspect you've changed me. You must have, or I wouldn't care if my toys killed you. I never cared before."

"I didn't change you," I said softly. "You changed. You decided what you wanted to do, not me."

She smiled, though the look was strange on her face, as if she wasn't used to it. "Perhaps. Now, you need to go. I can hear the fight, feel the death, and I suspect that as the one who started this, you are the one who will have to end it."

With that, the world took form around me again. I blinked and found myself back in the North Tower alone. Lilianna had left, taking her toys with her, leaving me there.

Her words forced me to my feet. We were finishing this all right now.

I didn't have time to take the bridge over and make my way through the other tower to the bottom floor, to risk running into guards who would only slow me down. Instead, I took the elevator to the bottom floor.

Larkwood could sue me for the damage I was about to cause, but when life closed a door, sometimes a person had to put a hole in the fucking wall.

* * * *

Knox

Everything ached. Brax enjoyed pointing out that I wasn't a fighter, but never did that feel as true as right now.

Yet, no matter how exhaustion tugged at me, no matter how much I hurt, I couldn't stop. Too much rested on us. With the other shades who had come, we had a shot, but that didn't change that we had to fight with everything we had.

At the very least, my incubus got to stretch itself out, to show itself for the predator it was.

A blast shook the ground, nearly knocking me from my feet, and I turned to find a shade standing there, flames surrounding her. Farther down was another who had taken the form of a bear and charged into a group of soldiers. Bowen kept his barriers up to repel the bullets and level the playing field.

It made it so the guards had to approach us, had to get close, which gave us an advantage.

Not that the edge guaranteed anything. It didn't take much to change the course of a fight like this. One lucky hit could alter everything.

"Enough."

It was strange how that one word caused every person to go still. Then again, the Warden always had plenty of power and had never been shy to use it.

Sure enough, walking out from the main building, was the Warden. She held a radio, and when she spoke, it rang out over the same speakers Kit had used to address the shades of Larkwood. "This is over."

"This is far from over," Kit answered, seeming impossibly larger, as if her appearance had set him off. So much for his normally unflappable exterior.

"It is," the Warden assured him. "Your little rebellion has gone further than I thought possible. You should be proud of doing what no one else has managed, but it ends here."

A roar echoed through the night, and a glance at Brax, his teeth bared, said he didn't agree with her.

She only smiled as though not worried about him at all. "Do you really think I would leave Larkwood with so few defenses? That I wouldn't expect shades to try this someday and have already put things in place to prevent it?"

"Well, even if you did, it didn't work," I answered. "You might plan well, but you underestimate others too often. You never thought we would actually work together."

She shrugged. "You're right that I hadn't expected the camaraderie you all have shown. It's proven to me that Larkwood will need to work harder to ensure no such bonds occur after we clean up this mess. Still, you are wrong if you think I didn't set up a plan."

She lifted her hand like a signal, and a ringing rushed through the space. The sound was high-pitched, the sort a person wasn't sure they actually heard or not. She then nodded at a North Tower guard beside her.

The man lifted his weapon, aimed it at one of the shades, and pulled the trigger. I jerked backward when it worked, when the bullet left the gun and sailed across the short distance, slamming into the shade's shoulder.

However, the Warden had made her point.

Whatever she'd just done had taken away Bowen's powers and our advantage.

"What did you do?" Bowen's voice came out unexpectedly angry. Then again, having a person's powers stripped away tended to piss someone off.

She pulled her shoulders back and stared out at as though she'd already won. "If you think I haven't been working on how to counter every last skill of yours, you are arrogant fools. I've known the defensive skills of brownies, and while others felt they weren't a true risk, I knew better."

"You think a few bullets will stop us?" Kit asked.

"A few bullets? No. I'm quite sure we have more than enough to put you all down."

I didn't bother to hide the anger swirling inside me. I'd been helpless for so long, a prisoner to my own fears, to my own needs, to Larkwood and to the Warden. I was done with that. If she wanted to shoot me, she could go right ahead. I took a step forward before speaking. "So what? Even if you kill us all, you haven't won. Larkwood is over with."

"Is it?" The smile on her lips sent chills down my spine. She was so confident, so sure she'd won. She crooked her fingers, and my heart stopped when a guard dragged a small body forward. He tossed the struggling girl to the ground in front of the Warden.

Soshi. She scrambled up and rushed to Bowen, her face showing small cuts and darkening skin.

"You thought we wouldn't find one girl? You thought you could get these files out and start some big public outcry? You thought you could sway public opinion when that has been my weapon for years?" She shook her head as if embarrassed by our hubris. "You've failed on every front. Without the barriers to protect you, my men will mow you all down. All those files, those secrets you thought would save you? They will never see the light of day. Your precious savior, Hera, is dead. Killed by my soldiers in the North Tower. This is over."

Her words struck me like a physical blow. Hera was dead?

I wouldn't put it past the Warden to lie, but something in the way she spoke, the smile on her lips — she told the truth.

I'd known that was possible, had thought I'd prepared myself for it, but as it turned out, there was no good way to prepare for losing someone so important to me.

"Here is what will happen," the Warden said. "My men will open fire in thirty seconds. Any shade who chooses to lie down will be spared. Make no mistake, there will be consequences, but you will live. Those who want to die in some pointless stand can remain on your feet and see how well you fare against bullets."

The shades looked around, as if searching for an answer from one another.

Would they fight? Give up? Go back to the darkness and emptiness that Larkwood was?

Not me.

I stepped forward, staring down the Warden. I'd cowered for too much of my life, hid what I was, feared it. I was done with that.

Hera had taught me to accept myself fully, and I wouldn't spit on her memory by throwing her lessons away now.

I'd do her proud, even if she was gone.

"Go fuck yourself," I shouted.

Just as quickly, the others joined me. Kit, Deacon, Brax, Bowen, shades I barely knew, they all gathered beside me. Even Wade came out from his spot, taking his place beside us, Moa and Aaron doing the same.

This was what Hera had truly accomplished. She'd brought us together, taught us to stop hating each other and to work together, had made us see that a future worth having was out there if we just stopped being so damned afraid.

The Warden smirked. "This works for me. It is like domesticating animals. You remove the ones who are too troublesome so the whole of the species becomes more docile. Ending you will make Larkwood stronger."

She raised her hand and the new guards all lifted their weapons. I wouldn't give in, though. I stared them down, unwilling to let them have the pleasure of seeing me quiver.

Before she dropped her hand, before the hail of bullets came, a blast so loud that it made me fall against Deacon's side rocked the ground.

It silenced everyone as we turned toward where it had come from — the North Tower. Debris obscured the view, made it impossible to see anything. Slowly, a figure appeared in that dust. It was nothing more than a shadow as it walked out toward us with unhurried steps.

As the dust cleared, as I got my first look at the figure, I couldn't stop my grin.

Hera was always a sight for sore eyes.

Hera

They're all alive.

Seeing that gave me the courage to keep going, to move forward. It wasn't hard to figure out what was going on based on the scene before me.

The Warden had guards lined up beside her, guns trained on the shades. It was the sort of ultimatum I expected from a woman like the Warden.

And yet, despite her threats, despite her willingness to carry them out, the shades stood tall. They faced the Warden with every bit of courage I had come to expect from them. Not just those I knew, either. The others, those who had come to help, they stood in defiance as well.

It humbled me, reminded me of how strong they really were.

Even when things looked hopeless, they hadn't given in. They fought until the end no matter what that end would be.

Wade grinned my way, the first to recover from shock, and I smiled back at him. Still, no one else moved.

Which was probably for the best. The last thing we needed was for the Warden to decide to make a rash move.

"You really need to learn when to call it quits," the Warden said, her words barely containing the anger inside them.

I looked over at Soshi, who had taken a spot pressed against Bowen's side. The fear in her eyes was clear, and even if I wished I could tell her it would be okay, I couldn't.

"Larkwood won't last," Deacon said. "It will fall. May not happen today, but it *will* happen."

"No, it won't. I've kept this place running for thirty years. It will stand long after all of us are gone."

"You think that because you only know about violence to keep others under your thumb," Knox called out. "The thing is, if you corner someone long enough, they'll eventually bite."

"I'm not afraid of that. I will do whatever it takes. I don't care how many shades have to die for that."

"People will care," Wade said. "They aren't as bloodthirsty as you are."

"You're right—they would care. People are soft because they don't know what's really out there. They don't know what we're up against. If they did, they'd understand how important my work is. That's why I will ensure that none of them ever find out. They can live their happy, ignorant little lives and I will make the hard choices that need to be made."

"I don't know about that." Moa's voice made me turn to find her pointing at the gate to Level 3. It opened and a group of people pushed through. I didn't need to recognize them because the large cameras they held screamed reporters. Along with them?

Mom and Dad?

I hardly believed my eyes as I looked at them, as I saw the mass of people making their way through the gates and gathering on the edges of the open, bloodstained dirt.

Another glance at Moa showed a smile and nod toward my parents, which explained it. Moa must have contacted them ahead of time, must have asked them for their help. They certainly had the connections and power to gather people like this.

Why hadn't Moa told me?

Because she hadn't known if they'd actually come, and she didn't want to hurt me if they didn't.

The Warden narrowed her eyes. "You're making a very dangerous mistake here, Mr. and Mrs. Weston."

My father stepped forward, his booming voice carrying. "I made my mistake when I listened to you, when I believed the things you told me. I abandoned my own daughter because I was afraid, and I won't be a coward any longer."

"You know what we are up again," the Warden said to my mother as though she could convince her more easily. "Out of anyone here, you know what they're really like. You know the sacrifices that have to be made."

My mother shook her head. "I can't make these choices on my own, but I can say that people deserve the right to know the truth. This will go to the public, but this time, the citizens will vote with the truth, with knowing everything and making a real choice."

The Warden pressed her lips together, then spoke to the guards around her. "This changes nothing—kill the shades. We'll deal with the fallout later."

Except, no one pulled a trigger.

Then again, this had been the point. It was easy to do evil things in the darkness, to assure oneself that the actions were justified. It was different when others saw, when someone had to own up to it.

It seemed none of the guards were quite willing to kill a bunch of unarmed shades — including children — while on film.

It wasn't that they were good people who didn't want to kill people. Instead, I suspected they just knew that once they crossed that line, once they fired on unarmed people, they wouldn't be able to easily come back from that.

The Warden turned and shouted at her men, but none followed her orders. It was the first time she appeared so fragile, so alone. Without the might of Larkwood behind her, without the ability to hide what she'd done, she had no power.

She walked forward, toward me, and I followed suit to meet her at the center.

"You think you've won? I told you the truth, tried to make you understand *why* what I do is important, but even after that, you still don't get it. You still don't understand what's at risk." She sighed, looking every day of her age suddenly. "Well, you have changed things, I'll give you that. One way or another, Larkwood will never be the same after today." She reached into her pocket, and warning bells went off in my head.

Even still, I couldn't react fast enough. She pulled a small round device from her pocket. Her words before came back to me, when she'd said they'd made devices as small as palm-sized orbs. "Believe it or not, everything I've done has been to save us all. Someone has to be the villain, someone has to do the hard things people don't want to do, and I'm happy to make that sacrifice."

"*It's over,*" I mouthed to her.

She nodded. "It is for me, but this is all bigger than I am. So, if you're determined to show the public the truth, let's make sure they see what needs to be seen."

Her words hit me, coming together so quickly that I went to reach for her. It was too late, though. She used her thumb to press the button on the round device, and a cracking echoed around us.

I closed my hands on my ears, trying to shut out that noise, but it was gone as soon as it happened.

A shimmering tear had appeared right where the device had been, making it hard to see her through it. Still, this wasn't the tear I'd seen before in the video. Or, it might have been better to say it was similar, but whereas only shadows moved in the last one, something came through it this time.

I saw the beast of the Warden's nightmares, the thing like a starving, mange-covered bear as it slid through the shimmering space.

It didn't belong in our world, that much was obvious. It seemed at odds with everything around, and it locked its eyes on the Warden.

I recalled what she'd said about her mark, about the thing stalking her, and I had to admit…she was right. The thing didn't give a damn about anyone else, about anything beyond the Warden.

And she didn't run. She didn't try to escape it. She stared back at it, no tremor to her voice when she spoke. "Go on. You've wanted me for all these years, and it's finally your chance."

The beast's tail twitched, and it waited only a moment before it dove forward on her. It happened so fast I struggled to believe it, to follow. It took the Warden and headed back for the tear.

I rushed forward, wanting to stop this. I didn't care what the Warden had done—I wouldn't leave anyone to such a fate.

A hand wrapped around my arm, yanking me backward. I didn't understand why at first until something that resembled a tentacle swung toward me from the tear. I fell against a hard chest, pushed away to find Deacon there, having saved me.

Still, the delay was enough for the beast to leap back into the tear, taking the Warden with him, her pained screams like daggers.

Kit stepped forward and raised his hand. He grasped the tentacle, the thing releasing a sharp, panicked noise just before ash fell from Kit's hand. It was as if that had let the thing know to retreat, because it pulled the stub back and the tear closed, the silence falling around us as if it had never been there at all.

I wanted to collapse. My knees threatened to give out as the reality hit me.

We won.

After everything, when I was so sure we'd fail, we hadn't.

It made me turn to look around, at the men I loved, at the shades who had risked their lives to help, at my friends who had stood with me, at my parents who supported me in the end.

I'd thought Larkwood had stolen everything from me. I'd said before that they had taken my life, my voice, my future.

Standing there, however, I realized the truth for the first time. Larkwood had cleared everything away for me. It had taken what I had, but as it turned out, nothing I had was worth keeping.

Larkwood might have changed my life, but *I'd* decided what to do. I'd picked my own path, decided who I wanted to be, and that was something *no one* could take away from me.

I stared up at Larkwood, at the building that stretched up and into the night sky, at the monster that had haunted my dreams for the last year.

I knew my path, and I'd make damn sure this place was used for good.

Larkwood belonged to us all now, and we'd make it into the place it should have always been.

Epilogue

Knox

Hera flopped down on the sofa and let out a long sigh. I should have felt bad at just how tired she looked, since I'd had a part in it, but I just couldn't find it in myself to do so.

"Larkwood never changes, does it?" My voice made her snap her eyes open. "It's been three months since we took over and yet this place is still exhausting. Or maybe you just need to go to bed earlier."

She pressed her lips together at my smart-ass comment. *"And whose fault is it that I didn't get enough sleep?"*

I shrugged as if it hadn't been my naked body and eager hands that had made her lose all respect for the coming morning. It was hardly all my fault, not with how tempting she was. Besides, she'd decided to go on a business trip, which had taken her away from Larkwood for four days.

It turned out four days was *far* too long to go without seeing or touching her, and I'd made up for it last night.

I went over to the coffee maker and grabbed one of the cartridges, then popped it into the machine. "I have the next interview set up for Friday."

"With who?"

"A morning talk show. I prefer sticking with news programs, but Wade pointed out there are a lot of people who don't watch traditional news. I figured it would be a good way to reach some of them."

My own words made me stop. I really had changed over the past months, hadn't I? I sure hadn't expected to take over the public relations department of Larkwood, yet here I was.

"This is an uphill battle," I said after a moment as I added creamer and sugar to the coffee. I handed it over to Hera without a word as an apology for keeping her up so late.

She nodded in thanks and brought the cup to her lips. *Damn it, how can she tempt me even with that?*

"The footage from that night did a lot, but we can't expect people to change what they'd believed for centuries in a single night," I said to get back on topic so I didn't end up trying to strip her down again. Even my incubus had started to take notice.

Hera met my gaze and nodded to prompt me to keep going. With the coffee in her hands, she couldn't sign back.

"Don't get me wrong, it's working. Six months ago, these people would never even consider speaking to me, and now they're reaching out. I know it's for ratings, because we're the hot topic right now, but if just one person hears the interview and it makes them rethink their stance on shades, it's worth it."

Hera stared at me just before a smile crept across her lips. A glint there in her hazel eyes told me *exactly* what she was thinking.

And it once again made me wonder how a man could get this lucky. It was hard to think that it had been less than two years ago I'd felt hopeless, trapped, as if nothing in my world would ever change. I'd accepted that I had no real life, no future, no chance at anything more.

Then, somehow, Hera had come into my world and changed that all. She'd taught me that I wasn't the monster I'd thought I was, and she faced down my fears right along with me.

Which meant when she stared at me with those lustful eyes of hers, I couldn't just ignore it.

I lifted my eyebrow and curled my lips into a seductive grin. I dropped my voice to a low, intimate whisper. "Have you forgotten I can smell you, songbird? After not getting enough sleep last night, I would have thought you'd be sated today, but it seems not."

She tore her gaze away, her cheeks bright red.

She's too much fun to tease.

I took her cup and set it on the side table in the office, then slid my hand behind her neck to pull her closer. "If the coffee isn't doing enough to wake you up, I have another idea..."

"*That will just wear me out more...*" she argued, though I didn't get the feeling she was putting up too much of a fight.

"Then you can take a nap afterward. Think of it as my way of ensuring good sleep for you." I leaned in and brushed my lips against hers. The touch was a question, like it always was with us.

I never pushed her. After so many years of feeling pressured into things I didn't want, I always ensured to never put anyone else in that place. It meant even when I embarrassed her, even when I drew her in closer, even when I knew damn well what she wanted, I let her cross that last line.

And she always crossed it. Today, she slid her leg over my lap so she straddled me, then took my lips in a full kiss.

I groaned as my hands found their way to her waist, squeezing tight. We'd come so far together, overcame so many fears that had held us back. She'd allowed me to enjoy this connection in a way I didn't think I'd been capable of. She'd taught me to trust, that there were people who wanted me for who I was and not what I could give them.

"I love you," I whispered against her as I turned us, laying her flat on the couch. I broke the kiss so I could stare down at her. "You're everything to me."

She slid her arms around my shoulders and tugged me down, against her. She didn't need words to answer me, to wash away the fears that still lurked inside my head. Instead, she simply accepted me—*all of me.* My kind self, my fears, my incubus, everything.

She gave herself over to me.

Who needs sleep?

* * * *

Wade

I glanced at the clock on the wall and snorted softly. Hera was late.

Again.

She'd taken to her new position as Director at the newly reformed and upgraded Larkwood Academy. She'd resisted the new job, of course, but after all she'd done, all she'd risked, no one else could do a better job.

Well, maybe someone who understands how to read a schedule.

"Don't worry," I assured Soshi when she frowned. "She'll be here."

Soshi nodded, glancing toward the other three kids seated at the table. In the past, the Warden had never given a damn about meeting people new to Larkwood. That was yet another example of the changes Hera had made.

The door opened and Hera rushed in, looking frantic and disheveled.

And what was it about that that made me all the more smitten with her? Sure, I liked when she was cool and collected. I couldn't deny my less than pure feelings when she'd faced off against the Warden after blasting a hole in the side of a building like a total badass, but *this* woman was just as tempting.

Hell, I think I loved every last side of her and that was the real problem.

Her cheeks were red as she turned to look at me, and boy did that tell me a bit.

Such as the way her clothing was askew, that the flush on her skin covered her chest, and her breathing was hard.

I'd seen Hera in that condition enough to easily tell what exactly had made her late, and I couldn't stop the way it made me want to toy with her. Not to mention that she still smelled like Knox, with his pheromones hanging off her.

"Hey, Hera," Soshi said with her normal bright smile.

One of the other kids elbowed her, then whispered, "You can't call her Hera. That's the *Director*. Call her Ms. Weston."

"Soshi here gets special privileges, and you're late, *Ms. Weston*." My tone with that name made it perfectly clear I was mocking her. I dragged my gaze over her slowly and lowered my voice as I moved past her, whispering into her ear so only she would pick it up, "You missed a button. Also, tell Knox to not leave hickeys where they show. They give me ideas that aren't appropriate in front of kids."

She turned her back to the kids and looked down to find that I'd been one-hundred-percent right. She fixed the buttons quickly, her lips moving as she probably cursed both Knox and me.

I turned away from Hera, to find Soshi with her back straight. She took her position looking over the kids of Larkwood seriously. In fact, she certainly reminded me of Bowen. Not many dared to bother those under either of their protection.

"I gave them a tour of the school," Soshi said.

"Good job." I took a seat at the large table.

"Welcome to Larkwood," Hera wrote and held it out for them to see.

The words chilled me like they always did for a moment. I'd heard them when I'd arrived—we all had—but they had been a threat back then. They'd been terrifying. They'd warned me that I had no future.

Now, however, we'd changed that. Shades came here because they wanted to. Sometimes they had no other place to go because they were kicked out, some needed help to control themselves, some simply wanted to be with others like themselves where they didn't feel the need to hide anything.

Whatever the reasons, though, it was always voluntary, and they stayed only as long as they wanted to.

I nodded toward the newest children and introduced them one at a time. "This is Harriet Carrol, Mya Linchon and Jacob Rodgers. Today is their first day, so we're doing all the introductions."

"I showed them to their rooms and how to use the key cards," Soshi said. "I introduced them to their staff advisor."

"Who did they get?" Hera asked.

"Harriet has Layla, Mya has Brax, and Jacob got..." Soshi went quiet for a moment, as if she didn't want to say the next part. After a moment, she finished, her voice softer. "Kit."

I tried to smother my laughter as I asked, "Did you stay outside the room when you introduced them?"

Soshi shook her head. "No. It's my job to make sure they know where to go, so I went in."

"What did you think of him?" Hera asked Jacob, holding the writing pad out so he could read it.

He shifted slightly in the chair, but when he spoke, his voice was honest. "He's scary, but he seems nice."

Soshi's gaze darted away as if she wanted to argue that but knew better. Then again, Soshi had been there during the big fight. She'd had a front-row seat to exactly how dangerous Kit could be. That sort of thing stuck with a person, especially if they didn't otherwise know that person.

"He isn't nice," I said, to which Hera kicked me under the table in the shin *hard*. I grunted but otherwise didn't let on what she'd done before going on. "But you couldn't ask for a better advisor. He's been helping shades here as long as this place has been around. He's not much fun, and he never gets pop culture jokes, but you won't find a person who will work harder to help you than he will."

Hera went still, a line between her eyebrows appearing as if the words surprised her. Then again, none of us had had the best start, and if someone had told me two years ago that I'd end up in a relationship with not only a woman but *those* four men? I'd have asked for some of whatever drugs the person was on.

Yet, we'd ended up there, and I could admit the truth that Kit—along with the others—were good people I was grateful to be able to rely on.

Then, in true me fashion, I ruined all the goodwill I'd earned by opening my mouth. "Plus, if you make him *really* mad, there is this vein on his temple that throbs. It looks like the Mississippi River."

Jacob stared, eyes wide, before breaking into a laugh.

Because I was ridiculous, but I also knew how to put others at ease.

"So now you're on a tour of the classrooms, right?" I asked.

"That's right."

"Well, Harriet, Mya, Jacob, if you need anything, you can go to your advisor or right to me. In fact, you can even talk to *Mrs. Weston* here anytime you want to."

The kids nodded, then rose and followed Soshi out of the room.

"Her help has been indispensable," I said, my gaze on the door they'd closed behind them. "I'm surprised Bowen is allowing her to stay here, but I'm not about to rock the boat. I don't think I could have handled all the intake without her."

Hera turned toward me. *"You would have done fine."*

"Maybe," I said, unconvinced. "But I'm still grateful. I think having someone around their age helps the process."

I remembered how alone I'd felt when I'd first arrived at Larkwood, and all the old people in the world could have told me it would be fine — I wasn't about to believe it unless I heard it from someone like me. That was why I was so passionate about my position as intake manager. I handled all new residents, but I always had a special interest in creating the programs for younger shades, after all I'd gone through.

My gaze moved to Hera's collarbone despite the mark being hidden beneath her shirt. "I can't believe you were late to a meeting because of a little afternoon delight. You do realize that is highly unprofessional, right?" Even as I scolded me, my voice held no censure.

"Technically, I was late because I was taking a nap."

"Yeah, well, Knox sure can wear a person out, can't he?" I chuckled, then removed the gloves I still wore most of the time. I'd learned to control my powers, at least with those I trusted, but it still took effort on my part. When out in public or around anyone except Hera, Knox, Brax, Deacon and Kit, I still chose to wear them. If nothing else, they made me more comfortable.

I reached out and set my bare skin against hers, the touch gentle, indulging in what I'd been denied for so long.

"The new resident who will be here in a few days is only four," I said to try to distract us both.

"Four?"

I nodded. "It's a boy. I'm not even sure what he is, honestly. The results are all inconclusive. We should have Kit look at him when he gets here."

"You think he's an elder?"

"It's all I can figure. We've seen more of them lately."

"Or maybe Larkwood used to hide them more?"

I shrugged, the idea unpleasant. I was sick of Larkwood's secrets. "That's possible. This place still has more than its fair share of secrets, after all."

She tapped my hand with her finger, drawing my attention back to her as she lifted her eyebrow, a sure sign to keep going.

I let out a soft laugh. "I should know better than to hide anything from you, huh? The new shade, named Orion, we're handling transfer paperwork from a group home."

"Group home?"

"Seems his parents sent him there when he changed. Because he isn't fitting nicely into any categories, no one realized he was a shade. They just knew he wasn't behaving the right way, so they got rid of him."

The story pricked at my own scars. It was too common a story, having families who opted out the moment they realized their precious kid wasn't the perfect being they'd wanted them to be. Those sorts of scars lasted for a person.

I shook his head to clear away my own negativity. "So he's technically a ward of the state. I don't like taking in cases like that, because it feels too much like forcing them to be here, too much like the old Larkwood, but I think we're the only ones who can help him."

Hera's expression softened as she reached out and caught my hand, squeezing tightly. Her support meant the world to me, a reminder that I wasn't alone, that I wasn't isolated from everything else. She understood me—my good parts and my not so great parts—and she still wanted me.

I'd never felt this, not even as a kid. It had taken walking through hell to realize not only my own worth but to accept that there were people in the world who would love me unconditionally.

When I glanced back at Hera to find a familiar, hungry look on her face, I smirked. "Is Knox losing his touch? Because I'd figure you'd be finished after him."

She was obvious as she tried to hide her embarrassment at my words—I loved getting a rise out of people *way* too much, which meant Hera was forever trying to not give in. Of course, I lost my upper hand the moment she grabbed the front of my shirt and pulled me toward her.

And I went willingly.

It was the way of the world. If Hera called, I came. If she wanted, I gave. The amount of power I had, the things I could do, they didn't matter a bit when it came to that woman.

She set her free hand on my cheek, and I flinched for a moment as I often did when touched. I'd gotten better about touch but a part of me couldn't shake all of those old wounds, those old fears. As soon as it happened, though, I turned his head and pressed a kiss to her palm as if in apology.

"Well," I whispered to her, "if you're not done, it's not like I can really deny you…" I sank to my knees as I spoke and pulled off my other glove as well, then ran my hands up her bare legs, teasing her at the hem of her skirt. I didn't look away at all, pinning her with my gaze as I moved one hand up the inside of her thigh until I stroked over her cunt through her panties.

Still, I kept the touch soft, reverent. "When I first saw you, I never would have thought we'd end up here." I pressed a kiss to her knee, ignoring the way she squirmed when the touch was enough to excite her but not nearly enough for what she wanted. "I was terrified of the world, of myself, of letting anything near me. You gave me a place where I didn't have to feel that, and I'll never be able to thank you enough for it."

I teased over the line of her panties but didn't dip beneath them, didn't give her all she wanted.

"You make me feel like I'm not that bad. No matter what else happens, no matter who else throws me away, when you look at me like this, when you touch me, you make me think I wasn't a mistake."

Telling her these things wasn't easy. I didn't much like baring my soul or revealing my weakness, but she deserved that and more. After everything she'd done for me, after how much she'd helped me grow, she should know how important she was to me.

Of course, I couldn't stand being serious for long, so I curled my lips into a smirk, ready to throw some sarcasm onto the conversation to keep it light.

She must have read my expression for exactly what it was, because she seemed only too happy to take the upper hand again. She slid her fingers into my messy hair, using it to pull me forward. Instead of toward her lips, though, she guided me to the hem of her skirt.

God, I love this girl.

I darted my gaze from what was clearly her goal to her eyes, unable to help my reaction to her. I fell for her more each time she took control like this, when I could shut off my brain and just fell. She lifted her eyebrow like a challenge, and I smirked before sliding her skirt up to fully expose her.

Her schedule was already behind for the day...

Might as well make her a little more late.

* * * *

Brax

I can't believe I'm waiting for a woman.

I was a berserker, I put fear into almost any person I met, and yet here I was, sitting in my office because Hera was over an hour late.

I'd hate the woman if I didn't love her so damned much.

I sighed and fought the urge to tap my foot on the ground. I had plenty of work to do, and I could have canceled with Hera, but the ability to see her was *far* too tempting. After missing her over the past few days, I wasn't about to lose out on my chance to see her now.

When she finally arrived, rushing into my office as if we were still in the old Larkwood and she might get in trouble for being late, I made my opinion *perfectly* clear with my glare.

She peered around the empty office and frowned. *"I thought we had a meeting with someone."*

"We did. An hour ago." I crossed my arms and said nothing else.

"Sorry," she signed back. She didn't go on, didn't try to explain it away or make excuses for her behavior.

Then again, Hera wasn't the type to make excuses. She owned up to what she did, took responsibility for it.

And I was pretty damned sure Wade had a part in her lateness, given she'd had a meeting with him before and she had the glow of a woman who had been enjoying a few orgasms.

I snorted but didn't call her out on it. Instead, I kept on topic about why she'd come to my office. "I dealt with the meeting. It was a representative from Jasmine Academy out of Texas."

"What did they want?"

"I think they're hoping to get our approval."

She frowned. *"I thought they'd be trying to threaten us."*

"Public opinion is changing. The laws are next to change. They want to get us on their side so when that all happens, they've got alliances. They want to not get in trouble when everything comes to light and maybe even keep their jobs."

Just talking about it made me rub my temples to ease the headache that worsened with each word. I'd taken over a position whose name I'd already forgotten. I handled missions that occurred outside of Larkwood, running and training a group of shades who could handle about anything the world threw at them.

It meant I handled it when we found an illegal shade holding area, when we got word about shades who needed help. While humans weren't allowed to hold shades normally, there were far too many private 'collectors' who enjoyed showing off rare types in what amounted to a zoo. So far, we'd avoided hitting academies to keep us off the bad side of the law, but I had no doubt that was where we'd get to eventually.

I had no doubt that in time, we'd have to face the other academies, because people in power never gave it up without a fight.

Working in a group, leading a team, they were skills I'd never had before. I'd always looked out for myself and Knox and cared little beyond that, but I couldn't deny a strange sense of fulfillment when I worked with others. I liked them relying on me and I liked feeling as if they had my back.

"*I hate politics,*" Hera signed.

"Me too," I admitted. "That guy even setting up an appointment with *me* instead of Knox says he was hoping for something underhanded. Otherwise he'd have stuck with the PR department."

"*So why did he come to you?*"

I leaned back in my chair, rolling my shoulder to ease an ache there. I'd gotten back the day before from one such mission, and I'd spent a little time in Medical afterward.

I let out a soft laugh at the worry in her expression. "You can't hide anything, you know that? I'm fine."

"*I heard you had to get treated.*"

"I just got my arm twisted bad—nothing to worry about. I'll be healed up by tomorrow."

She pressed my lips together, as if she didn't care for the answer. She always worried too much, always felt I was too cavalier about my own safety. While she rarely tried to lecture me much, she was too honest to hide her feelings from her face.

And a pathetic part of me really liked that worry.

I let out a soft sigh. "You really are worried, aren't you?" He held out his hand. "Come here."

She crossed around to my side of the desk, and I pulled her into my lap with a quick grab of her wrist. I held her tight, letting her hear the steady beat of my heart to reassure her.

"You're about the only person in the world that worries about me," I said, my arm wrapped around her, my hand on her hip. "Everyone else is, at best, indifferent and more often terrified of me. You though? You not only don't fear me, you actually worry about me."

I caught her chin and pulled her in, taking her lips in an aggressive kiss. Then again, I wasn't ever gentle. If she wanted softness and romance, she needed to get that from someone else. From that first night when I'd crawled into her bed and we'd had what could only be described as desperate hate sex, I'd always touched her with a passion I couldn't hope to hide.

I wasn't rough because I didn't care about her, but because I did, because I couldn't help it, because I needed her so much I couldn't control myself around her.

And for the first time, I trusted someone enough to accept me entirely, even the difficult parts, even the violence that was so much a part of me, a part others had always rejected.

And she gave in to me as she always did, somehow using her sweetness to stand against my darker urges.

When I went to pull her even closer, I winced. I tried to hide it, but Hera was *far* too observant.

She pulled back and zeroed her gaze in on my side.

"It's nothing," I assured her.

She leaned away to grasp the hem of my shirt and pull it up, finding the large bruise across my side that I'd tried to hide from her. When she met my gaze again, she lifted my eyebrow to ask me, *'You call that nothing?'*

"I'll heal by tomorrow. It's just a bruise."

The look on her face melted me. It was so damned earnest. Despite the power she wielded—both due to her powers and because of her position at Larkwood—she never let it go to her head. It hadn't twisted her, made her cruel and uncaring as it so often did to people.

Instead, she had this expression of guilt, as if each scratch and mark on me were a failure she had to claim and carry with her. She wanted so badly to protect those around her, even when we weren't people who needed much protection.

Just how was I supposed to deal with that? She crawled under my skin, an attack I couldn't even hope to resist or stand against.

I let out a soft laugh at just how whipped I really was. "You look tired. Maybe we should just relax for a bit, hmm?"

She gave me a look that said she thought I was an idiot. I didn't even need her to move her hands for me to guess what her thoughts were. *You're the one with a bruise the size of Texas and you say I need a rest?*

Even still, I wrapped my arms around her and pulled her against my chest, reveling in the way she fit there perfectly. She was warm and soft and sweet—all things I'd been denied most of my life. The movement aggravated my shoulder and my side, but fuck it, I didn't care. She soothed and healed me more than any amount of rest ever could.

"You work too hard," I whispered. "I know you've got a lot to do, but you need to take care of yourself, too."

She pressed her finger against my side—not hard enough to really hurt but enough to remind me of the injury and make her point. *Back at you.*

I snorted softly and tightened my arms around her. "Fair point. Of course, I'm still pretty damned careful.

I didn't used to be because what was the point? What the fuck did it matter if something happened to me? Now, though? I've got something worth coming back to, so I'm very cautious."

I wasn't the type of man to give declarations of love, so she'd better enjoy this rare moment of honesty from me. My life before her hadn't meant much of anything beyond trying to keep Knox and I alive. Looking back, I wondered if I wasn't reckless on purpose, as if I were just looking for a way out of it all.

That was over with, though. This last mission had sent me to the home of a well-known drug lord who had taken to keeping shades as pets. Before Hera, I'd have attacked that place alone and reveled in each bullet I'd taken. Now, though? I'd planned our attack carefully, avoiding every injury I could, desperate to make it back to Hera.

I hadn't wanted to see the worry or guilt on her face if I got seriously hurt.

She wrapped her arms around me, as if to ask me to never let her go, to assure me that she wasn't going anywhere.

"Let's take a little break," I said, shifting to get more comfortable. I wouldn't have figured having an adult in my lap would ever be comfortable, yet here we were.

All it took was her warmth and scent and my eyes already felt heavier.

Our relationship had started out rocky, to say the least. We'd hated each other until that hate had morphed into something just as passionate but less hostile. Everything we did, we did to extremes, which was why I cherished times like this so much.

I'd never had another person I could just let my guard down with, someone I could just be with like this. It was a debt I knew I could never pay off but I'd spend my life trying to.

I held her tightly as she closed her eyes, as her breathing evened out and she drifted off. I pressed another kiss to her head, then whispered the truest words I'd ever spoken. "I love you, songbird."

* * * *

Deacon

"*I'm sorry,*" Hera signed as she jogged up to me, even though with how far away she was, it mostly looked like frantic waving.

When she reached me, I actually tapped my foot. "Do you have any idea how late you are?"

"*Pretty late,*" she signed back.

Hera could get out of trouble with that smile of hers with almost anyone. Wade and Knox sure as fuck spoiled her, giving in the moment she batted her eyelashes. Brax wasn't as obviously whipped, but he gave in pretty fast, too. Kit didn't give in so much as seemed old enough he didn't get riled up about the stuff she did.

I wasn't as easy for her to distract, though. In fact, a part of me enjoyed our push and pull.

"Yes, you are," I said, my arms crossed. "You need an assistant."

"*I don't need an assistant,*" she argued, the same talk we'd had a few times.

"Of course you do. Every Warden has had one—"

"*I'm not a warden,*" she signed, interrupting me with the intensity that said she didn't like the term.

Which I understood. It held a lot of bad feelings, which was why she'd changed her title here, to try to show she didn't plan to run Larkwood as it had been run before.

"I know that, but your job remains similar. You're running yourself ragged trying to do everything on your own and it's dumb. Why don't you make Wade be your assistant? He like taking your orders."

"He's busy with intakes. Besides, I can handle this."

"No, you can't. No one could. You aren't sleeping enough, you're constantly late for meetings and you're working through every weekend. It can't keep going on like this. I'll look over the records we have and suggest a few qualified shades who would serve as good assistants."

Her expression said she wanted to continue to fight with me. Hera tended to take on too much, to not ask for help even when she really needed it. I'd watched her run herself down trying to deal with every last problem here all on her own, doing far more than the previous Warden had done. I'd found that sometimes, she needed a firm hand for her own good. Thankfully, she eventually gave in to me.

She moved her hands in a grudging acceptance. *"Thanks."*

I nodded, then moved onto the reason for our meeting. "Now, the issue at hand. The North Tower."

She turned to look up at it, anxiety appearing in her features. Everyone probably felt the same way about it, like it was this looming dragon that watched over the rest of us, waiting for a chance to swoop in and fuck us all over again. No matter how long it was since it had caused us pain, we couldn't shake the fear that it could still swipe out at any time.

"I've gotten a lot of requests for people to get access."

"I'm going to strongly suggest against that," I said.

As the new head of security for all of Larkwood, what we did with the North Tower fell right into my area. While we didn't have the issues we had before, since we didn't treat the shades here as prisoners needing guarding, we still needed people who kept the peace.

Fights happened between shades and people up to no good sometimes tried to gain access to Larkwood. I was in charge of keeping Larkwood safe, of ensure the people who chose to come here didn't have to worry.

"It's going to take a long time to go through this place," I said as I gestured at the tower. "The Warden kept the records for the North Tower out of the main servers, so we still have no idea about all the projects. Even the files for the old projects could be extremely dangerous if they fell into the wrong hands. We can't give people access until we know what's there. I wish we could just burn it all down," I muttered.

Hera hesitated as if she knew she should tread carefully. *"We can't do that. While most of what they did there was horrible, there could still be projects that help shades."*

I sighed. "I know we can't, but I really wish we could. I think I'd sleep better knowing this place was just ashes."

Hera moved close enough to lean against my side. *"We'll figure out a way to safely document it all, then we can make sure it can't ever hurt anyone again."*

I nodded and took her hand in mine, needing to feel the warmth of her skin. It wasn't nearly enough, though. The thoughts of the nights alone while she'd been gone hit me, made me realize it had been far too long since I'd gotten to touch her.

Still, I kept my mind on the task and pulled her in through the door we'd placed where Hera had blasted through the wall. Having outside access on the ground floor made sense.

I held her hand tightly, not sure if I was reassuring her or myself—probably a bit of both. The North Tower had been hell for us both.

"Lilianna has full access to the elevator, the floor she lives on and both the top and bottom floors. I had Wade lock access to all other areas of the tower," I explained.

"Did that annoy her?" She had to take her hand from mine to sign and I immediately missed the touch.

"I don't think she cares. Course, I'd bet if she wanted access, she could get it. She's still got a few of her *'toys'* there." I didn't bother to hide my feelings about her or her powers. "She's going to be a problem."

"She's Kit's daughter." Hera shrugged as if that explained everything. It sort of did. As Kit's daughter, it wasn't as if we could just throw her out. *"Besides, she's a wendigo. There isn't a lot to be done about one."*

"I don't like it," I muttered. "Kit is one thing—he's earned my trust. She's twisted, though."

"She was raised here—she's never known anything else."

"So was I." I didn't like to think about my time there, about growing up in that hell, but that didn't change it had formed me too. I might have been twisted, but not in the same way. Lilianna didn't seem to give a damn about anything or anyone else. She spent almost all her time locked up in the North Tower with her toys. No wonder people didn't trust her.

Still, Hera's frown reminded me that she was right, too. Lilianna might be a problem, but it wasn't one we could find a solution to right now.

"We'll leave it alone for now," I said.

She turned toward me, her eyebrows furrowed. I normally liked to circle around topics until we figured something out, beating at it until the answer became clear.

I gestured toward her face. "I don't like arguing with you when you're this tired. If we're going to fight, it's no fun if you're not at your best. Besides, I didn't meet you here to talk about Lilianna."

"What are we here for?"

I opened my mouth then snapped it shut. After a moment, when she just stared at me, I sighed. "You were gone for a week, Hera."

"Yes, I know."

I didn't go on for a moment, annoyed that she didn't get it.

Her eyes widened. *"Did you set up a meeting just so you got to see me?"*

"You've been running yourself down lately, and I'm busy, too. We've got plans tonight, so I didn't think I'd get any time alone with you if I didn't do something drastic."

I wouldn't have been surprised to have her angry that I'd wasted her time, that I'd scheduled a meeting just because I missed her. She was busy enough already, and maybe it was selfish to force another thing on her to-do list for today. Instead, however, Hera gave me a smile that completely melted me.

Which was strange. I'd grown up at Larkwood, raised—if you could even call it that—by scientists and guards in the North Tower. The only way I'd survived had been to harden myself, to remove every last bit of softness from me. That was the shit that got a person killed here.

Then I'd met Hera, then she'd somehow worked her way beneath the defenses I'd built around myself. It had annoyed me at first, especially as I stopped being able to ignore her, but that hadn't changed the course.

In fact, I couldn't picture me acting this way — especially with the slight warmth of my cheeks that made me think I was blushing — before I'd met her. She'd given me a place to be this person.

Hera slid her arms around me and pressed her forehead to my chest. I gave in to the touch, wrapping my arms around her and pulling her tighter against me.

My little trip down memory lane took me back to meeting her, to seeing her that night when she'd changed and nearly died. Maybe it was missing her that had me speaking softly. "You asked me before why I saved you, and I didn't have an answer. Fuck, I don't know if I have one now, not a good one, but I can at least say I did it because I couldn't not do it. The moment I heard your siren's scream, the moment I laid eyes on you, something pulled me closer. I couldn't walk away, couldn't imagine seeing the light go out in your eyes. You changed everything for me that night."

She pulled back enough to look up at me, letting me see her hazel eyes. I ran my fingers through her hair, then cupped the back of her neck. The fact she let me touch her with my hands, even knowing how much damage they had done, always astounded me.

She went up to her tiptoes, leaning against me, and claimed my lips in a soft kiss. I groaned, then returned the kiss, tightening my arms around her to pull her closer, to trap her against me.

Hera had changed the course of my life in so many ways. I'd felt trapped, not by Larkwood but by what I was, unable to leave but unwelcome to stay, either. Hera had opened my eyes, had shown me that I could change that and have something more, something better.

And despite all the odds, the risks, the fallbacks we'd suffered, Hera had given me the strength to keep going. She'd stood beside me, which had let me push through all of that to end up here.

So I kissed her back, as if I could explain to her with this touch just how much she meant to me. I couldn't talk sweetly to her like Wade or Knox, but she and I spoke a language all our own.

The North Tower had tortured us both, but we'd stood together and outlasted it. It seemed fitting to be here now, standing here free, without the chains of this place on either of us.

All that pain we'd survived and endured had led us here. I wouldn't change a single minute of that, because the taste of the woman I loved made it clear that it was far beyond worth it.

* * * *

Kit

Smelling food was always a strange thing to me. I had no appetite—at least for regular food—which meant the scent didn't spur some desire to eat. In fact, in the past few months, I'd gained an appreciation and knowledge from cooking.

Perhaps it was a strange hobby from someone who couldn't truly enjoy the things he created. Still, watching Hera eat the thing I made fulfilled some strange part of me.

Which was why I'd come to her place early to start food for this evening, especially since I knew she'd be running late. I had access to her schedule, and I'd noted that each meeting she had came later and later, as if it had started out bad and snowballed out of control.

I smiled as I checked the oven, grateful to have a full kitchen. The new quarters that Hera had taken had many advantages over her old ones. She now stayed in the main tower rather than the residential one, having moved into the Warden's old place. She'd resisted it at first, but in the end, the need for more space and security had won her over.

Living in the main tower put her closer to her work as well, so she didn't have to run back and forth constantly. Besides, this place had multiple rooms, which was useful. Despite having our own apartments still, we'd all sort of taken a room in her place as our own and spent most nights here.

The door opened and I turned to find Hera rushing in, her hands flying in what was no doubt an apology.

When she looked over at me, out of breath, I couldn't help the way my heart seemed to beat faster. How was it possible to feel such fondness toward another person?

"You are nearly two hours late," I said, throwing out the information like a challenge.

"*Sorry,*" she signed again. "*The day got away from me.*"

I sighed at her apology. Despite our time together, she still often took my words as colder than I intended them to be, thinking I was angry when I wasn't. "It's fine. I started dinner for you so we wouldn't be behind schedule."

She caught my hand and squeezed softly as a thank you. It told me what I'd already known—she was nervous about tonight and would have been upset for it to have been thrown off by her lateness.

I never smiled much, and even now I was certain my lips didn't curl up. Still, a softening of my expression at her gratitude wasn't something anyone else got to see. Hera had a glimpse to a part of myself that I didn't hide from others on purpose, it was simply a part no one else could draw out. I didn't feel safe enough with anyone else for this softer part of me to come to light, for me to experience this.

And it was a sensation I didn't know if I'd ever grow used to.

"You don't eat. Can we trust you to cook?" she asked, her grin saying she enjoyed teasing me.

And really, who else would dare tease a wendigo of my age? *Adorable.*

"I don't need to eat to know how food is prepared. I also had extra chairs brought and put leaves into the table to make room."

She glanced at the large table as she worried her bottom lip. *"I've never had so many people here before,"* she admitted.

"Larkwood isn't the sort of place where many have family dinners."

She stood back up and faced me, the light in her eyes saying she'd been thinking. *"We should do a family night."* At my lifted eyebrow, she went on. *"A lot of shades here haven't seen their family in a long time, but not all of them have bad relationships. Maybe we should do a real get-together, like an open house."*

"Do you think anyone would attend? I recall visitation days here, when shades who had no one to speak to trudged through the day. I wonder if such an event would not cause more heartache than good." I recalled Hera when her family had stopped contacting her, the way visitation day had worn on her week after week.

I didn't want to see other shades suffer that same disappointment.

"What about a big event that we all attend? Humans and shades could come, and it could serve as both a way for shades to see family but also as a way for people to see what Larkwood is now. If shades don't have family willing to come, they'll still get that same feeling of belonging from everyone who does come."

I tapped my finger against the counter, blinking slowly as if working through the idea. Finally, I shrugged. "That could be a good idea. We should consider trying it in the next few months. If it goes well, we can implement them regularly."

Again, I found myself impressed by Hera. She was young—especially when compared to me—but she was smart and capable. She'd faced down so much and never lost herself in it all. She'd been the right choice to take this place over, to direct Larkwood and change it into what it should have been.

She saw the world differently than I did, and when she came up with ideas like this one, it reminded me of it. Only Hera would consider hosting large family gatherings to make the shades here feel they were not alone. No matter how much time passed, I suspected she would never stop astounding me.

Something about my expression seemed to affect her, because she turned away as if to hide her face.

Which immediately set off that possessive wendigo side of me, the one who cherished my bond with her, who wanted her to hide nothing from me.

I walked up behind her, pressing in tight, trapping her between me and the counter. I brushed my lips against her ear. "Haven't I told you before not to run from me? My control only lasts so far, and as it turns out, you fray it considerably."

I recalled when she'd run from me in the forest, when I had entirely lost myself, when I had taken her for the first time. I could still feel the softness of her skin, the way she had pressed into the dirt from our combined weight, the way she'd given herself to me entirely.

She shuddered as I teased her ear, but didn't fight at all. Instead, she tilted her head as if in surrender, exposing her neck to me.

I hesitated, then pressed my lips to the skin above her racing pulse. "You trust me even when it isn't smart to do so. Even when everything inside you should scream for you to run from me, you don't. You humble me by accepting me fully, in a way no other person has ever done. I hide nothing from you, and even then, you don't reject me." I traced along her throat with my tongue as she leaned more against me.

"You should lock doors," came a new voice that made me yank away. Then again, who wanted their daughter to catch them in such a position?

"It *was* locked," I told her.

"Not well enough." Lilianna looked toward the clock above the stove. "I am on time."

The way she spoke reminded me that she was every bit my daughter. Even though we had grown up very differently, it seemed that some things must have passed to her in her DNA. She was blunt and honest to a fault. Hopefully, in time, she learned some amount of tact.

"Sorry," Hera signed, then glanced at me to translate. *"I was running late."*

"And everyone else?"

"Probably caught up with security measures and work. I told everyone we would sit down at six, but they could arrive at five-thirty."

"You should have been clearer." The strange thing was that Lilianna's words, while clearly pointing out where she felt we had failed, held no real censure. She said them as if the obvious solution that we should have seen for ourselves.

It made me nervous, as it always did. I had not spent as much time with her as I would have liked, trying to not push my presence on her and giving her the space to come to me. She would have to fit into society, to learn to work with humans and other shades, but she struggled to understand anyone else or value their opinions or views. She had to find her own way, but I hadn't ever realized how painful parenthood was when I could not step in and fix everything for her.

"I'll make it more clear next time," Hera signed to end the fight before it could go very far. No doubt she did so for me, so Lilianna and I didn't argue or cause tension.

Instead, Hera moved around behind Lilianna to take a stack of plates to the table. When she glanced back over, she met my gaze from where I stood behind Lilianna.

I didn't have to say a word—she could easily read my expression. *You got lucky. I'll have you later, once everyone leaves.*

Her breath caught, and I had no doubt that the redness on her cheeks was due to excitement.

Lilianna moved her gaze between the two of us then narrowed her eyes until just black slits watched us. No doubt she understood the relationship between Hera and I, but she'd never addressed it. I wasn't sure if she cared at all—she rarely spoke about her personal thoughts or feelings.

At the very least, she didn't seem bothered by it.

The sound of the door opening broke Lilianna's scrutiny. In walked Knox and Brax. They were both well dressed, though wore similar nervous expressions.

"Wait!" Wade shouted, rushing in behind them, not that either other man even slowed let alone acknowledged him. He panted, then hit Knox on the back as they were best friends. "You didn't hear me, but I was trying to catch up."

"We heard you," Brax said with a glare when it seemed Wade would slap him on the back as well.

Wade must have taken the threat seriously because he slid his fingers through his hair instead of trying to touch Brax at all. Wade had also dressed up, though he'd forgone the full suit, going for slacks and a long-sleeved button-up shirt instead. It probably fit better, since a suit might have made him look like a teenager wearing his father's clothing.

He looked at Hera, then smirked. "You haven't gotten ready yet."

Knox let out a laugh. "You were late this morning, too."

"She needs a keeper," Deacon said as he walked in from the hallway, pulling at the cuff of his shirt to straighten it beneath his suit jacket. "She's been running behind all day."

All the men ganged up on her, something that seemed to fluster Hera even more.

Of course, the slight grin to each made me suspect they had been responsible for her lateness.

A knock on the door turned my focus that way, but Wade opened it before anyone else needed to respond. Aaron and Moa walked in, the same quiet discomfort they often had despite three months at Larkwood.

Well, not a full three months. They came and went, both helping to teach different classes and to create connections between Larkwood and the human world. Moa held a large platter, the scent telling me she'd cooked, while Aaron had a bottle of wine in his hand.

The two approached Hera and handed the items over, relaxing at her presence. While having humans around made me uneasy, Hera's smile made it more than worth enduring. The extra security to ensure their safety seemed a small price to pay, and the two had stood by us even when all had appeared lost. They'd earned their places both at Larkwood and at our table.

The ticking of the clock on the wall reminded me that our time was not without limits.

I set a hand on Hera's hip, making her jump. When she looked up at me, I nodded toward the bathroom. "You should go change and get yourself ready. We can handle setting the table and finishing dinner." I pressed a kiss to the top of her head.

As she walked toward the other room, my heart sped again. Before I'd met her, I hadn't thought myself capable of this feeling, hadn't known I could desire and crave a person this much. As a wendigo, I'd always wanted control of others, but Hera was the first person I ever loved so much that I gave her freedom.

She hadn't saved me from my darkness — that would always be a part of me. She'd done something even more impressive. She'd faced that darkness and still accepted me, still cared for me, still loved me.

It was something I hadn't thought possible, which was why I would spend all my years trying to pay her back for it.

And I'd use all the power at my disposal to keep her safe. The last thing any person who dared to threaten the happiness we had found here would be an enraged wendigo, because she'd given me a life worth protecting.

Hera

I followed Kit's request, jumping in the shower for a quick rinse-off before putting on the outfit I'd set out. I'd picked a black dress with lace detail, something that straddled the line between my two lives.

It wasn't designer or fancy the way the old me would have worn, but it wasn't the simplistic outfits I'd grown used to in my life as a shade. Instead, this combined both those people, which I'd tried for the past months to do. It was flirty and sweet and subtly sexy. I paired it with low heels and kept my makeup simple, applying only mascara and some lip balm that had a sheen to it.

One last glance in the mirror made me figure I'd done what I could. I told myself to relax, that this wasn't anything special, but I doubted lying to myself would do anything.

After waiting as long as I dared, I exited my bedroom to find the living room full of movement.

Bowen and Sohi had arrived while I'd been in the shower, the two common enough guests that they fit right into my space and company. Bowen, Kit and Knox worked in the kitchen, moving food into serving dishes that they then handed off to Wade and Soshi to take to the table. That left Brax, Deacon, Moa and Aaron speaking to the two people we had thrown this dinner for.

My parents.

My mom and dad stood there, appearing entirely uncomfortable. Whether that was due to not having seen me yet or being at Larkwood or having shades surround them, I had no idea. It was probably a mixture of both.

My mom looked toward me, her eyes instantly glistening as if she were ready to cry on the spot. She squeezed my father's hand, who followed her gaze to me. He didn't react quite the same way, but the harshness of his expression softened.

I'd spent little time with them after the fight, after the guards had given up and we had won. Everything had been a mess that night, and I'd had plenty of issues to deal with. Injured shades, injured guards, frightened people, the risk of a follow-up attack—those had all taken my attention.

I'd hugged them both, said think you and they'd let me go. If anyone understood what rested on my shoulders, they would, since they'd both lived with high-pressure jobs. They'd dedicated their lives to their careers, which meant neither had put me down when I'd had to do the same.

Since then, we'd done a few video calls, but this was the first time seeing them in person. Worse, the times we had spoken, we'd kept everything surface-level, as if none of us knew what to say beyond that.

How did people address the past? How did they move forward without tripping over the things that were already over? I didn't want to tell them everything I'd suffered, didn't want to burden them with that.

What did I get out of their guilt? How did them feeling bad help me at all? Having them show up that night said everything about how they'd changed, how they'd learned and accepted me. They'd risked a lot to come to my defense the night of the attack. Sure, Moa had been the one to tell them about it, but they'd made the choice to follow, to help, and that told me all I needed to know.

We all took our seats at the large table, with my parents seated across from me. Moa and Aaron sat to each side of my parents like a security blanket and buffer. Lilianna sat at the far end of the table, near Kit, no doubt so he could play buffer for her. Still, having her there, no matter how awkward she was, pleased me. She was family even if she didn't want to be.

Kit didn't talk about her openly, wasn't the sort to admit to tell me how he felt, but I could see how his face softened each time he saw her.

Everyone else filled in the open spots, the table small enough that we all sat arm to arm. At least it meant no one would need to shout to be heard.

"This is wonderful," my mother said after taking a bite of ham, the words hesitant as though she wasn't sure how to speak to me anymore.

"Kit made it," I signed back automatically before remembering they couldn't understand it.

Wade spoke up, translating for me.

My mother laughed softly, though it held discomfort. In her calls, she'd mentioned an ASL tutor, but I knew just how hard it was to become fluent. "That doesn't surprise me. You never cared for cooking." Her voice trailed off but then she added on quietly, "and I never really took the time to teach you, I guess."

The regret of those words came through loud and clear and made me think about all the things we'd missed out on.

Her and my father because they were busy and me because I hadn't understood how important and fragile family actually was. Now, however, I'd come to realize that family was imperfect, that it was frustrating at times but that there was nothing more important in the world.

We all failed miserably, all carried around wounds and snarled when others prodded them. I'd been afraid of the world, afraid of speaking up for myself...afraid of myself. Wade felt as if he were forever unwelcomed, Deacon thought he would never find others like him, Kit feared he wasn't capable of making anyone happy, Knox hated what he was and Brax thought no one could accept him without fear. My parents had been devastated by the idea of losing their daughter and had thought it easier to believe me dead than to face the heartbreaking truth. Lilianna had grown up alone, told she was a monster. Bowen had needed to come to terms with the risk of losing others and Soshi needed to learn to trust. Even Moa and Aaron had had to travel a hard path, choosing between what was easy and what they felt was right.

We were all broken in our own ways, but sitting together like this, looking around, I finally understood.

Family wasn't about perfection. It wasn't about finding people who had no problems, about always doing the right thing. Instead, it was about finding people I wanted to fail with, people who supported me, who I would sacrifice and risk anything for.

And I'd found them...

I peered around the table, feeling an ease I'd never thought I'd find, a level of acceptance I didn't think was possible.

Larkwood had tried to destroy us all, and it had left its mark on each of us. Instead of letting it win, though, instead of tearing each other apart or giving in, we had fought for ourselves and for one another.

A smile touched my lips as I stared at the others. I'd had my voice stolen by people who wanted to keep me docile, who thought they could control me, and while I'd never get what was taken back, I was finally okay with that.

I'd found something so much better. I held up my drink and tapped my nail against the glass to draw the attention of everyone at the table. The room went silent as everyone else mirrored my action.

I swallowed hard, then smiled, lifted my glass and nodded toward them all, toward the family I'd found, the one I cherished, the people who had helped me to survive the impossible and grow into who I was now.

And when they smiled back, when they accepted me with my faults and strengths alike, I knew the truth — we didn't need words to understand exactly how we all felt.

Larkwood was different because *we* were different.

We had stood up against the system created to keep us quiet, to use us, and we'd changed it all. I'd turned

Larkwood into a force for good, and if anyone dared to threaten it ever again — we'd fight together.

And there was no one else I'd rather fight beside.

Want to see more from this author?
Here's a taster for you to enjoy!

The Devil's Luck:
A Devil of a Time
Jayce Carter

Coming March 2023

Excerpt

My name is Loch Lacey, and I am sexually attracted to red flags — the more of them shoved into a vaguely man-shaped form, the hotter and dumber I get.

I'd say that trait would end up killing me, but it already had. Five years ago, I'd let some fuckwit tell me pretty lies and sold my soul for his benefit, which left me spending my afterlife here in the Chasm as my punishment.

And even though I should have known better, a part of me saw the man across the bar, Tyrus, with a flashing neon sign above his head that said *Death Two Here*. I didn't believe in love at first sight but fuck if 'my future bad decision at first sight' wasn't a thing.

Tyrus sat at his normal table in the back. He ran this place — much like he ran many of the businesses here. Whereas most bosses, especially ones with as much on their plate as Tyrus did, would half-ass the actual day-to-day headaches, he never seemed to. He was *always* here.

Right now, he talked to someone else, his arm out on the back of the bench as if to prove himself in charge. *Talk about posturing.*

Of course, Tyrus was all about his posturing. He liked to play the game and from what I'd seen, he excelled at it.

"Another?" The bartender, Koya, put a new drink down in front of me before I got the chance to answer. Then again, my empty glass suggested I needed more. I didn't have a whole lot of talents, but I could drink most people under the table while staying on my feet. Call it a gift from a life spent trying to escape the ugliness of my reality.

I nodded in thanks, then brought the new glass to my lips. The liquor burned, but I didn't so much as flinch as I swallowed down a gulp.

"Hey there, pretty thing. You new here?" The unfamiliar voice made me struggle to resist the urge to roll my eyes like a petulant child.

I turned on my barstool to find a damned behind me, his body already twisted beyond recognition. He had horns that curled back from his temples and bright red eyes, his face having shifted into a muzzle. When I'd died, five years ago, the thought of talking to something as terrifying looking as him would have sent me screaming. Now, however? I was used to it.

Fangs, feathers, claws, scales? Big fucking deal. So long as they didn't drool or spit acid on me, I didn't much care.

"Nope," I answered before taking another drink and peering out at the dim bar again.

The Chasm was *always* dark. Even inside, even with lighting, it never got bright enough. Trying to do puzzles here was a fucking losing battle. It made me wonder if the very air here absorbed the light.

Wouldn't surprise me. Seemed yet another way to remind us all that we were the bad guys and this was our punishment.

"But you still look human—you can't have been here that long, then," the man added on.

I gave him a side-eye because I'd heard this shit before plenty of times. People showed up in the Chasm in two forms—as damned or as demons. They all looked human at first, but the damned quickly twisted into monstrous forms. They grew fangs and claws and became animalistic. Demons, on the other hand, kept their human body. They had another form, a demonic one, but they didn't have to take that. Demons were rarer and more powerful, putting them above the damned.

I still appeared human because I'd been one of the few who arrived as a demon rather than damned.

"Nope," I assured him. "Been here in this depressing paradise for five years."

"So why haven't I seen you?"

"Because I've been really fucking lucky so far?"

He narrowed his eyes until they looked like some cheap Halloween decoration, nothing but a red spotlight staring out from his not-at-all human face. "You're mouthy for someone who just got here."

"Again—didn't just get here. Why don't you go look for someone who might actually find you charming?" *Like there's anyone who would...*

He leaned in closer, bringing his face just in front of mine. His breath was hot and smelled of rotting flesh. "You need to learn how this world works. People survive by clinging to someone more powerful. You'll lose those looks of yours before you know it, get twisted into something just like the rest of us, so why not sell that pretty little human body while it's still worth something?"

My stomach didn't even roll. Was that how far gone I was already? That even this disgusting thing whispering into my ear in the middle of a bar, suggesting things I'd *never* take him up on, didn't even warrant any stomach churning? Not at least a rumble or threat of vomiting all over him?

I really am jaded, aren't I?

I'd suffered with assholes like him plenty of times, damned who took one look at my unmutated form and wanted to own and break me. I knew what I looked like, which was exactly the same as when I'd died. I didn't have to dye my hair green anymore, since it was like that when I'd taken the bullets that had killed me. I still had the small tattoo on each of my cheeks, hadn't grown more than my pathetic five feet in height, and didn't put on or lose weight. Basically? At death, we ended up stuck. It made me feel bad for those who died with not-so-great trends like shaved-off eyebrows or shitty tattoos.

On the plus side, I'd shaved the morning I'd died, so no worries about body hair. I had to find the silver lining where I could, or the dreariness of this place would get to me.

"Hard pass." I brought my drink to my mouth again, letting the heavy glass smack him as I did so.

At least that caused him to lean back and give me a bit of space.

"Who are you bound to? I'll just buy your soul off them."

The name caught on my lips. Talk about an answer I hated to give. Then again, that was how the Chasm worked. People didn't wind up here because they were bad people—though, to be fair, most of us were—but because we'd all sold our souls. Just admitting that I didn't own my soul made my mood plummet.

And given I was this far into a bottle on a...Tuesday night? Yeah, my mood was already dragging ass.

"I'll find out," he assured me. "And I can be *extremely* persistent. You'll be mine by the end of the week, and I can't wait to fuck up all that soft human skin. Bet you won't look so pretty when I'm done with you."

"I would personally recommend against that," came a deep voice that made the man freeze. He turned slowly, as though if he took long enough, he'd find something other than what he expected behind him.

Except it didn't change. No matter how long the man took, Tyrus stood there, his dark eyebrow lifted in an obvious challenge.

"She yours?" the man asked, a waver in his voice that made it clear he wasn't rising to that challenge.

"No."

"Then why do you care? Unless you're enjoying her right now, in which case, I'll fucking wait. I don't want to step on any toes."

"Hardly," Tyrus said with so much disgust in his voice that I was pretty sure I should feel insulted. I might not be sultry or sexy, but he didn't need to say that as if I were some rotting carcass. "She belongs to Gorrin."

And there went the color from the man's cheeks. In fact, forget some parting snarky shot—the man was lucky to stay upright as he fled the bar just as fast as his little legs could carry him.

"Coward," Tyrus muttered as he watched the man leave, then turned toward me. "Why didn't you tell him about Gorrin? Mentioning his name would have resolved this instantly."

"Somehow, it bothers me to admit being owned. Imagine that?"

Tyrus leaned against the bar beside me, giving me the chance to see him up close. How was it that someone could look that dangerous, even dressed in a suit, as civilized as a man could appear? He had tan skin and dark features, with deep brown eyes and black hair slicked back in true gangster style. He had facial hair that rode the line between being well-maintained yet still looking like he had a five-o'clock shadow.

He was terrifying in a wholly unusual way, and when he stared at me, I felt as if he saw me naked.

No, *worse* than naked. I could deal with people seeing bare skin—what did that matter? Plenty of people had seen my tits and I wasn't conceited enough to think they were special in any way. The left was better than the right, but neither were real superstars. Tyrus saw deeper than that, though. He peered into my soul—what a shitty turn of phrase since I'd sold that already—and saw things I wanted to keep hidden.

"You wouldn't deal with people like that if you gained your own power and made your own name," Tyrus added on.

This again? Seemed it was lecture time yet again.

I took another drink, hoping the burning liquor would dull my senses and the conversation. "I'm fine."

"No, you aren't. In the Chasm, the only things that matter are power and connections. You need to obtain both to survive here."

"I'll do that about when hell freeze over, which it hasn't in five years, so I think I'm safe."

"This isn't hell."

"Close enough. I'm not about to go around stealing souls just to make myself more powerful."

"It isn't stealing — it's bartering. When you were still alive and human, did you not exchange money for goods and services? You do the same here. The only difference is that we use souls as currency."

I thought back to how I'd ended up here, to when I'd sold my soul, to that crushing regret when I'd realized it had all been for nothing. The memory threatened to close my throat, but I shut my eye and took a deep breath to push it all away.

The Chasm wasn't the sort of place to show weakness, and certainly not in front of a Demon Lord like Tyrus.

The four assholes who ran this place — Tyrus, Gorrin, Hale and Yazmor — held the souls of nearly all the damned between them. This gave them the power to stand mostly unopposed. They ruled the Chasm through fear, threats and a good old heaping of violence just to really flavor the whole thing.

"Thanks for the completely unsolicited advice, but no thanks. I'm good."

"You really aren't. You have stagnated here for five years. You've survived this long only because of your connection to us — that won't save you forever. It is an imperfect defense that chips away each time you use it. Eventually, it will crumble, and you will have to stand against your threats on your own. You can either be moral or you can be strong. You will have to choose between the two." With that, he peered at Koya. "That is her last drink. She does not need to be drunk on her way home."

"Didn't think the Devil cared."

"I am not a devil."

"Could have fooled me," I muttered as I gulped down the rest of the liquor and slammed the glass down on the bar top.

Tyrus said nothing else before he turned on his heels and headed back to his table. The other man still waited there patiently, telling me Tyrus had left his meeting to intervene on my behalf. It made his words sting more and irritated me worse than the cheap liquor.

And yet that annoyance didn't stop me from noticing the way he filled out his suit... Most men I'd known who wore such outfits mixed different colors. They'd have a black suit with a white shirt and red tie — something to create a balance. Not Tyrus. He paired a black suit with a black shirt and a matching tie.

It wasn't how he looked that garnered the fear and respect of others, though. It was his power, his demon form, his absolute ruthlessness that had earned him his place at the top. I'd yet to see that other side of him, and honestly? I never wanted to. Seeing my *own* demon form had shocked me enough when I'd first arrived here.

I peered back at Koya, who offered me an apologetic smile. "Sorry, Loch. If it were anyone else, I'd say fuck it and give you another, but I'm not about to piss the boss off."

"Thanks anyway, Koya." I shrugged and slid from the bar stool, the world shifting as I moved for the first time in a few hours and more than a few drinks.

Guess Tyrus hadn't been wrong about cutting me off.

Koya set something on the bar, and for a moment, I smiled. Had he given in to my meager charms?

Of course not. Instead of more alcohol, a cup made from a small skull sat there, the dark liquid inside no doubt coffee. "Should help clear your head a bit," Koya said.

"Thanks." I picked it up and took a drink. When I'd first arrived, the idea of drinking from a skull would have grossed me out. Funny how quickly things can become normal for people.

Demons and damned and skulls had been nothing more than Halloween jokes for most of my life, but now? Totally average. In fact, a day where I didn't see anyone brutally murdered would strike me as odd.

I headed toward the door, coffee in hand, ignoring the weight of Tyrus' gaze. Something about the way he watched me always let me know it was him even if I wanted to pretend otherwise. No matter how distracted, how busy, I always felt the weight of his gaze.

But I refused to look backward and acknowledge it, because men who were bad for me had already fucked up my life *more* than enough.

I could fuck it up all on my own now, thank you very much.

About the Author

Jayce Carter lives in Southern California with her husband and two spawns. She originally wanted to take over the world but realized that would require wearing pants. This led her to choosing writing, a completely pants-free occupation. She has a fear of heights yet rock climbs for fun and enjoys making up excuses for not going out and socializing.

Jayce loves to hear from readers. You can find her contact information, website details and author profile page at https://www.totallybound.com

Home of Erotic Romance

Sign up for our newsletter and find out about all our romance book releases, eBook sales and promotions, sneak peeks and FREE romance books!